Praise for *The Sweetest Remedy*

"A page-turning, emotional, and romantic journey of self-discovery. Jane Igharo beautifully celebrates the powerful ties that link families and the legacy of love that unites them."

—Chanel Cleeton, *New York Times* bestselling author of *The Most Beautiful Girl in Cuba*

"*The Sweetest Remedy* is a journey around the world into the complex and wonderful intricacies of family. Igharo gives readers a story filled with love, humor, and the magic of belonging. Reading *The Sweetest Remedy* will have you calling your family, updating your wardrobe, and looking for your passport!"

—Denise Williams, author of *The Fastest Way to Fall*

"*The Sweetest Remedy* is a stunning story about family, love, and what it means to belong. Jane Igharo has a knack for writing bold, heartfelt stories and this one is a joy from start to finish!"

—Saumya Dave, author of *What a Happy Family*

"Jane Igharo does it again in *The Sweetest Remedy*! Igharo masterfully weaves together family drama, romance, and acceptance into this gorgeous, unputdownable novel."

—Kaia Alderson, author of *Sisters in Arms*

"This well-paced, multi-narrator tale expertly marries romance with a moving story of family and identity. Readers will be impressed."

—*Publishers Weekly* (starred review)

"An engrossing work of women's fiction."   —*Booklist*

Praise for *Ties That Tether*

"Lovingly written and heartfelt. *Ties That Tether* is a beautiful exploration of culture, family, and romance. Azere's journey to find her own voice should resonate with anyone who's ever felt trapped between conflicting worlds and expectations."

—Helen Hoang, *USA Today*
bestselling author of *The Heart Principle*

"*Ties That Tether* takes the reader on a rich, emotional journey. A big, bold story about finding ourselves amidst the struggles of family loyalty, honoring one's culture, and the endless facets of love. Loved every glorious moment of this book!"

—Jennifer Probst, *New York Times*
bestselling author of *Our Italian Summer*

"[An] intriguing examination into the dynamics of family relationships and what it means to have pride in one's culture and heritage. It also holds some unexpected twists and turns that will keep readers engaged until the end." —Associated Press

"This exploration of identity, love, and loss in the context of an interracial relationship feels authentic and bittersweet, yet hopeful all the same." —*BookPage*

"Happily ever after is hard-won and satisfying in this #ownvoices romance." —Shelf Awareness

"Igharo's debut beautifully depicts the tension between self-determination and the desire to live up to family expectations. . . . Clever and heartwarming storytelling. Readers will be rooting for Azere from the very first page." —*Library Journal* (starred review)

"An unexpected and heartfelt romance about true love and the sacrifices we make for it."

—Sonya Lalli, author of *Serena Singh Flips the Script*

"*Ties That Tether* was a roller-coaster ride from page one and holy cow did I love it. Jane Igharo chronicles Azere's journey in such a beautiful, wrenching, and relatable way. As Azere struggled to find a balance between her love life, her own happiness, and the expectations of her family, I went through a whirlwind of emotions—and I adored every minute of it. I laughed and teared up and cheered and yelled. Best of all, Jane Igharo delivers a happily ever after that made me smile until my cheeks hurt. I tore through this amazing book, I couldn't read it fast enough."

—Sarah Smith, author of *Simmer Down*

"A Nigerian immigrant herself, Igharo tackles issues like immigration, cultural identity, and interracial dating in a compelling way. While a love story at heart, this book is so much more than that. It's a must-read for your summer vacation."   —Betches

"A wonderful fall romance with immense depth, *Ties That Tether* seizes you from the very beginning."   —Shondaland

"The best part of this book for me was Azere and her mother's relationship. It is so fraught with the immigration experience. . . . To read this book is to read it for the tenderness of the romance and for the immigrant experience, to feel your heart soften and your throat clog with tears, and to celebrate the resilience of the spirit. As Rilke has said, 'To love is the ultimate human task.' So celebrate the love between the protagonists and within their families as you turn the pages."   —Frolic

"With deft writing, snappy dialogue, rom-com movie references throughout, and a delightful cast of characters, *Ties That Tether* is a wonderful romance and the start of a long career for Jane Igharo."

—Fresh Fiction

"Igharo brings a great deal of heart to Azere's internal conflict as she navigates two cultures. This emotional debut marks Igharo as a writer to watch."   —*Publishers Weekly*

TITLES BY JANE IGHARO

WHERE WE END & BEGIN

Jane Igharo

BERKLEY ROMANCE

New York

BERKLEY ROMANCE
Published by Berkley
An imprint of Penguin Random House LLC
penguinrandomhouse.com

Library of Congress Cataloging-in-Publication Data

Names: Igharo, Jane, author.
Title: Where we end & begin / Jane Igharo.
Other titles: Where we end and begin
Description: First Edition. | New York: Berkley Romance, 2022.
Identifiers: LCCN 2022004871 (print) | LCCN 2022004872 (ebook) |
  ISBN 9780593440230 (trade paperback) |
  ISBN 9780593440247 (ebook)
Subjects: LCGFT: Novels.
Classification: LCC PR9199.4.I37 W48 2022 (print) |
  LCC PR9199.4.I37 (ebook) | DDC 813/.6—dc23
LC record available at https://lccn.loc.gov/2022004871
LC ebook record available at https://lccn.loc.gov/2022004872

First Edition: September 2022

Printed in the United States of America
1st Printing

Book design by Elke Sigal

To the giver of stories, who picks the right teller.

PART I

PART I

CHAPTER ONE

The plane landed, and Dunni's rapid heartbeat slowed. As the pilot announced the arrival in Lagos, a prolonged breath eased out of her along with a whiff of alcohol, courtesy of the wine that had made her anxiety manageable.

Dunni had recently developed a fear of flying. And the person responsible for that fear was her grandmother—her Iya Agba. The seventy-eight-year-old woman, known within the family for dreaming sinister things that somehow came true, had called Dunni five times in the last month, detailing five different scenarios where Dunni died.

A plane crash had been one.

The logical part of Dunni's brain, the part that had gotten her a PhD in genetics, had dismissed the dreams. The other part of her brain, the part that kept a detailed account of her grandmother's predictions, had been terrified, paranoid, and irrationally cautious.

Dunni often described her grandmother as someone who lived with one eye in the present and another peeking into the future, spiritually straddled between two periods.

Iya Agba dreams, and her dreams come true. History held the proof.

When Iya Agba was a child, she dreamed her primary school teacher died in an *okada* accident.

He had.

On the eve of her wedding, she dreamed her husband-to-be died of a heart attack days after his sixty-fifth birthday.

He had.

Iya Agba dreams, and her dreams come true. It was a known fact, especially to that other half of Dunni's brain that relied on historical proof. But she tried to ignore history and her upbringing in a country where there were always two narratives—the natural and the supernatural. Dunni had lived in America for twelve years, where she had studied molecular genetics, pursuing a career as a research geneticist. She had learned to rely on the practical, the explainable. But now, back in Nigeria, with her grandmother's warnings resounding in her head, practicality suddenly seemed unattainable, further from her reach than it had been before, a continent away.

She rolled her suitcase along and stopped once outside of the airport. It was evening, the sun partially beneath the horizon. The dusty harmattan air moved through the weightless chiffon blouse that flapped against her body. The paved ground beneath her feet was a source of comfort and security. For the first time since leaving Seattle, she breathed easy and felt the fullness of air through her nose and mouth, noting the difference between what she had inhaled in America and what she inhaled now—a dense mugginess infused with the scent of dry earth and flavored with something invisible yet so particularly Nigerian.

Trimmed hedges lined the walkway she stood on; the green shrubs complemented the pale red of the ground. Dunni missed this aspect of Nigeria—the soil, its color, and even its stubbornness, how it clung to anything and everything. It was definitely resilient.

She'd spent twelve years away from her home and from him.

She scanned her surroundings to ensure he wasn't there. It was stupid. Like her, he was thirty now. For twelve years, she only ever thought of him as a boy. But he must have changed. His lean face and slender physique were probably fuller now, either with muscles or fat. The scanty hairs on his chin, the ones she used to count without going past twenty, must have multiplied, carpeting his face with an unruly thickness. She even suspected his fair complexion had darkened. Then she suspected, with no evidence, that he could be the black-market dealer hollering at travelers, telling them he'll give good prices for currency exchange—dollars to naira and vice versa. That could be him—Obinna.

Could it?

Maybe she wouldn't recognize him. But what if she did? What if something in her—something that had stayed the same for twelve years, frozen in time—recognized him? Would that familiarity in her—the one that was both comforting and taunting—recognize the same familiarity in him, something kindred between them?

She hoped not.

Dunni had four days in Nigeria, and if Tiwa wasn't her best friend, she would have declined her wedding invitation and sent an expensive present instead. She was here only out of obligation.

"Madam! Madam Dunni!" The voice came from behind, a gruff projection that disturbed Dunni's thoughts.

She turned around and studied the man jogging toward her, his round face older and more worn than she remembered. "Paul?"

"Yes, ma. It's me." His feet fell to a slow stride as he neared her and caught his breath. "Welcome, ma." He sucked in air greedily, then pushed it out as if he no longer had use for it. "Welcome home."

"Thank you, Paul. It's good to see you." She examined his face and noticed the hard lines that tugged on his smiling lips and the corners of his eyes. They hadn't been there twelve years ago. "You look . . ."

"Like an old man." He laughed, and his round belly jiggled along with each chuckle. "It's the consequences of time. What can we do but embrace it?" His mouth closed, and he assessed her. "But look at you. You left home a girl and have returned a woman." He shook his head and pressed his lips in a regretful smile as if offering condolences for the loss of her youth, something he might consider a tragedy. Or maybe the true tragedy had been the way she'd lost it.

As her family's driver, Paul had always been there—at the forefront, uncomfortably watching things unfold while trying to appear like he saw nothing and heard nothing. Sometimes, however, he was pushed into the chaos and forced to be an unwilling participant. That day, twelve years ago, when it all happened, that was exactly what he'd been. Unwilling, forced to do something her mother had made him do.

Dunni wondered if he still felt guilty. He had, all those years ago. She remembered that days after the ordeal, he'd driven her to the airport. She was eighteen at the time, leaving home to attend university in America. Her parents hadn't accompanied her to the airport. It had been only Paul and her in the car. Her stare connected with his in the rearview mirror, and she saw his eyes, full of remorse.

"It wasn't your fault," she had told him, because she felt he needed to hear it.

Some people knew how to handle their guilt—how to rearrange the order of an ordeal and direct blame at someone else or redefine their guilt as sympathy pains. Paul did not know how to do any of that. He needed someone to do it for him, so that day, Dunni had.

"What happened wasn't your fault," she'd told him.

"But I should have . . ." Paul choked on his words, then cleared his throat until his tone was steady again, professional as it ought to be. "I should have done something to help him."

"My mother would have sacked you if you had. You have a family to take care of." She looked through the window as the distance between the car and the airport shrunk. "Just stop. Stop apologizing."

"Yes, ma."

Dunni still remembered arriving at the airport and checking her phone, while Paul pulled her luggage out of the trunk.

"Madam Dunni," he had said. "Is everything okay?"

"I need you to do something for me." She looked at him. "It's important."

He nodded briskly, eager to make amends for what he had done just days ago. "Anything, ma."

"I need you to check on him." For the first time since knowing Paul, ten years, she had touched him—gripped his hand, squeezed firmly to convey how desperate she was. And she was. The action—foreign to them both—was more telling than saying *please*. "I've called him, but no answer. He knows I'm leaving today, and still, I've heard nothing. You know where he lives. Go to him, check how he's doing, tell him I'll find a way for him to join me in America. Tell him I love him. Please." She added the word for good measure. "Please, Paul. Do this for me, and say nothing to my mother."

"Madam, of course," Paul had said. "I'll do as you've asked. And I won't say a word to big madam." That was a vital part of the request—one that would secure his job and Dunni's head.

"Thank you. I'll call you once I land." She released her grip and entered the airport.

She left Nigeria that day to attend Princeton University. But she had a plan. They had made it together—Obinna and her.

She would attend university abroad as her parents wanted, and they would stay in touch—talk on the phone and send emails. Dunni would hire an immigration lawyer and find a way to bring Obinna to America on a student visa. He was smart; he had excellent grades. He would join her months later. They would live in the apartment her parents bought her. They would study hard during the weekdays, visit American landmarks during the weekends, and make love as often as they wanted. And after they graduated, they would get married—a small garden ceremony with the eccentric group of friends they had grown to call family. They would have three children or maybe four, just to even out the number. They would be happy. They would be together. That had been the plan. But it never happened.

Dunni spread out her fingers and looked at the scar that split across the center of her palm; it broke through creases to forge a path of its own. He had a similar scar. They'd made it together—broken their flesh in order to mend their fates. Back then, she believed it would be enough, that a binding promise would secure their planned future. But she'd been wrong. She turned her hand and looked at the engagement ring on her finger. She'd been so very wrong. It hadn't been enough. In fact, it had meant nothing at all.

She expelled a deep breath and coached herself to forget the past.

Twelve years without seeing him or speaking to him. Four days in Lagos to attend a rehearsal dinner and a wedding. Then she would be back in America—an ocean and continent away from her past. It sounded simple enough, but she felt unsettled somehow—disturbed by the anticipation of something unknown.

You shouldn't have come here. The thought occurred to her, and rather than dismissing it or combating it with positive thoughts, she agreed with it.

No. I shouldn't have.

CHAPTER TWO

When the black gate slid open and revealed the Lekki estate, Dunni became more certain she had made a mistake.

The house had changed since she last saw it. Her mother had hired architects to reconstruct the traditional features of the pillared building into something contemporary with large windows and glass railings. It looked less like a home than it had before.

Paul drove through the opening, and the car's wheels trundled over the interlocking concrete pavers. If Dunni's mother felt motivated to renovate something, it should have been the pavement. She should have had the small squares hauled out— anything to forget that Obinna's blood had once been there, pouring out from the gash on his back, covering the patterned ground, and seeping into the slim cracks of the interlocks.

"Madam Dunni," Paul said.

She met his eyes in the rearview mirror, and it suddenly felt like it had all happened yesterday. She hated that. In America, the memories eventually grew stale—lost their vividness until they were shadows lurking in the back of her head. But now, back in Nigeria, back at her family's house, sharing a knowing look with Paul through the rearview mirror, the memories seemed to take shape again. And Dunni felt like a child coloring, bringing the details of a horrid picture to life.

"Madam, there is a very nice hotel near here. If you would prefer—"

"It's okay, Paul." She inhaled deeply and held the breath before releasing it. "Take my bags to the guest room." She opened the car door, and the soles of her sandals slapped the pavement as she walked toward the front door.

The instant Paul entered the house with a suitcase and a duffel bag, Dunni heard her grandmother's taut voice; it trembled as she asked Paul questions, confirming he had truly picked Dunni up from the airport—all of her and not parts of her under the ruins of a blazing plane. When Paul answered the question—the same one multiple times—she shouted, "Hallelujah!"

The elderly woman appeared at the front door—her skin like roasted chestnuts, her petite physique made hefty by the folds of wrapper around her waist. Dunni thought it was intentional, the way her grandmother doubled up on the *ankara* fabric—an attempt to make her figure as big as her personality.

"*Ololufemi.* My darling." She sang in Yoruba then translated to English, a pattern she continued while dancing toward Dunni, waving her hands and shaking her waist. "*Ayo mi.* My joy. *Omo baba olowo.* The child of a wealthy man." Her arms looped around her granddaughter and tightened. The action looked less like an embrace and more like an attempt at preventing something from slipping away.

"Iya." Dunni hunched slightly and pressed her face into the curve of her grandmother's neck, inhaling the scent of baby powder and peppermint on her creased skin. This was the only reason she had chosen not to stay in a hotel. "I've missed you. So much." She'd last seen her grandmother six months ago in Seattle. It had been too long.

"My dear, I have missed you far more." Her palm flattened and stroked the back of Dunni's head. "You didn't tell me you were coming. Why?" She pulled away and frowned.

"I didn't want you to worry. After all the dreams you've been having, I—"

"Exactly. The dreams. How could you get on a plane after everything I told you? How could you take such a risk? Eh?"

"Tiwa is getting married."

"And so?" She braced her hands on her hips or on the layers of material that gave her a false weight. "Tiwa is getting married. Does that mean you should come and die?" She pressed her eyes closed after saying those words and murmured a prayer, retracting the statement. When she looked at Dunni, her lips relaxed and expanded to a weak smile—a voiceless apology. "You came alone?"

"Yes."

"Why? You could have at least brought Christopher."

"He couldn't make it—work."

Dunni felt the weight of the engagement ring on her finger,

as she often did. It was heavy and not in the playful way newly engaged women pretend their diamond is too massive and is therefore weighing their hand down. The ring on Dunni's finger was heavy like a tumor—like something that didn't belong on her body. She felt also, along with the weight of the ring, the need to lie, to answer a question even though it hadn't been asked.

"Everything is great. We're doing great."

It's what people expected to hear from her, and in the last two months—since Christopher got on his knee and slipped the ring on her finger—she had learned to tell this lie and many variations of it. "We're so happy. I'm so excited about the wedding. I can't wait." But each lie left her mouth bitter, and she wanted to wash out that taste with the truth.

"Come. You must be exhausted."

Dunni followed her grandmother into the house, a house she hadn't entered in twelve years.

With no expectations of what the interior would be like, she was not surprised it no longer looked like the house she grew up in—no more curtains draping doorways, patterned throw pillows against cozy couches, massive vases filled with thick bamboo sticks, or walls the warm hue of a prairie field. It was different now. Her mother had created a castle of glass and crystals, with a white-and-black palette that perfectly conveyed her views of the world. Everything looked fragile, like simply breathing put something in jeopardy of shattering.

"Your mother made changes," Iya Agba said, her tone harsh as she spoke of her daughter-in-law. "It looks like we live in one of those *yeye* glass balls that you shake."

"A snow globe?"

"Yes. Those things." Her lips curled upward as she hissed. "At least she left my room alone. Thank God."

"Is she here?" Dunni asked. "My mother?"

"No. But she should be soon."

"What about Daddy?"

"He is in Abuja. Did you tell them you were coming?"

Dunni shook her head. "I only spoke to Paul, so he could get me from the airport."

"I see." Iya Agba pursed her lips, her mouth full of words she contained with a forced smile. She clearly wasn't done reprimanding Dunni, but let the matter go. "Anyway, go take a bath and get settled. I'll prepare you something to eat."

"Iya, I don't want you fussing and stressing yourself. Let one of the staff do it. I'm sure my mother has at least three on duty."

"I am old, not on my deathbed." She frowned and the loose skin around her eyes overlapped. "I am very capable of cooking for my granddaughter."

"Of course you are."

Agreeing was the only reasonable response. No matter how much age piled on Iya Agba, causing her back to hunch just a little, her bones to ache, and her stride to slow, she never admitted to being old and no one dared make the assertion to her face.

"I look forward to whatever you'll cook." Dunni pressed her lips to her grandmother's cheek then ascended the floating stairs, her firm grip leaving fingerprints on the glass railing.

"Madam." At the doorway of the guestroom, Paul stood

with the composure of a soldier. "I've put your things inside. Is there anything else you need?"

"Nothing. Thank you." She placed a hand on his arm, and he stiffened then relaxed. She'd only ever touched him once. Maybe the contact triggered him to recall the exact moment and the request she'd made. Maybe he feared she would make another request that would put his job in jeopardy. "Have a good night, Paul."

"Yes. You too, ma."

⁓

Dunni stepped out of the shower stall and pulled the protective plastic cap from her head. Her hair fell free. The long locks stuck against her damp back and bare shoulders, the parts the towel around her chest didn't cover. She looked in the rectangular mirror that stretched above two vessel sinks and considered how to wear her hair tomorrow for the rehearsal dinner—curly, straight, up, or down. She busied herself with options for a few minutes because it was the most trivial matter in her life and for just a little while, she wanted it to be the most important.

After five minutes of deliberation, she decided to wear it down and curly.

When she stepped out of the en suite, she flinched in surprise, or maybe it was horror. After brief consideration, she concluded: it was definitely horror.

"Mother. Hi."

Dunni hadn't seen her mother in over a year, since the last

time she came to America for a social event. They rarely spoke on the phone, and it suited them both fine. They didn't whine about hardly seeing each other or missing each other. They weren't that kind of mother-daughter duo.

"Dunni." The middle-aged woman sat on the edge of the bed, her back straight, one leg crossed over the other. She wore an emerald-green pantsuit that made her look tall and lean even while she sat. "What are you doing here?" She tilted her pointy chin, which was more pronounced because of her messy-yet-stylish topknot bun.

They looked alike. Eerily alike. Their skin was the same tawny shade of brown sugar, their lips small and plump, and their eyes had a slight tilt at their ends. When Dunni looked at her mother, she didn't see traces of herself. She saw a goddamn reflection. And even when she was a continent away, she was never really away from her mother.

"Tiwa Jolade is getting married this weekend. I'm here for the wedding," Dunni said.

"I know she's getting married. I'm attending the wedding, but I assumed you weren't."

"She's one of my closest friends," Dunni explained, slightly annoyed. "Of course, I wouldn't miss it."

"And you didn't think to tell me you were coming? Do you know how that makes me look? My daughter, who has been abroad for years, comes into the country, and I'm absolutely oblivious to it. I had to hear it from the help."

"You're worried about what the staff will think of you?"

"I am worried about what they will say once they leave this house. You know how they like to talk. I don't want them saying I'm an inattentive mother."

Dunni couldn't think of a reason the term would bother her mother. If being branded an inattentive mother concerned her at all, it should have been during the many times she left Dunni and her older brother, Jeremiah, in the care of housekeepers while she traveled abroad, sometimes for weeks on end. She didn't care what people said about her then, and she certainly didn't care about the welfare or whereabouts of her children. And Dunni was sure that had not changed. It was exactly why she hadn't felt obligated to inform her mother of her travel plans.

"If you're coming into this country and my house, I deserve to know. It's really simple etiquette."

"Of course. I'm sorry." It was the only suitable response, the only means to ending the conversation. "It won't happen again, Mother."

Dunni said the word—*mother*—with a stiffness in her tone. It wasn't a word loaded with much warmth, and she liked to emphasize this by pressing down on the syllables and drawing out the *r* just a little. It was a title that further established the boundaries of their relationship and reminded them of what it was and what it would never be.

"So, how long are you staying?" her mother asked.

"I'll be gone in four days."

"Oh. I see." She rolled her shoulders, the tiniest gesture to indicate the answer discomforted her. "And Christopher? He couldn't make it?"

"He's working," Dunni answered.

"How is he?"

"Good. He's good."

They fell silent. Dunni waited for her mother to ask another question. They looked at each other—a challenge in Dunni's eyes and an unwillingness in her mother's.

She didn't ask the question. She never did.

It had been twelve years. She had uprooted Obinna from Dunni's life, but there was still an aspect of him she couldn't get rid of. He was still there—between them, the question she refused to ask.

"Well. I should leave you to rest." She stood and slipped her hands into her pockets. "Good night, Dunni." She turned and walked out of the room, the clack of her heels an uncanny echo in the corridor.

Dunni stood still with a firm grip on the towel around her chest. There was a scream inside of her, one she had been holding in for years. Whenever she saw her mother, she felt it claw in her throat like an animal unearthing itself. But each time, she clenched her teeth and buried the scream because even if she released it and shouted at the top of her lungs, her mother would never hear her.

CHAPTER THREE

Dunni changed her mind and wore her hair straight; it fluttered against her cleavage as she walked. It was a mild evening, which was ideal considering the rehearsal dinner was in the garden at the Jolade estate. Two long tables were side by side, below tree branches with lanterns dangling from them.

Dunni stood on the concrete steps and watched the guests below sip cocktails. She knew no one. If she'd stayed in touch with friends and classmates while in America, maybe she would have known one person or two. But she had stayed in touch with only Tiwa. They'd grown up together; their fathers were business associates and good friends. Even when Tiwa went off to boarding school in London at sixteen, they'd stayed in touch—texting and speaking on the phone frequently until they went to university and had the liberty to fly between London and America for visits. They were extremely close. That was why Dunni was in Nigeria against her better judgment and her grandmother's warnings.

A server approached her, and she grabbed a champagne flute. She drank slowly. Her eyes wandered above the rim of the glass and searched the garden for the happy couple. Another server approached her and presented a platter of hors d'oeuvres, which she waved away before taking a hasty step off the stairs. Her heels sank into the grass, and the goblet in her hand tipped over. Champagne poured out, thankfully missing her dress as it drenched the manicured grass.

"Don't go hurt yourself *o*."

The voice came from behind—stern with a combination of a British and Nigerian accent Dunni had secretly always envied. She turned around and saw Tiwa, whose red lips stretched in a smirk.

"If you fall and chip a tooth now, I suppose you'll sue me."

"Well, you're having a garden party and didn't even bother informing your guests, so they could wear the proper footwear," Dunni challenged, with her own smug smile. "If I sustain any injuries during this event, you'd be totally liable."

"Not when I mentioned it was a garden party on the invitation." Tiwa crossed her arms and jutted out her chin. "But I'm guessing you didn't read the details. Did you?"

"Um . . ." Dunni thought back to receiving the invitation in the mail, glancing at the major details—date, time, location—before occupying herself with something else. "Oops. I guess I might have skipped that detail." She winced as if the truth stung.

"For Christ's sake. There were even flowers on the invitation—like a ridiculous amount of flowers."

"I thought it was just a part of the design. Brides like flowers and all that stuff."

Tiwa shook her head while observing her friend's unbalanced stance. "What am I going to do with you? Huh?"

"I don't know. Love me?"

"Yeah. I think that's all I can do. Come on. Give me a hug."

Dunni carefully stepped forward, the empty glass still in her hand, and embraced her friend. They giggled like they were children again, without a worry in the world.

"Wow." Dunni pulled back and really took in Tiwa's appearance—the white halter dress with a pearl-encrusted collar. The weightless silk material hugged her delicate curves and flowed to her feet. "You look fucking incredible."

"I really do," Tiwa said confidently, as if her attractiveness was law—indisputable. "You look damn good yourself." She considered Dunni's champagne-colored wrap dress. "Love that color on you."

"Thanks. And I thought you were making a grand entrance—that's the only reason I didn't stick to Naija time."

"Well, I wanted trumpets and the whole nine yards, but Dayo wanted to save all that for tomorrow, so we're keeping it simple tonight. But on another note, I still can't believe you came alone. I mean, I'm happy to see you and all, but I was really hoping you'd bring my—"

"I know, I know." Dunni sighed. "But you'll just have to settle for me. Now, will you please take me to the groom-to-be. I can't seem to spot him."

"He's somewhere around here. Come on."

Dunni took a step forward, and her right heel plunged into the grass, causing her to slope awkwardly. The softness beneath her four-inch shoes had the same effect as sinking sand.

"How about you change your shoes before going any further." Tiwa held Dunni's arms, helping her stand upright. "I can't have you falling and busting your head on the fountain. I'll have one of my sisters help you to my room. I'm sure there's a pair of sandals you can wear." Tiwa spotted Dami, her younger sister, not too far away and waved her over.

"Hey," Dami said when she reached them. Her Afro was the most ostentatious part of her appearance. It was big and perfectly rounded, with vibrant flowers and butterflies peeking out of it. It might have been a hard look for anyone else to pull off, but she looked exquisite and whimsical, especially with the sheer floral dress that fell in ruffled layers over her thighs. "Dunni, how's it going? Haven't seen you in forever. Heard you got engaged. Can I see the ring?" She took Dunni's left hand and examined the pear-shaped diamond. "Wow. It's stunning!" She squealed and looked up, expecting the bride-to-be to share her excitement.

"Yes, it's such a beautiful ring. I'm so lucky." Dunni spoke with a steady smile. Usually, the smile wavered, tugged down by a frown. But this time, it stayed in place. She was relieved. Maybe she was getting better at lying. Maybe one day, she would get so good at it, it wouldn't feel like a lie anymore.

"Can you please take Dunni to my room?" Tiwa asked her sister. "She needs a change of shoes."

"Yeah. Sure." Dami led Dunni toward the French doors. "So, when's the wedding?"

"Next year. June."

"Oh my God. It's October now, so you have less than a year. I bet you can't wait, right?"

"Yeah. I can't wait."

❧

Dunni returned to the party in a pair of sandals, the same shade as her dress. With a steadier balance, she approached Tiwa and her fiancé, who stood with two other people.

"Hey." She brought her lips to Tiwa's ear so her whispers were audible. "Thanks for the shoes. You're a lifesaver." Her attention switched to Tiwa's fiancé. With his shaved head and groomed beard, he looked somewhat like the Nollywood actor Richard Mofe-Damijo. He was fifteen years older than Tiwa, but they were a good pair—each equipped with something the other lacked. "Dayo, I haven't said this in person yet, so congratulations. I'm so happy for you both."

"Thank you." He gave her a single air kiss. "I'm so happy you could make it. How's the family?"

"Great. Everyone's great. Unfortunately, Christopher's working. His schedule didn't allow him to make the trip, but he sends his regards."

"No problem. Let me introduce you to some of our guests, some of our good friends." He directed her attention to a lean, tall man. "This is Ade, the son of Governor Edochie. He just started his own advertising firm."

"Congratulations," Dunni said, extending her hand. "And nice to meet you."

"It's a pleasure." Ade smiled and shook her hand. "And thank you."

"This is Gigi," Dayo continued, gesturing to a woman with an edgy, androgynous look. "She's Nollywood's latest rising star."

"And soon to be legend." Gigi presented her hand and grinned. "Nice to meet you."

"You as well."

"And this is Dunni," Tiwa said proudly. "One of my oldest friends. She just completed a Ph.D. in genetics and works in Seattle as a research geneticist. She isn't only beautiful, she's brilliant."

Dunni couldn't help laughing and blushing. "That's the nicest introduction I've ever received."

"Just spitting facts."

With the introductions out of the way, Dunni felt less tense and less alone than she had initially.

"Nicholas!" Tiwa called out, and waved in an undefined direction. "Another one of our good friends just arrived—an hour late." Now she addressed the group. "I swear, he's never on time for anything."

"That's because he first has to decide which girl to bring along." Ade chuckled.

"It doesn't look like he's with anyone tonight," Tiwa confirmed. "Strange."

"Yeah. Very strange." Gigi tilted her shaved head upward and inspected the dimming sky. "Funny. Pigs aren't flying."

The entire group, including Dunni, laughed. When Tiwa warned the butt of the joke was getting closer, they grew quiet.

"Just a little heads-up." Gigi brought her lips to Dunni's ear. The alcohol on her breath was as potent as her perfume. "You're gorgeous, so he'll probably . . . definitely hit on you. Yes, he's handsome and wealthy. But here's a word of advice, resist. Trust me. You'll thank me later."

Dunni giggled because she assumed Gigi was still making fun of this Nicholas character.

"Seriously," Gigi asserted. "I'm not joking." The heavy, smoky makeup that rimmed her eyes added an unsettling element to her stare.

"Um . . . I'm engaged." Dunni raised her left hand and presented the proof, and Gigi laughed as if she'd heard something completely absurd.

"Honey, if he wants you, that pretty piece of jewelry won't stop him. Trust me."

She'd said that twice now. *Trust me*. But Dunni was skeptical. She'd only just met Gigi and was unsure if her warning was warranted or a consequence of the drink in her hand.

"Dunni," Tiwa said, "this is Nicholas, a good friend of ours."

No longer willing to deliberate on Gigi and her advice, Dunni turned away and looked at the man Tiwa introduced, the man she'd called Nicholas.

"Nicholas," Dunni whispered the name, but it felt wrong rolling off her tongue. It felt wrong because it wasn't his name. It wasn't what she used to call him. "Obinna." That was his name. It rolled off her tongue like something sweet—gone and she wanted another taste. "Obinna." She said it slowly this time, relished each syllable, the ones she hadn't uttered in years. Until

now. And just simply saying that name was like conjuring something imagined into existence. "Obinna." Say it three times and
it appears, an urban legend whispered even on the cusp of fear.

"Wait. You two know each other?" Gigi asked, a subtle slur
in her speech.

"Yeah." Obinna cleared his throat and exhaled as his stare
rested heavier on Dunni, unflinching, unblinking, inquiring.

He looked different, a notable contrast from the boy Dunni
once knew. Regardless, something in her—something that had
stayed the same for twelve years, frozen in time—recognized
him. That familiarity in her recognized the same familiarity in
him, something kindred between them.

"I'm so confused right now. What's going on?" Tiwa had
an unusual urgency in her tone. "How do you two know each
other?"

"Dunni and I are . . . um." He moved his lips as if weighing
the impact of his words. "We were—"

"Excuse me." Now more than ever, Dunni was grateful for
the shoes Tiwa had lent her because they allowed her to leave the
garden swiftly, without falling flat on her face.

CHAPTER FOUR

Dunni didn't recall the details—the turns taken to get to this part of the house, an office with high bookshelves covering two walls. She closed the door, bent over the grand mahogany table, and expelled air with the same force she used to inhale it.

It had to be a dream. Yet, she was desperate to believe it was real. Even if it hurt, she wanted it to be real—something more than memories.

Just him, tangible.

The door creaked, and her head snapped up. When it opened completely, Obinna appeared.

Their eyes connected.

Dunni's heart pounded erratically. Her hands shook even though she clenched them. Flutters were rampant in her stomach. Perspiration wet her skin.

WHERE WE END & BEGIN

"Hi."

That was the first word he had said to her in twelve years; it was simple and underwhelming. There was a lot they could talk about, shout about, and even cry about, but then Dunni said, "Hi."

And there was a moment of silence where they looked at each other, their eyes getting reacquainted and comfortable with the new versions of themselves.

She was curvaceous now in places she hadn't been before—her hips and ass. She had the full breasts she didn't have back then, and her natural hair was braided beneath eighteen inches of straight, black weave. There was a tattoo on her shoulder blade, a name that was precious to them both, etched into her brown skin.

He was more handsome now than he had been then—his physique both lean and muscular, his clothes coordinated and undoubtedly expensive, the trimmed hairs around his lips definitely outnumbered twenty. His skin was fairer than it used to be, smooth and unblemished. She presumed it was because he no longer worked under the sun, selling rice and stew alongside his mother. There was something else about him, something he didn't have before. Dunni noted it in his bearing as he strode into the room and shut the door. He was confident, assured. And this new temperament took her aback. She tensed, unsure of what to expect with them alone.

"Dunni," he said quietly, "relax."

"I am relaxed." Her eyes, which darted between him and the closed door, proved she was not. "I'm just not sure what you're doing, Obinna . . . or Nicholas. That's your name now. Right?" She assessed him while working through her confusion.

"That has always been my name. You just preferred calling me Obinna. Remember? So, don't act like I've taken on a whole new persona."

"Well, haven't you?" She didn't know what to think. "What are you even doing here?"

"At a party, mingling with the likes of Tiwa Jolade? That's what you really mean to ask. Isn't it?" He laughed—brief and dry. "It's been twelve years. Did you really expect to come back to Nigeria and find me exactly where you left me—selling rice and *ofada* stew in the market? Did you think I wouldn't evolve and make something of my life?"

"Honestly, the thought never really occurred to me." And that was the truth.

Whenever Dunni thought of him, she didn't envision a grown man with a career and success. She thought of the boy she'd known and loved. Occasionally, she even imagined the life they could have had together. But she never imagined him as he was now. There was a Montblanc watch on his wrist, and she was aware of how much it cost. His beige summer suit had a Ralph Lauren crest embellished on the breast, and his brown suede loafers had the letters *LV* engraved on their small, golden buckles.

"I thought you were above all this," she said.

"Above what?"

She eyed him, glancing at the items with expensive tags.

"Nice things? Luxury? Comfort? Money?" He chuckled again, with an edge. "You see, that's the thing about you rich people. You romanticized poverty as good and pure and hum-bling." He shook his head. "Well, there's nothing good about be-ing unable to feed yourself. There's nothing good about being so damn poor, I was unable to afford the medical care that could have saved my mother's life. There's nothing good about being humiliated by my girlfriend's mother because she deems me street trash, unworthy of her daughter."

Dunni stumbled back as if everything he'd said balled up like a fist and pummeled into her.

Obinna's gaze dropped to the floor. His features softened. In an instant, he was no longer the confident man sporting ex-pensive labels. He was the eighteen-year-old boy, pushing him-self off the concrete squares that paved Dunni's family estate. Shards of broken glass surrounded him. Dunni appeared when the scene was already in progress. Clueless, she looked between her mother and Obinna. She asked questions, but no one an-swered. When Obinna stood, there was blood on the ground; it rushed through a gash in his back. It drenched his shirt. Dunni attempted to run to him, but Paul's firm grip stopped her. She thrashed around and commanded him to let her go. He did not. His job depended on it.

"Obinna." Now, Dunni took a step toward him. "I'm sorry." She didn't think twice about placing her hand on his cheek be-cause, despite the stubble that prickled her palm and the jawline that was stronger and more defined, he was still the boy she knew and loved twelve years ago. "I'm so sorry about your mother. And for what happened that day. I wish—"

"Stop." His thumb brushed over her cheek and gently wiped

away tears. "It wasn't your fault. I've told you this before. Remember?"

She did. Days after the incident, she had snuck out of her house and gone to his. He'd told her then. And she had believed him, but immediately after she left, he had cut all ties with her—stopped responding to her phone calls, text messages, and emails. So whatever guilt she had dispelled, she reclaimed.

"I thought you did," she whispered. "I thought you blamed me because you just . . . you just disappeared."

"Dunni, it's complicated. But it had nothing to do with me blaming you. Nothing at all. Do you understand?"

She nodded, and then it happened naturally—the way their foreheads fell against each other's. She didn't realize the proximity of their bodies until she breathed him in.

When they were younger, he smelled like the *ofada* stew his mother sold in the market. All the ingredients of the rich, red stew were embedded into the fabric of his clothes. Now, he smelled like a man—like the natural and artificial spices a skilled perfumer combines and bottles up. She liked it—this new leathery, smoky fragrance. It had the same warmth and comfort as the fragrance of home cooking.

"Dunni, I can't believe this is you. I can't believe I'm looking at you right now, touching you." He smiled. "I'm hoping this isn't one of my vivid dreams."

He'd been dreaming. About her. The admission shocked Dunni, but what was more shocking was everything in his eyes, everything that should be dead after twelve years but wasn't.

"I've more than missed you," he said. "*Miss* really isn't the right word." He cupped her hand, the one on his cheek. Then he felt it, the bulge on her finger. "What is this?" He pulled back and examined the jewelry. "You're engaged."

"Um . . . yeah." She drew her hand back. "I should go. Back to the party. It was good to see—"

"Wait." He pinched the short bridge of his nose and exhaled. "Just wait. Can we have a minute to talk?"

"It was good to see you again." She completed the sentence he'd interrupted, her tone leveled and professional. "I'm glad you're doing well."

Seconds ago, they were standing so close. It had been easy to fall into such an intimate position. It would be reckless to allow that to happen again. Even though gears turned inside Dunni and angled her body toward his, she couldn't let it happen once more.

"We can't just leave things like this." There was an anxiousness in Obinna's eyes and even in his jerky, uncoordinated movements. "Please. Let's talk."

"Take care of yourself." She went against the gears spinning inside her and headed for the door, bearing the discomfort of resisting what seemed natural.

Tiwa stood at the far end of the hallway, a hand perched on her hip in a demanding pose. "Where in the world have you been?" she asked when Dunni reached her. "I've been looking for you. Is everything okay?"

"Yeah. Of course. Sorry about that. I just needed a moment."

"Okay. And what was all that about—between you and Nicholas?" She squinted and edged close. "Seriously. I'm curious. How do you two know each other?"

Dunni had shared many things with Tiwa but had never spoken about Obinna. It was much too complicated and painful. "We went to the same secondary school. That's all."

"Aw." Tiwa pouted. "Were you guys high school sweethearts?"

"Um . . . yeah. Sort of." She admitted to just a fraction of the full story but decided to give nothing else away.

"Aw. Cute. But that was a long time ago, so who cares? No need to be bothered. You're engaged and he's . . ." She pondered, then sighed. "Well, Nicholas is doing whatever he does. No need to feel awkward 'cause of a silly high school fling. Besides, you've never even mentioned him to me, so how serious could it really have been?" She took Dunni's hand and led her to the garden. "Now, let's get back to the party. I'm not done showing off this dress."

If Tiwa knew the whole story, she would understand that what Obinna and Dunni had was far more than a high school fling.

It was everything love stories shouldn't be.

CHAPTER FIVE

THEN

Every morning, before Obinna went to school, his mother prayed for him. Usually, she asked God to protect her only child in five or six sentences that rounded up to the same meaning. Obinna was familiar with the routine, yet today, he ached to break it.

"Ma, I'm going to be late *sha*," he murmured under his breath. The olive oil on his forehead that his mother had used to draw the sign of the cross dripped and trailed down the bridge of his nose. He rubbed it off with the back of his hand and opened an eye to peek at the front door. Today, he would walk through it and go beyond the ordinariness of Obalende—the area, the people, and his life there that were as mundane as his mother's morning prayers. He would escape it all today. Well, if his mother would wrap things up. "Ma, I have to go *o*. It's my first day. I can't be late."

"Shh," she said sharply, her hand flat on the crown of his shaved head. "In Jesus's name, every evil eye will be blind to Obinna. Jehovah God, cover him with your umbrella and bless him. He shall go and return safely."

Obinna bit his tongue and forced himself to endure the prayers of his overly religious and equally superstitious mother.

Religion and superstition. His mother had an even dose of both, making her a fanatic woman who believed in God and feared the occult. Her fear made her suspect everyone for her misfortune, and her faith made her certain there was only one solution, one remedy to the many catastrophes in her life—prayer.

Months ago, when Obinna told her a wealthy man had come to his school and chosen him—the brightest student in his class— for a scholarship at a private school in Lekki, she hadn't given Obinna credit for working hard. Rather, she'd attributed the good news to her prayers.

"Prayer aligns a man with his fate," she'd said. "Out of all the schools he could have gone to in Lagos, he went to your own. This can only be God. He has answered my prayers."

It annoyed him how much his mother prayed, how much she believed in God, as if her faith and devotion were currency she could exchange for miracles. If that were the case, their life wouldn't be what it was.

Whether his mother admitted it, Obinna's hard work had gotten him the scholarship to one of Lagos's best secondary schools, a school filled with the children of politicians and entrepreneurs, a school his mother could not otherwise afford. He was excited about the opportunity—excited and terrified and tired of his mother's prayers.

It ended eventually with a sound "Amen" from her, followed by a fainter one from him.

"Okay. Let me look at you." She took a step back to inspect him and then another forward to adjust his burgundy coat and tie. "You look sharp. Handsome."

He shoved his hands into his pockets and rocked gently on his heels. "Thank you."

He was no longer eager to walk out the door, to leave her. She was excited, like he was, but also worried. And he knew why. The ordinariness of Obalende was safe. They lived on the first floor of an old two-story flat. Their church wasn't far off, and neither was the market where his mother sold rice and *ofada* stew. She had already made her serving for the day. Usually, she started cooking early in the morning—chopping and grinding, then frying before boiling. The strong aroma of tomatoes and *tatashe* never woke Obinna because it was there, in their one-bedroom home, perpetually. He had grown so accustomed to it, he could no longer detect it. But with a sniff in his direction, others could.

In his neighborhood, people knew him as the son of the woman who sold rice and stew. His mother had a reputation that preceded her, not only because of the aroma that lingered on herself and her son, but because she was an excellent cook. Customers gathered around her shed six days a week. She worked excessively, and even though Obinna's scholarship lightened her financial burden, she still had the rent to consider. The annual fee of ninety-five thousand naira was due in three months. It was a lot of money. Obinna did his part to contribute by working alongside his mother on Saturdays. Sometimes, he even hawked *abacha*. This was their life. It wasn't an easy one, but even with its hardship, it bore a comfort and familiarity. Where Obinna was going had neither of these things.

"Be careful," his mother told him. "Stay out of trouble." Even with her stern stance, her hands firmly planted on her hips, there was a gentleness in her eyes, a plea she did not voice. "If you come to this house with fire on your head, you will put it out with your own hands. Do you hear me? Don't bring any trouble to my doorstep o."

"Yes, ma." And he meant it sincerely.

She was already dealing with a lot, but she handled it well. The bags that sagged beneath her eyes were the only proof of her fatigue. When Obinna's father was still around, things were better—far from perfect, but better than they were now. He was a mechanic and a dreamer, eager for so much more than the life they managed. He spoke of America often, so sure his fortune was on that side of the world. Obinna remembered the night his parents argued when they believed he was asleep.

"Go to America to do what? Eh?" his mother had asked his father, her hushed tone strained as she fought the urge to shout. "Aren't there millionaires in this very country—wealthy and successful people? Do they have two heads? Don't they have one head just like me and you?"

"Mama Obinna," his father said tenderly. "There are better

opportunities there. People are making it in that country. I will go, and once I am settled, I will bring you and Obinna."

"God forbid," she hissed. "I have heard how they are killing black men in that country. And now you want me to deliver my son to them, so they can kill him for me, *abi*? *Tufiakwa*. Obinna is not going to any *yeye* America and neither are you. If God wants us to be millionaires in this country, we will be it. And if he wants us to be paupers, so be it. His will be done."

"But—"

"Eh!" She'd cut him off, no longer whispering. "Papa Obinna, just mind yourself *o*! Mind yourself. Don't let the devil use you to disturb my peace this night. Just mind yourself. I've already said my own."

After that night, there were no more talks of America. But months later, Obinna's father packed a bag and slung it over his shoulder. "I won't let poverty kill me in this country." He had hugged Obinna but had not dared touch his wife, who glared at him without saying a word. "The plan is to go to Europe first and from there, America. I will contact you once I get there and hopefully, send money shortly after."

He walked out the door that day, with no intention of getting on a plane that would take him to his destination. He couldn't do that without a visa. He'd found other means, dangerous means that didn't guarantee his feet would ever touch American soil, and maybe they hadn't. Two years had gone by, and they had not heard a word from him. Maybe he hadn't made it. Many didn't make those sorts of journeys. Or maybe he had and had forgotten about them. Either way, Obinna's mother never spoke of it.

She only bore the responsibilities he left behind. And with this, Obinna knew he couldn't add to his mother's load.

"Don't worry," he told her. "I won't cause any trouble."

She pressed her lips and looked at him for a long while before nudging her head toward the door. "*Oya*. Go. Don't be late."

His steps were reluctant, but he left eventually. He got on a public bus that took him to a side of Lagos he had never been to before.

⁓

At only seventeen, Obinna lived his life with low expectations. He didn't have faith like his mother, and the Sunday mornings and Wednesday evenings they spent in church had not changed that. He was practical. And when he wasn't practical, he was pessimistic. He found these two options left very little room for disappointments. Today, however, his expectations increased almost automatically. The environment he was in inspired it; it inspired hoping and dreaming and wanting. In fact, it demanded it.

"If you are here, within these walls, it means you are extraordinary. Therefore, you have a responsibility to do extraordinary things," the school's headmaster said as they walked through the immense campus.

The tour consisted of a warning disguised as a routine speech for new students. The contempt in the headmaster's gaze marked the difference. Obinna, who had no intention of causing trouble, listened halfheartedly. The setting—the pool, the basketball court, the science laboratory, and the tennis court they were now walking past—distracted him. *Am I dreaming?* He'd asked himself that several times already and still couldn't believe the answer was no. He wasn't dreaming. This was his life now—his school. Trimmed grass surrounded the large beige building that didn't have a coating of grime or chipped paint. The school was remarkable and so different from his last.

"Mr. Arinze."

Obinna heard the sharpness in his name and suspected the headmaster had called him several times already. He turned from the tennis court and faced the stout, gray-haired man, who wore a well-tailored suit that made him appear more powerful and imposing than he probably would have without it. "Yes, sir?"

"Have you been listening to me?"

"Yes. Of course, sir." He rushed out the words and hoped they were convincing. When the expression on the headmaster's face revealed they weren't, he conceded. "I'm sorry, sir."

The headmaster sighed, then turned Obinna's attention to the person standing in front of them. "Meet Miss Damijo."

This time, Obinna's attention was exactly where it was supposed to be. Frankly, he couldn't imagine it being anywhere else. He froze while watching her, scared the slightest movement would cause her attention to shift elsewhere, away from him. He didn't want that to happen. And it didn't.

They looked at each other. And he thought that strangers shouldn't look into each other's eyes like this—so invasive, so bold, and unwavering. But they did. And his heart moved in a way it hadn't before. The quickness scared and excited him. When the corners of her lips lifted in a smile, he did something unexpected.

Obinna thought of his mother. Rationally, he should have thought of love at first sight. It was a concept that suited the situation perfectly. But he thought of his mother. "Prayer," she always said, "aligns a man with his fate."

How many prayers had she said? How many *amen*s had he said in response, in agreement? Countless. His mother believed prayer had aligned him with the opportunity to attend this school, and that was his fate. But something intangible convinced Obinna otherwise. And even though he didn't have faith as strong as his mother's, even though he was practical and pessimistic, he didn't deny the conviction that his fate was not this school.

It was her.

"You can call me Dunni," she said, extending her hand to him.

He took it, and that simple act—hands touching—activated something inside him, something that had always been there but lain dormant. He didn't know what that something was, but it was alive now, pulsating with a vigor he had to adjust to by breathing more deeply, with a lot more intention because he suddenly forgot the simple mechanics of inhaling and exhaling. A handshake had done that. *A handshake.*

"Miss Damijo's father is the reason you're here," the headmaster said.

Obinna didn't understand that bit of information. Unwillingly, he let go of Dunni's hand and turned to the headmaster. "I don't understand what you mean, sir."

"Her father is the gentleman sponsoring your education here."

"What?" Obinna turned to Dunni. He hadn't met the man who'd been so generous. His headmaster at his former school had only called him into his office to tell him the news. Since that day, he'd wondered what had provoked a man to be so kind to a stranger. He still wondered. "Why? Why did he do it?" The question was for Dunni, but the headmaster answered.

"Every year, he picks a first-class student from an underprivileged school and sponsors their last year of secondary school. This year, you are the lucky student."

"He wanted me to give you this," Dunni said, handing Obinna a white box. "It's a laptop. He thought you might need one."

"Really?" A computer. He'd always wanted one, always envisioned his fingers moving quickly against the keys. He imagined all the things he could accomplish with it and took the gift while saying multiple thank-yous.

"Miss Damijo will escort you. You both are in the same class." The headmaster's hand dropped on Obinna's shoulder. "Have a good first day and remember everything I said."

"Yes, sir. No problem, sir."

"Mm-hmm." He eyed the pair then turned and strolled toward his office.

They were alone. Obinna and Dunni. He liked their names side by side. They went well together—the perfect pairing, like bread and butter or *boli* and groundnut.

"Class is this way. We have biology."

He walked alongside her, watching from the corner of his eye. Her long braids swung against her back as she moved. Like him, she wore a burgundy blazer; it fit her slim figure perfectly, and so did the pleated gray skirt that flapped against her knees. She was beautiful, and there was something about her—a fierceness that came across to him so clearly. He liked it. Very much, in fact. He suspected she was the golden girl of the school, someone people feared and admired. He instantly felt the need to measure up—to be good enough, someone deserving of someone like her. He wished that in a matter of seconds, he could add weight and muscles to his naturally slim build and polish the blemish of a rough life from his fair skin so it could gleam as hers did. He wished he had the confidence and swag of a man who had enough, who had a lot. But wishes remained just that. And he remained unchanged.

"You have something on your head," Dunni said, her stride slowing. "On your forehead."

"Oh?" He touched his forehead and felt the oil his mother had used to pray for him. Embarrassment made his cheeks grow hot, especially as Dunni stopped walking and faced him.

"What is that?"

"Um . . ." He didn't want to tell the girl he'd just met about his religious and superstitious mother who sold rice and stew for a living. But Dunni's unrelenting stare proved she wouldn't walk away without an answer. "Olive oil. My mother uses it when she prays for me."

Gradually, Dunni's straight lips curved upward. When she started to laugh, Obinna was caught between marveling at the sound of her laughter and cowering behind the rectangular hedges that aligned the walkway.

He had ruined everything. Why hadn't he lied? He could have said anything, no matter how outrageous.

"I can't believe she does that—douses you with olive oil." Her shoulders shook as she giggled. "My grandmother does the same."

"Huh?" Obinna had not expected that. "Really?"

"Yeah. In fact, she carries a small bottle of olive oil in her purse in case she needs to pray on the go."

Obinna chuckled—amused and stunned. "Seriously?" He didn't admit his mother often stuffed a small bottle in her bra because, in the comparison of overly religious relatives, his mother would likely appear more unhinged. Maybe that information was best reserved. "That's extreme," he said instead.

"Yeah. Well, my grandmother is a little strange. Some might even say, very strange."

"Oh? Why?"

"Well, she has these dreams or premonitions." Dunni shrugged, and her laughter stopped completely. "I don't know what to call them. But she sees bad things—people dying and stuff. And somehow, her dreams come true. So she prays a lot." After her last words, Dunni blinked sharply. "I have never said that to anyone." Her stare turned accusatory as if Obinna had dug inside her and pulled those words out himself, violated her privacy.

He noticed this and thought of apologizing, even though he had done nothing wrong. Maybe he would follow the apology with a promise to never repeat her words to anyone. Those were good options and maybe the most sensible ones, but a question bothered him.

"Why? Why haven't you ever told anyone?"

Dunni dropped her head and chewed her bottom lip. "Well." She looked at him, and her gaze softened. "You know how people can be—judgmental, afraid of something they don't understand. I don't want them giving her any labels."

Yes, Obinna knew how people could be because his mother was one of those people. He was not. "You have nothing to worry about, Dunni." He liked her name—the way it felt on his tongue, the way it sounded in his ears. It was a Yoruba name and probably an abbreviation. But he was Igbo and uncertain of the other missing parts. It didn't matter. He would take the name as it was. He just wanted to say it again—get a better feel of it, like when rich people swish wine in their mouths before spitting it out. "Dunni."

"Yeah?" She looked at him expectantly.

He rushed to string a few words together, to appear like he wasn't a madman chanting her name. "I . . . um . . ."

"Here." She leaned into him and brought her thumb to his forehead. "You didn't get all the oil."

Obinna stood erect, frozen, stupefied. Gently, she rubbed his forehead, her eyes engaged with his, a playful smile tilting her lips. Obinna's toes curled, and his breath hung in his throat.

"Your mother really packs it on." She laughed softly, then stepped back.

Inwardly, Obinna struggled but eventually found his voice. "Yes. She's incredibly generous. Unfortunately."

"She does it because she cares about you. While my grand-mother does it because . . . well, when she anoints someone, it's usually because she's had a bad dream about them. She prays to stop it from happening."

"And does it work—the prayers?"

Dunni shook her head. "Never. My grandmother always says that the future has already happened, and we're just trying to catch up to it." She huffed then turned away and continued along the path that led to the school's entrance. "Come on. We're already running late."

Obinna walked beside her, at ease. Before he'd met Dunni, he was practical and pessimistic. Now, he wanted to broaden his narrow perspective and adopt the narrative that there was an alternate reality—years away—where he and Dunni were together, a couple, maybe even married. If the future had already happened, then every step they took from now on would lead them to exactly where they were meant to be.

And maybe, it was with each other.

CHAPTER SIX

Dunni sat in front of the vanity in her room and clipped on pear-shaped diamond earrings. She thought of wearing something less ostentatious but decided the jewelry would act as a distraction from her drowsy, puffy eyes.

She hadn't slept the previous night. She'd returned from the rehearsal dinner in a daze and had lain in bed, reliving the moment she and Obinna saw each other; the moment they spoke; the moment they touched.

At dinner, she'd acted composed. Obinna had disappeared after their encounter in the office, so maintaining a calm guise had been easy. Though, when she returned to her family's house that night, closed her bedroom door, turned off the lights, and curled under the covers, she broke down. She muffled her cries with a pillow and her screams with two pillows until her eyes dried out and her throat grew sore.

Now, she stared at her reflection and hoped the flashy earrings would distract people from her exhausted and distraught state.

"I see you're almost ready for the wedding." Iya Agba entered the room and sat on the edge of the bed. "You look beautiful."

"Thank you." Dunni met her grandmother's gaze in the mirror, and then her stare shifted to the small bottle the elderly woman held. "*Rárá*. You are not putting that on my head."

"Just a little *na*." She twisted her hand against the cap and broke the seal on the bottle. "It won't be noticeable at all."

"Iya, I have a full face of makeup. You are not putting olive oil on my head—no matter how small." The sternness in her eyes and tone conveyed her seriousness.

"Okay. Relax. I will wait until you return." Iya Agba tightened the cap on the bottle. "But our time is so short. The wedding is today and then tomorrow, you are leaving. You didn't even spend time with me. Eh? Is that how you are?" Her thin lips shriveled into a tight pout. "Is that how you treat me?"

Dunni turned in the swivel chair and faced her grandmother, a woman she loved dearly but saw rarely. "My flight is at night, so we can spend the day together."

"And what would we do?"

"I don't know. Anything you want to."

"Okay." She smiled. "Well, I want us to go to church and see my pastor. He will say a quick prayer for you."

Dunni had fallen into a trap set by a sly old woman.

"Iya Agba—"

"I've already made the appointment with him. I've told him

about the situation—the dreams I've been having. I've been praying myself, but maybe we should see a pastor this time."

This time. Dunni heard the expectation in those words—the hope of a better outcome. The other times her grandmother prayed and smeared olive oil on foreheads yielded no results. Things had played out just as she had seen. This time would be different. Well, at least she hoped the intervention of a pastor would make it different.

"This pastor is a very powerful man of God," Iya Agba said. "He will pray for you and anoint you. Whatever the devil is planning won't stand. In Jesus's name. Amen."

Dunni watched her grandmother blankly. This was the aspect of Nigeria she had not missed while in America—the way everything linked to the supernatural. No matter what religion a person was—Christian or Muslim—they acknowledged this otherworldliness, and growing up, Dunni had too. How could she not with a grandmother who accurately predicted future tragedies? How could she not when many Nollywood films depicted long-nailed witches plotting and chanting in covens, *babalawos* stirring concoctions in calabashes, and *mami watas* taking the guise of innocent and beautiful house girls?

How could Dunni not acknowledge this otherworldliness when it was woven into her culture—the reasons many were prayerful as well as paranoid? It seemed impossible until she moved to America. Within months there, she'd realized that Americans focused only on the visible, the explainable. A classmate got fired from a part-time job, and he'd credited it to downsizing. Another got into a car accident and had simply attributed it to being at the wrong place. In Nigeria, however, there would have been multiple spiritual explanations. A relative in the village working alongside a *babalawo* to afflict family members would have likely been the winner; it was a popular narrative.

Dunni wanted more practical answers to life. That was why she had found solace in her studies—in things she could place under a microscope, in explanations and conclusions that were multifaceted yet within the bounds of logic. Because of this, she wanted to discount her grandmother's dreams. But more than that, she wanted to believe a promise made between two young lovers and sealed with blood meant nothing.

Her eyes lowered to the flesh-colored scar across her palm. She'd felt a brief surge of energy beneath it yesterday, the instant her eyes locked with Obinna's. Though, she had attributed it to adrenaline—a probable scientific explanation. It was easier for Dunni to wholly lean on science as she had for years, but as the granddaughter of a woman who saw events before they occurred, Dunni knew, regretfully, that sometimes, science told only part of a story.

CHAPTER SEVEN

The wedding guests wore a forest-green *aso ebi*. The color complemented the rich brown of Dunni's complexion, and her one-shoulder mermaid gown flattered her physique. While most of the women wore a *gele*, Dunni did not. Her hair, slicked behind her ears, fell over her back in waves.

She had put extra effort into her appearance—coated her lips with a ruby-red shade, dusted a bronze shimmer onto her cheekbones, and attached false lashes that made her eyes bold and smoldering. All this was for him. Though she didn't want to admit it and denied the thought each time it crossed her mind.

She scanned the Gothic architecture of the church and admired the clean wedding décor because, of course, she would never admit searching for him. When the music started, her eyes stopped roaming.

The bridesmaids—Tiwa's three sisters—ambled down the

aisle, one after another. They wore white strapless gowns with a short lace train, and anyone who thought the color would take away from the bride was silenced the moment Tiwa stepped through the double doors. Guests stood and gazed at her, mesmerized. The long-sleeve dress was exquisite, with the upper half completely encrusted with pearls and crystals and the lower half a full skirt of charmeuse silk. She approached her groom in a graceful stride, a bouquet of red roses in her hands. When she reached the altar, the congregation retook their seats. That's when Dunni's eyes caught his.

Obinna.

They were on opposite ends of the church, separated by the aisle. But even with the distance, they shared a look that was deep and intimate. Dunni recalled the first time they had met. They'd shared a similar look, and her body had responded as it did now—skin heating and tingling and nerves gnawing at her insides. All those years ago, it hadn't been love at first sight. There was a simplicity in that phrase that didn't fit the situation. She had felt something else, something beyond the reach of understanding. Now twelve years later, she felt another *something else* and struggled to name it. She wondered briefly if it could be attraction or maybe even love—the remnants the years had not wiped away.

Yesterday, as they looked at each other with their foreheads touching, Dunni had seen it in Obinna's eyes—what should have died twelve years ago but had not.

It hadn't died—not for him.

And maybe not for her.

CHAPTER EIGHT

THEN

Obinna stepped into the classroom cautiously—one foot inside and then seconds later, the other followed. He tested his weight against the floor to ensure it wouldn't break through and take him under like in one of his nightmares where he fell endlessly. The firmness beneath his feet further confirmed he was not dreaming. With that sureness, he faced the students whose inquisitive glares were fixed on him.

"Miss Okafor." Dunni addressed the young woman in a gray pantsuit. "This is Obinna."

"Yes. Of course. I've been expecting you." She left her position beside the whiteboard and extended a hand to him. "Welcome to Lekki Secondary School."

"Thank you, ma." He shook her hand firmly. "It's good to be here."

"And we're happy to have you. Why don't you tell us a little about yourself? What school did you attend prior to coming here?"

"St. Paul Secondary School, ma."

"And your parents? What do they do for a living?"

That question. Why did she have to ask that question?

Obinna glanced at his classmates, who he assumed were the children of wealthy, influential people. In a school like this, it was more than likely. People like him couldn't afford to come here. Unless through a scholarship. He looked at Dunni, and a wrinkle formed between his eyebrows. He wished he had a different answer, something that would help him blend into her world.

"Go on," Miss Okafor pressed, eager to resume her lesson. "We're waiting."

Obinna thought of lying, but the idea didn't sit well with him. A lie implied he was ashamed of his mother, who worked tirelessly to keep him clothed, fed, and sheltered. And he was not.

"My mother is a street food vendor." He looked at Dunni, then he turned to the teacher before finally facing his new classmates. "She sells rice and stew."

A loud snort came after a period of silence. It didn't shock Obinna. He'd expected it.

"Two years ago, it was the son of a tailor. Last year, it was the daughter of a carpenter. This year, the son of a street food vendor. Rice and stew." A boy who sat at the back of the class chuckled. He was bulky, but in a way that made him appear wealthy. He looked like someone who was well fed, someone who had surplus to eat, including the expensive American foods sold at franchise restaurants. He looked like someone who had tasted a hot dog and a hamburger and even pizza—all the things Obinna had never tried. "Dunni, your father's charity cases always make the first day of school more entertaining."

"Emeka, enough!" Miss Okafor scowled and braced a hand on her hip, the perfect stance for the scolding she seemed prepared to give. Though, she didn't get the opportunity because Dunni spoke instead.

"Shut up, Emeka." Her tone possessed a sternness and authority Miss Okafor's hadn't. "Whether his mother sells food on the street or sits in an office, what does it matter? You know what they say, there's honor in honest labor. Make sure your father, the businessman"—she threw air quotes around *businessman*—"gets the memo."

A series of *oh*s and chuckles resounded around the room, but Obinna was no longer the butt of the joke.

Emeka shrunk in his seat. He glowered at Dunni, his face tense as if sustaining the sting of a firm slap. Dunni met his stare without flinching and smirked, undoubtedly taking pleasure in his humiliation. When Emeka looked away and took a sudden interest in the textbook on his desk, the class roared with laughter.

"Okay. That's enough," Miss Okafor shouted over the chaos. "Everyone settle down! Now!"

The students released a few soft chuckles before going quiet.

"Dunni and Obinna, please take a seat."

At the two-person desk stationed in the back of the class, they sat side by side. Obinna, stunned by what Dunni had done, stared at her.

"Rice and stew." She glanced at him. "I guess that explains why you smell like that."

"Um . . . smell like what?"

"Like home," Dunni whispered. "Home cooking."

Obinna grabbed his jacket and lifted the collar to his nose. "I don't smell anything." But obviously, she did. Did it bother her? Could she stand sitting beside him? "I'm sorry."

"No. Don't apologize." She smiled and shuffled along the bench they sat on, nearing him. "I like it."

Obinna frowned, but as his confusion receded, his lips extended into a smile. Dunni was certainly odd. She was also mystifying. And though Obinna never had the patience for puzzles nor an interest in them, he suddenly had a generous portion of both and wanted to devote them to collecting fragments of Dunni and piecing them together.

He wanted to know her.

⁓

Obinna's former school didn't have a lunchroom. Usually, students ate in the schoolyard, leaning against the eroded building, sitting on the cracked steps or on the football field with patches of yellow grass sparsely scattered over red soil. The lunchroom at Lekki Secondary School was similar to the one in *High School Musical*. When Obinna was younger, his neighbor bought a pirated copy of the movie and lent it to him. Obinna watched the movie several times within the two weeks he was permitted to borrow it, and he remembered how the two-story lunchroom had circular tables and the school's name painted on the wall with bright colors as it was here. With the similarities, he expected everyone to break out in song. Of course, that did not happen.

As he walked between the tables, clenching his small flask, he felt a strange pinch of isolation—one he had never felt before. He didn't know where to sit and wondered who, among the students peering at him disparagingly, would accept him into their fold. He had watched several American movies that reflected this exact scene. Maybe he would end up eating his lunch in the bathroom like most of the characters did.

"Hey."

The soft voice jolted Obinna from his thoughts. Dunni stood to his left, smiling. He hadn't seen her since their biology class. After it ended, they'd gone their separate ways—she to mathematics and him to English. Seeing her again sent a surge of relief through him, and his stiff shoulders dropped.

"Hi," he said with a collected tone he hoped hid the degree of his relief and elation.

"Come. Sit with me." Dunni walked to an empty table at the back of the cafeteria, and he followed and settled down beside her. "So. How's your first day going?" She pulled a small container from her lunch bag and flipped open the lid, revealing a portion of spaghetti.

"It's going well." Obinna followed her lead and placed his flask on the table. When he twisted the cover open, soft steam escaped and meandered before disappearing. "This place is nothing like my old school. The classrooms, the teachers are . . . better." He dug a spoon into the flask and mixed the red stew with the white rice. After chewing and swallowing a spoonful, he noticed Dunni staring at his food.

"That looks and smells . . ." She bit her lip and met his gaze. "Did your mother make that?"

He nodded.

Dunni abandoned her plate of spaghetti and shifted near him. "Can I try some?" She took his spoon before he could answer. "Do you mind?"

"Um . . . no. Go ahead." He looked at the spoon in her hand. His spit was on it. Though, that didn't seem to faze her.

She scooped the red rice and shoved it into her mouth. "Mmm." Her eyes rolled upward as she chewed. "Oh my God."

"You like it?"

She bobbed her head. After swallowing, she laughed. "Sorry. You must think I'm such a *longa* throat."

To that, Obinna laughed harder. "I think you're the furthest thing from that." He moved his flask to her. "Here. Have as much as you like. I don't mind."

Dunni studied him; her gaze darted between his dark eyes and his lips that had a light sheen of red oil. "Why don't we share," she suggested. "Unless you'd like to switch and have my lunch."

He looked over her shoulder and examined the spaghetti coated with a pale sauce and speckled with green leaves. "No offense, but that looks tasteless."

"Trust me," Dunni said, "it is."

They laughed, and maybe their laughter was contagious, or maybe it was the influence Dunni seemed to have, but people gradually occupied the empty seats at their table. One person talked about their summer holiday in Amsterdam, and another complained about a teacher who'd assigned homework on the first day of school. And what Obinna thought would have been an awkward conversation between him and his peers, was light-hearted banter and jokes that weren't at his expense. And he knew it was all because of Dunni.

Emeka, with his chest puffed out, marched to the table as if trying to assert his position as big man on campus. He looked from Obinna to Dunni and shook his head. "So because I was joking with your friend, you just wanted to bite my head off? *Shebi*, Dunni? Why do you always have to overreact? Why does one plus one always have to equal ten with you? Someone cannot even joke with you? Eh? Is that how you are?"

Dunni took the spoon Obinna extended to her and focused on the piece of beef at the bottom of the flask; she pressed the edge of the spoon against it, trying to split it in two. When she succeeded, she scooped one half into her mouth and chewed while watching Emeka with a blank stare. Everyone waited for her reaction, even Emeka, who had given his version of an apology by crediting his rudeness to a joke. Now, he waited for her forgiveness, her acceptance, her permission to sit.

When Obinna first met Dunni, he sensed a fierceness in her and suspected she was someone people admired and feared. Now, he was certain of it.

She rolled her eyes and groaned. "Emeka, just sit down and stop talking. *Haba!* That's your problem. You talk too much. In fact, your tongue must be tired. Close your mouth and let it rest. Eh? At least for one minute."

The crowd at the table chuckled, even Emeka. He shoved and imposed his large physique between two people. "Obinna," he said, "be careful with this girl o. Her own is too much. She will just be dishing out insults anyhow."

Obinna watched Dunni lean back and sip from her water bottle, a satisfied grin across her face and a hand on her stomach. "No," he said, meeting Emeka's stare. "I think she dishes out exactly what's fair."

Everyone laughed at Emeka, who rolled his eyes.

But Dunni did not. Her expression didn't give away her amusement or anything at all. But under the table, her legs lost the tension that held them upright. They relaxed. One tilted and met Obinna's leg. His heart broke out into an uneven flutter, and then slowly, with caution and anticipation, he rested his leg against hers.

They stayed that way throughout the lunch period, knees touching under a crowded table.

CHAPTER NINE

Tiwa Jolade's wedding was notable, not only because of the weight her family's name carried in Lagos, but because she had married a man fifteen years older than her, a man who had been her late father's friend. News about their relationship had been buzz-worthy—the hot topic among elite Lagosians. Now, with a marriage certificate that legitimized the relationship, buzz dwindled among guests who lost enthusiasm to gossip and judge. Most had hoped for a spectacle—perhaps Tiwa's mother objecting to the union like a domineering mother in a Nollywood film. That had not been the case, and for some, that was a disappointment.

At the reception, Dunni sat at a table for six—Gigi to her left and an empty chair to her right. A place card rested in front of the vacant seat, atop the folded white napkin. Dunni avoided reading it, too afraid of disappointment and too unnerved by her secret expectation. Instead, she admired the lush décor—the grand banquet hall adorned with jewel-toned flowers and hanging greenery. Two large circular tables, one hosting the bride's family and the other hosting the groom's, had an opening in the center where a tree came through—its trunk an interlacing twine of gold metal rather than stiff wood and its green shrub bursting with lilac wisterias, ruby roses, and pink peonies. Lights twinkled between the vibrant flowers and gave the illusion of fireflies. On a long table with tall flora centerpieces and candelabras, Tiwa and Dayo sat with their bridesmaids and groomsmen on either side of them.

While bringing her third glass of champagne to her lips, Dunni looked at the empty chairs at the table—the one beside her and the one Ade had vacated minutes ago. He'd been in and out of the hall, receiving phone calls. Without his constant "Hello? Can you hear me now?" Dunni caught the conversation between the two young women also at the table. Though their words became more audible the instant the music stopped for the MC's comical commentary.

"I still can't believe she married him—her father's friend," one said, her glossed lips pursed downward.

"*Abi?*" The other eyed the newlyweds in the manner a window-shopper eyes something they want but cannot afford. "It's pure madness."

When they realized the absence of music had exposed them, they dropped their eyes and shrank in their seats.

"It's obvious their happiness is paining you. It's just eating you up, isn't it?" Gigi said, casually swinging her champagne flute. "But if you can't swallow your bitterness and be happy for them, then please find the nearest bridge and jump." She brought the glass to her plump lips, which were coated in a cherry-red shade. There was a sharpness in her gaze as she sipped slowly, an unspoken threat that didn't need the weight of words.

The two women, lacking the nerve they possessed when the music pulsated, occupied themselves with their cutlery. One picked up a fork and tucked it under the bed of *jollof* rice she hadn't touched since the server placed it in front of her. She chewed the grains of rice, then pushed them down with a tight jaw as if swallowing the bitterness Gigi had referred to.

Dunni turned to Gigi, who wore the content expression of a mother who had successfully disciplined her children. "Okay," she whispered. "I think I want to be you when I grow up."

Gigi laughed in the same languid manner with which she'd sipped her drink. She coughed up one chuckle and seconds later, coughed up another, and then more came out in a lively burst. Gigi's laughter had a certain quality, something that implied she was at ease—unbothered. Dunni's laughter hadn't had that quality in years, so she found herself admiring Gigi until something shifted in the corner of her eye.

After releasing a deep breath, she turned to the chair beside her, the one that had been empty for two hours but wasn't anymore.

"Hi," she whispered.

"Hi," he said.

That one word always seemed to linger between them, before they gathered the nerve to say more. For a moment, it was enough—simple, cordial, and casual. But then the moment passed and there was a demand to say more—to confront each other, offer explanations, and reveal truths.

"Nicholas." One of the women who had been bashing the bride and groom sat to Obinna's right. She angled her body toward him and leaned forward, her cleavage displayed before its only intended audience. "I've been waiting for you." Her teeth grazed her bottom lip. "Where have you been hiding?"

"Um . . ." Obinna turned from Dunni reluctantly. "Cynthia. Hi. I was caught up with some things at the office. Unfortunately."

"Yeah. Truly unfortunate." She narrowed her dark, long-lashed eyes. "But you're here now, so let's make up for lost time. Yeah? After all, Nicholas, we haven't seen each other in ages."

Nicholas. Dunni hated the way Cynthia pronounced the name, sensuous and slithering as if licking each syllable. But more than that, she hated the name itself. Obinna, she knew well. She remembered all the details of that boy—his awkward, shy disposition and even the contours of his lean body. He was an image she'd framed and hung on the walls of her mind for years.

Nicholas was a stranger. Dunni didn't know this man. It seemed like he was a song she had forgotten the lyrics to. She had only the melody, the one she'd hummed for years. But she needed the words. She needed to know Nicholas.

Why couldn't she be content with the fraction of him she had? Why did she want more? Why did Cynthia's shameless flirting bother her so much? *Why?*

If Dunni understood the inner workings of her mind, then

maybe she could have prevented what happened next. Perhaps dissecting her logic and isolating the distinctive *why* could have helped her restrain her emotions and control her motor skills. But the lack of understanding caused her hand to slip under the table and fall on Obinna's leg.

He turned from Cynthia swiftly—his spine straight and his wide eyes on Dunni. Her skin flushed with warmth as his alert eyes turned sultry. When his hand slipped under the table and fell over hers, her body tensed with need.

It was still there . . . this thing between them—chemistry, attraction. How? After being apart for more than a decade. After the distance he kept despite promising never to. After she accepted the marriage proposal of another man. How could there still be this thing between them?

"Um . . . guys." Gigi placed a light hand on Dunni's shoulder. "Maybe pretend, at least for a little while, that it isn't just the two of you at this table or in this room."

Gigi's soft tone brought Dunni to her senses, and she withdrew her hand. "I . . . I'm sorry," she told Obinna. Her voice shook, unsteady as she tried to piece a lie together. "I didn't mean to . . . do that. It was an accident."

Obinna slanted his head, and his assessing gaze shifted over her delicate facial features. When he seemed satisfied with his inspection, he straightened his head. "Dunni, even after all these years, I can tell when you're lying to me."

"Years?" Cynthia blurted. "You two have known each other for years? How?"

"Secondary school sweethearts." Gigi tapped her fingers

against her phone screen. When she looked up, she smirked at Cynthia. "By the looks of things, it's safe to say your chances with the eligible bachelor are slim to none."

"Oh, please." Cynthia's friend, whose *gele* had shifted to an awkward angle on her head, snorted. "Secondary school. That was ages ago. Besides." She focused on Dunni's finger. "You're engaged. No?"

"Yes. I'm engaged."

"Well, congratulations." Cynthia scooted closer to Obinna. "So." She propped an elbow on the table and placed her chin in her open palm. "Tell us about this lucky man. What's his name?"

"Christopher."

"Oh. And what does Christopher do for a living?"

"He's a doctor—a pediatric surgeon." It was stupid of Dunni to entertain Cynthia's passive cattiness, to answer her questions. But she didn't stop. She answered each one—not for Cynthia but for Obinna. Even with the sadness that washed over his features, he had to hear this. He had to know that, despite what she had seen in his eyes yesterday and what she'd felt seconds ago, nothing could happen between them.

"And how long have you and your fiancé known each other?" Cynthia went on.

"A year."

"Aw. Almost as long as Nicholas and I have known each other?" Her fingers traced the gold embroidery on his green *agbada*, and he didn't cringe or flick her hand away.

Dunni felt a sickening churn in her stomach.

"We met through a mutual friend," Cynthia carried on. "I

still remember how he looked at me, how he couldn't keep his hands off me."

"Gosh. Would you do us all a favor and just shut up?" Gigi released an exasperated sigh. "Nicholas has basically fucked his way through half of Lagos, so stop acting like you two had an epic romance. Seriously. You're embarrassing yourself and nauseating the rest of us."

Dunni went rigid. She looked at Obinna, prepared for him to deny what Gigi had said. But he avoided her eyes—the sign of a guilty man. The stomach-turning sensation she'd felt earlier intensified. She stood, grabbed her purse, and rushed through the banquet hall, moving between servers who balanced empty plates on trays.

With the length of her gown in her hand, she came down the imperial stairs, and her heels clicked against the foyer's glimmering marble floor. She paced at the base of the stairs. Her hands shook. Her breaths were short, matching her brisk heartbeat.

How many women had there been after her? How many had he made love to? How many had slept in his bed and woken up to him every morning? How many had he loved, while she struggled, unable to completely give herself to any man, even one as good as Christopher? Obinna had carried on with his life while she bore so much. More than he would ever know.

Behind her, footsteps descended the stairs. She hoped it wasn't him. She needed a moment to compose herself before returning inside. But then the footsteps stopped, and she knew.

She felt him, even though he hadn't touched her.

"Dunni," he sighed her name. "Let me explain."

She spun around and scoffed. "I hate you."

"No, you don't," he responded coolly.

"Don't tell me how I feel. You don't know."

"Of course I know. It's been twelve years, but you're still Dunni. My Dunni."

"Don't call me that. I'm not . . ." She glanced at her engagement ring. "I'm getting married."

"I know." He rubbed his forehead, then huffed. "But you can't marry this guy, Dunni. We both know that."

"Seriously? You, of all people, have no right to tell me that."

"I'm just saying—"

"No!" Her voice roared with an unexpected force. This had been inside her for years—a festering mixture of resentment, anger, and heartache that now erupted. "You disappeared! You left me! I called! I wrote emails, and nothing! For twelve years. Nothing. Not a damn word."

He opened his mouth, but she didn't give him the opportunity to speak.

"And don't you dare say you didn't get my emails because I know you did. I know you read them."

She had installed an application in her account that notified her when a recipient opened her email. So she had been aware each time Obinna opened one of her extensive letters, begging him to contact her, explaining she had something very important to tell him, stressing she was in trouble—in serious trouble. Each one opened. And not one reply.

"Why didn't you answer them?" Like air leaking out of a balloon, anger left her voice and it shrunk to a whisper. "Why did you just disappear? Why did you leave me? We had a plan." After all these years, she just wanted answers. Going on about how much she hated him when she didn't accomplished nothing. But maybe answers would. Maybe answers would give her closure and help her be the kind of woman Christopher deserved. "Please. Just tell me."

He blew out a breath. "I know I owe you an explanation."

"Then give it to me."

"I don't think we're in the right place for this discussion." He looked around the foyer, filled with wedding guests, some eyeing them. "We should go somewhere. Maybe to my place. We'll have privacy. Or maybe you would prefer a hotel?"

A hotel room with Obinna. It didn't seem like the right move. She shook her head.

"Then what about your place? I'm guessing you're staying with your family. Should we go there?"

"What?" she said, stunned he had suggested it. How could he think about going back there? Was he trying to prove something— that what happened that day no longer fazed him? Whatever his intention, it was a terrible idea for so many reasons. "No. Not there. We can't go there."

"Then my place?"

Dunni had asked for answers, but frankly, she wanted more of a drive-thru transaction. What he suggested required more than a simple exchange. Having no other choice, she agreed to it.

"We can go now if you like," Obinna said.

"What about the wedding?" She glanced at the double doors above the stairs.

"We attended the ceremony. That's the most important part, so I think we're good."

Dunni considered briefly, then nodded. "Okay."

They walked outside, and when the valet pulled Obinna's car—a silver Porsche Panamera—to the curb, she resisted the urge to ask questions. How he could afford such a luxurious car did not concern her. She settled into the passenger seat and looked at her engagement ring, remembering why she was in the car to begin with—to get the closure she needed to move on.

CHAPTER TEN

THEN

W hat now?" Obinna turned to Dunni, his eyebrows bridged in a frown.

"We'll get another teacher for the day," she said. "That's what usually happens."

They had received news from the school's receptionist that their biology teacher, Miss Okafor, was absent due to a family emergency. They would get a substitute teacher soon. At any moment, one would walk into the classroom and bring order to the students, who were taking full advantage of their temporary freedom.

It was chaotic. Everyone but Dunni and Obinna had exchanged seats and were talking about the latest films and the latest rumors circulating the school.

"The headmaster is probably going to teach," Dunni said. "He usually does whenever something like this happens." She looked at Obinna and smiled. "Hey. You didn't get all of it. Again."

She referred to the oil on his forehead. Usually, Obinna rubbed it off the moment he stepped out of his house. But in the past three weeks, since starting his new school, he'd been wiping only some off and leaving a slight sheen behind for Dunni. Just as he and his mother had their routine, he now had one with Dunni. She would look at him while settling into their shared seat, and her stare would rise to his forehead. "You didn't get all of it," she would say. Then she would lean into him and brush her thumb over the residue of oil, her eyes never leaving his.

"There." Her hand dropped, but she stayed close. "Let's get out of here."

"What?"

"Before the headmaster comes. Trust me. You'll thank me. He's such a boring teacher. You'll be sleeping one minute into the lesson." She searched his eyes. "So? Come with me?"

"Okay." He couldn't imagine saying anything else.

"Good. On the count of three, we run out," she instructed.

"Run?"

"Well, we certainly cannot stroll out. I'd rather not hear all the whistling and sexual innuendo from our classmates. Have you met the ringleader of foolishness, Emeka?"

Obinna laughed.

"Also, I don't want the headmaster to catch us mid-escape. So it has to be a quick getaway. We run on the count of three. Okay?"

Obinna nodded. This was exciting. A little terrifying, but

nonetheless exciting. What if they got caught? What if they got in trouble? What if they got away? What if they stayed away—together, alone for just a little while? The possibility and uncertainty thrilled him. He'd never felt this before—this strange mixture of fear and exhilaration. He liked it. And God help him, he liked her. So much.

"One." Dunni mouthed the word. She stood up, and so did Obinna.

"Two." She smiled and walked casually toward the door. Obinna followed.

"Three!" She shouted the last word, and they took off, running out of the classroom and then down the corridor, turning corners before stopping. "In here." She opened a door and shut it quickly once they were inside an empty room.

They had gotten away with it. Obinna looked at her, and they laughed.

"We have to be quiet," Dunni whispered, a finger to her lips. "We don't want anyone to hear us." She breathed deeply and stopped chuckling.

It took Obinna a little longer to settle down completely. "That was—"

"Fun?"

He nodded. It was. He looked around the spacious room. "Where are we?"

"One of the recreation rooms. We have school clubs in here. Sometimes, the drama group practices here."

"Oh."

Their laughter had been the perfect filler. Without it, Obinna would have to speak—carry an entire conversation. It wasn't like he hadn't done it before. But this time was different. This time, they were alone—not among friends in a classroom or a crowded lunchroom.

They looked at each other, both expecting something from the other.

"I—" They spoke at the same time and laughed.

"You go ahead," Dunni said.

"Thanks." He cleared his throat and hoped it removed the waver in his voice. "I've been wondering. Dunni is your abbreviated name. What's the full name?"

She frowned, as if disappointed by his question. Maybe she expected more. "It's Adedunni."

"Oh. Adedunni." He liked it, liked how the extra syllables made it more complex and beautiful. "What does it mean?"

"'The crown is honorable to have.'"

He smiled. Of course that was the meaning. "It's nice. I like it."

"Thank you. What about yours? What does Obinna mean?"

"Um . . . well, I don't really like my name." His stare dropped to his shoes. "I have another—a middle name. Nicholas." He looked at her again. "You can call me that. If you like."

"I like Obinna. What does it mean?"

He groaned under his breath. He didn't like the meaning of his name. He had once. But not anymore. "It means 'father's heart.'"

"Well, that's nice."

He shrugged.

"What? You don't think so? It honors your father."

"Well, he doesn't deserve to be honored."

They fell silent. Obinna waited for Dunni to say something, but she said nothing. It surprised him that she didn't immediately ask for more details. Didn't she want to pry into his life and find all the ways it was inadequate? She could compare his misfortune to her fortune. That's what people usually did when they learned about his father.

"Ah. So your father just left you and your mother—just like that? No word for two years? *Nawa o*. At least my father is with us. We might not have much, but at least he didn't just abandon us." A friend at his former school had said that to him—used Obinna's misfortune to appease himself. He'd always expected that reaction from people. Either that or pity. He had never gotten Dunni's reaction before.

"I'm tired of standing." She slipped off her jacket and spread it on the floor. There were chairs and desks pushed against the wall, but she lowered herself to the floor and sat. "Well?" She looked up at Obinna, an eyebrow arched. "What are you waiting for? An invitation? A handwritten letter? Unfortunately, I don't have a pen and paper. So you will have to settle for a verbal invitation." She cleared her throat and spoke in a British accent. "Dear Obinna, I bid you a good day. Will you honor me with your presence by joining me on the rec room floor? I would appreciate it greatly." She smiled. "Did that do it?"

Two things surprised Obinna—the fact that she hadn't pried and the fact that she had spoken in a very convincing British accent. "You're something else, you know that?" He pulled off his jacket, spread it on the floor, and sat facing her, their knees touching.

"People keep telling me that, and I'm not sure if it's an insult or a compliment." She didn't seem bothered either way. She fanned her skirt over her thighs, keeping the gap between her legs covered.

"It's a compliment," he told her. "It's definitely a compliment."

Because she was something else—something strange and complex, and he liked that.

"He's gone," Obinna said. "My father. He's gone."

Dunni hadn't asked. Maybe she would have eventually. But her initial reaction hadn't been to meddle. She hadn't been eager to hear what a mess his life was, and that made him want to tell her everything, so he did. He told her the entire story, and then he waited.

"What do you think happened to him?"

No one had ever asked that—not his friends at his old school, not the church members who masked their judgment and ridicule with false sympathy, and not his relatives. They only ever made assumptions. "He probably didn't make it. Pray for his soul. He probably found an *oyinbo* to marry him and got a visa."

Those were all probable scenarios, but none Obinna believed.

"My father promised he would send money once he got there. He promised he would bring us to join him." Obinna bit his lip and summoned the guts to say what he'd believed for years, but hadn't mentioned to anyone. "I don't think he ever planned on coming back for us or contacting us again."

Dunni scowled. "What makes you believe that?"

"He said something before he left." Obinna closed his eyes and recalled the details of that day.

His father had worn a gold chain around his neck and a cap on his shaved head. The chain was too shiny, too gold. It was fake. The hat was too small, but he wore it anyway. And his dark eyes were too bright for a man who was leaving his family; they weren't sad at all. In fact, they seemed relieved.

Obinna met Dunni's inquiring gaze. "Before walking out, he said, 'You are going to grow up to be a wonderful man, Obi. A better one than me.' He whispered it, so my mother wouldn't hear. That, along with the look in his eyes, and I just knew. I knew he was running away."

"That's crazy. I find it hard to believe someone can just do that—leave their family." Dunni shook her head as if kicking the thought around. "He must have loved you and your mother."

"I don't think my parents had that kind of love."

"What kind of love?"

Obinna rubbed a finger along his lip and thought of how to explain himself. "Okay. Have you ever seen the film *Titanic*?"

"Yes, like everyone on the planet."

"Okay. You know that scene when Jack gives Rose the plank and practically gives up his life for her?"

Dunni nodded.

"Well, my father would never do that for my mother."

"How are you so sure? Have they ever been in that situation?"

"No, but I just know."

"You just know?" She scoffed. "Come on. Give me more than that. Convince me *na*."

"Okay." He squinted and considered the best way to articulate his conviction. "It starts with the little things. My father never did the little things for her. Whenever they ate together, he always—and I mean always—took the last piece of meat. He never shared it, he never offered it to her. He would just eat it.

"Here's another example. One time, my mother's half sister had a baby. My mother didn't want to visit her alone. They didn't have a good relationship, so she asked my father to go with her—begged him to. And he refused. He said he was too tired. I could go on and on."

He didn't, of course. Otherwise, they would have been there all day.

"He never discomforted himself to make her comfortable. How could he possibly give up his life for hers? If you can't do the little things, how can you do something so big?"

"I see," Dunni said. "So they definitely didn't have that Jack and Rose kind of love."

"Not at all. But honestly, Jack and Rose were a little too intense. I don't want that kind of love."

"What kind of love do you want then?" She smiled. "I'm curious."

"I want an easy love."

"What's an easy love?"

"Boy meets girl. They fall in love. And bam." He clapped his hands just as he said *bam*.

Dunni threw her head back and laughed. "What in the world is bam? Sex?"

"What?" His face flushed. "No. Not . . . sex. Bam is they get married and have a family and live together happily. Forever."

"So let me get this straight. Boy meets girl. They fall in love. And bam?"

"Yes. Bam. Sweet, easy love. No complications. No obstacles. No stress." He smiled.

"Have you ever been in love, Obinna?"

His smile disappeared. "No. Not yet."

"Neither have I. But I don't think love is easy. I don't think it's supposed to be."

"And what gave you that idea?"

"I read a lot of novels," she said. "Romance novels."

Obinna resisted rolling his eyes.

"I know what you're thinking, but just listen to me." She shifted and sat on her knees. "In every great love story, right before bam—way before bam—the couple goes through hell. Boy meets girl. They fall in love. Boy loses girl. Boy realizes he can't live without girl, so he fights for her. Or maybe she fights for him. Or maybe they fight for each other. God, I love it when they fight for each other!" She rose to her knees and shuffled toward him, the jacket beneath her moving as well.

"They lose multiple fights, but they don't give up. They can't because something inside them—something stubborn and insuppressible—won't let them. So they fight. They're exhausted, but they don't stop. And then one day, it happens. They win. Bam!" She clapped her hands together and squealed, then giggled. "They live happily ever after. But if they don't go through those hurdles, how do they know it's worth anything? How do they know their love is worth having?" She placed a hand on either side of Obinna's face and sat on her knees. "I want to be worth something to someone. Enough that they'll give up everything for me. Enough that they will never stop fighting for me. And I want someone to be worth that much to me. That's the kind of love I want."

Obinna breathed rapidly, ran out of air too quickly, and gathered another dose only to run out again. Her excitement had triggered his. He stroked her cheek; his fingers curved against the slope of her cheekbone. He wanted to kiss her. He needed to before he lost his mind. He leaned forward, his lips inches from hers, and then the school bell chimed. Classroom doors opened and students rushed into the corridor. The commotion disrupted the moment, robbed them of their first kiss. Their foreheads inclined slightly and met. Briefly, they stayed that way—their heads touching, their breaths mixing, their eyes set on each other.

And he knew. Obinna knew he also wanted a love like that.

CHAPTER ELEVEN

The motion of the moving car had lured Dunni to sleep. Though when the Porsche stopped, she stirred awake. Sharp lines of light pierced through the haze coating her eyes.

"Hey," Obinna said softly. "We're here. At my place."

"Oh." She sat up and cleared her throat. "Sorry for falling asleep. I just needed to rest my eyes a bit." She was exhausted, having slept little the previous night. The glasses of champagne she'd had at the reception also deepened her fatigue.

"You seem tired."

"I'm fine." She pressed her lips together and suppressed a yawn that would confirm his statement. When the yawn dissolved inside her, she spoke. "Let's go inside and talk."

It was a little past eight at night. Dunni had carved out thirty minutes of her life for Obinna's explanation. That was all she could spare. She feared anything more would lead to some sort of emotional entanglement, and that could not happen. She pushed the car door open, stepped out, and her eyes expanded.

Dunni had slept through the drive, not envisioning what Obinna's home would look like. Though even if she had contemplated and settled on an image, it wouldn't have been the immense three-story building with geometric shapes and a flat, dramatically angled roof. Pot lights beamed against the white modern building and lit the walkway.

"This is your house?" Dunni tried to contain her astonishment, but it was apparent in the way her voice swelled.

"It is," he answered stoically, looking at the grand building with a neutral gaze as if it were nothing impressive.

How had he attained this? What steps had he taken to get here, to be the man he was now? What had happened after Dunni left Nigeria?

She remembered vividly how intelligent Obinna was. He'd been determined to attend university so he could make a better life for himself and his mother. He'd had dreams and the motivation and intelligence to make them a reality. And he had. At that moment, Dunni wanted to hold him and tell him how proud she was. She couldn't do that though, and not being able to acknowledge his accomplishment in a way that felt right hurt more than she expected.

"Let's go inside," Obinna said, walking ahead. He unlocked the door, held it open, and waited for Dunni to enter.

She stepped inside slowly; her heels clicked on the white ceramic floor, and the sound echoed against the silence. When he shut the door, she followed him, and with every step they took, lights turned on automatically and revealed the sophisticated, minimalist décor. They stopped at a large charcoal-hued couch—the only speck of color in the white living room. At the sight of the cozy furniture, Dunni's heavy eyelids drooped. She blinked and tried to clear the haze from her vision.

"Why don't you sit?" Obinna gestured to the couch. "I'll get you a drink. What would you like?"

"Nothing. I'm fine." Dunni sat, and her body loosened as it sank into the cushioned seat. "Let's just get to it, shall we?"

"Okay. Sure." He sat a respectable distance from her. Though after considering the space between them, he shifted closer.

Dunni didn't notice the proximity of their bodies. Her attention was elsewhere, on her heels that pinched her toes. She wiggled her feet, which did nothing to alleviate the discomfort. Impatient, she crouched and undid the buckles, then slid her feet out and released a loud sigh. For a moment, she forgot where she was and even whom she was with. Overcome by exhaustion, she rested her head back and closed her eyes.

"Dunni," Obinna whispered her name. "You're tired. You should sleep. Eh?"

She murmured sounds—whizzes, sighs, the beginnings of words that never formed.

"I'm going to put you to bed."

Some part of her—the part suspended between consciousness and unconsciousness, fading but at a slow pace—heard him and understood but couldn't bother with the formation of words. She didn't fight Obinna when his arms scooped her up, lifting and then cradling her body against his chest. The leathery, smoky fragrance on his shirt filled her nose and lulled her further. His weight shifted from one leg to the other as he climbed the steps. When his weight was balanced again, he walked ahead and stopped at a door that creaked open. He lowered Dunni onto a bed, her head atop a pillow, and she rolled on her side and curled into a ball.

"Good night. We'll talk in the morning."

"Talk?" She spoke through a husky sigh. "About what?" Just like that, she had forgotten her reason for coming to Obinna's home. Everything seemed muddled by exhaustion and alcohol.

"Talk about us, Dunni." He touched her forehead, brushed back strands of hair, and whispered words in Igbo.

It wasn't Dunni's language, but she remembered the little Obinna had taught her years ago. So as he spoke, part of her mind—the part spanned between consciousness and unconsciousness—became alert and translated what he had said.

Talk about how I have never stopped loving you. Not for a day, not for a second.

Dunni's eyes broke open, her fatigue temporarily suspended as she watched Obinna hunched at the side of the bed. She was speechless and at the same time, had so much to say. But she held each word back, and they weighed on her heart, made it pound with a sluggish ferocity.

Why did he always do that—complicate their situation by saying things he shouldn't? Yesterday at the rehearsal dinner, he'd admitted missing her. At the reception, he'd called her "my Dunni." And now, this. But Obinna wasn't the only one complicating things.

At the reception, she'd touched him—placed her hand on his leg. She had agreed to come to his home. Could she really put the blame on Obinna alone? Weren't they both responsible, their words and actions further entangling them, making it difficult to break away from each other?

"You should get some sleep." He stood and walked to the closet. He disappeared inside and returned with a white T-shirt. "In case you would like something more comfortable."

Dunni sat upright and took the shirt. "Thank you."

"Of course. Good night." He walked to the door but stopped when Dunni called him.

"My dress," she said. "I need help taking it off. The zipper. It's at the back."

He considered her deeply, then approached the bed and sat on the edge. When she angled her back to him, he pulled the zipper down. The dress fell open, and Dunni tensed, suddenly cautious. She spun to face Obinna and hoped he hadn't seen the tattoo on her shoulder blade. If he had, she would have to lie, and she was far too tired to invent something believable.

"We'll talk tomorrow." He was still on that subject. He hadn't seen it.

She sighed, relieved. "I'm leaving tomorrow—going back to the States. My flight is at night."

"Oh." His head dropped just as his tone did. "Then . . . um . . . we can talk first thing in the morning, and then I'll drive you home." He looked at her. "Is that okay?"

"Yes. Sure. Thanks."

It was there again, as it often was with them, the pressure to say something more, to penetrate the surface and get to all the mess their pleasantries and facade concealed so well. Of course, that would have to wait until the morning. It was best that way. Dunni needed to be fully alert for their conversation. She'd waited twelve years. She could wait one more night.

"Good night." He stood and walked to the door.

She watched him go, her heart still heavy with all the words she had not said. Something prompted her mouth to open and her lips to shape the beginning of a confession, but she stopped herself and shook off the impulse just as he left the room and shut the door.

"No more entanglements," she told herself.

But she was in his home, in his bed, pulling his shirt over her body, and she knew it was already too late.

CHAPTER TWELVE

THEN

Obinna had grown up associating the sun with certain emotions. On the days it shone mildly and allowed the wind to weave through its warmth, it was happy. On the days it shone with an unpardoning fierceness, the sun was furious and burned with the intent to kill. And because those days were often, Obinna had long concluded that the sun had a terrible temper.

Today, he felt the full force of its temper. Sweat slid down his forehead, settled on his eyelashes, and slipped through the gaps between the thin hairs before entering his eyes. He could only blink the moisture away. His hands were full, one holding an *uma* leaf and the other spooning rice onto the leaf. When he coated the bed of rice with *ofada* stew and topped it with two pieces of goat meat, he folded the edges of the green leaf into a perfect pouch and extended it to the customer. He repeated this as sweat glazed his face, too afraid to disrupt the routine he and his mother had mastered. She calculated the money customers placed in her hand while shutting down hagglers; her mind was sharp even with the unrest of the rowdy, impatient crowd.

Saturdays at the market were usually hectic. They served customers until their large coolers were empty, left with only a sheen of red oil and a few grains of white rice. They neared that goal as more people arrived at their modest shed that sat on the outskirts of the market, along the road bustling with cars, hawkers, and shoppers who all vied for space in an uncoordinated effort to reach their distinct destinations.

"Can I please have two-hundred-naira rice, ma? With two pieces of meat."

Obinna froze just as he attempted to start the order. He knew that voice—the buoyant tone, the way each word eased out perfect and unrushed without the dent of pidgin English. Over the past month, he had listened to that voice come through full, pink lips. He'd thought about that voice while dozing off every night and even bobbed his head to the memory of it while doing chores as if it were music worth dancing to.

Instantly, he became alert.

He broke his routine and looked at his mother, seated on the wooden stool beside him. Then Obinna looked at the girl who stood in front of his mother, a crisp thousand-naira note in her hand. She met his gaze and smiled, a smile so radiant, he felt a surge of heat inside of him, like someone had struck a match in his stomach. He swallowed, thinking the gulp of saliva would quench whatever was lit inside him. It did not.

"Hi, Obinna." Dunni's smile grew wider. "How are you?"

"Obi?" His mother arched a sparse eyebrow. "You know this girl?"

Obinna's throat was rough, parched from the heat he felt externally and internally. He couldn't get words out.

"We go to the same school, ma," Dunni answered, calm and respectful. "We're friends."

"Eh-heh." His mother considered Dunni and ignored the grumble of impatient customers. With her inspection complete, she turned to Obinna; her eyebrow arched higher, as if striving to form the shape of a question mark. "And what is your name, my dear?"

"Dunni, ma. Adedunni."

"Eh-heh. And are you also on a scholarship?" Even as she spoke, her eyes stayed on Obinna; her curved brow asked a question his body language would eventually answer.

Obinna became conscious of the simplest action. He measured the air he took in and ensured it was the perfect dose to make his chest fall and rise faintly, like a person who was not nervous. He kept his eyes on Dunni and hoped they were void and gave nothing away.

"No, ma. I am not on a scholarship."

"Eh-heh. Okay. Well, Obinna, what are you waiting for? Give your friend her food *na*."

He picked up the ladle and tried to dish the food quickly,

like he did with every customer. But his hand shook. And he knew he had given himself away.

His mother dropped her eyebrow and looked at the money in Dunni's hand. "No need to pay. I dash you."

"Ah. No. Please let me pay."

"No need. Keep *your* money."

Dunni, who didn't know to take offense by the words—*your money*—smiled. She tucked the bill into her purse and took the plastic bag Obinna extended to her. "Thank you, ma."

"No problem."

"Ma, can Obinna escort me to my car? It's not far at all."

Obinna almost choked on his saliva. Not only had a girl come looking for him, but she'd asked to be alone with him. He was in trouble.

"Why not? Obi, go. Escort your friend." Those words came out of his mother's mouth—calm, soft, pleasant—and he froze and waited for the punchline or a slap. "What are you waiting for? I said go. *Gaba.*"

He stood and walked with the uncertainty and awkwardness of a child taking its first steps. As he grew farther away, he looked back at his mother, but she focused on customers. Dunni's hand brushed his as they approached the black Mercedes, and he flinched, then shifted from her.

"Um . . . well, your mother is very nice." She acknowledged the space between them with a glance. "Tell her I said thanks again."

"Dunni." He watched her from the corner of his eye. "What are you doing here?"

"I was craving your mother's *ofada* stew. You mentioned the name of the market, so we drove around until I saw you."

They stopped at the car. Someone sat in the driver's seat. It was Paul, the man who drove her to and from school every day.

"I also came because . . ." She swung the plastic bag in her hand. "I wanted to see you. I . . . well, I missed you." Gingerly, she wrapped her fingers around his. "I really missed you, Obi."

They had never held hands until now. Since he started school a month ago, it had been subtle things—hands grazing as they walked side by side, knees touching under a table, the glint in their eyes and smile on their faces communicating what they had yet to. Now, they had taken such a big step in a market with his mother only a few feet away.

His mother. Was she seeing this? He turned around and received the answer.

The demanding customers didn't shake her attention. She gawked at Obinna and Dunni, fixated on their touching hands. When her eyes finally met her son's, he winced.

When Obinna was younger, it had taken him a few lessons to learn how to read his mother's eyes. One Sunday afternoon, when he was eight, he and his mother visited relatives. They offered him *jollof* rice and his choice of a cold drink—Fanta, Coke, or Sprite. Obinna hadn't looked at his mother for approval. Eager, he ate the food placed in front of him. That evening, when they got home, his mother pinched and twisted his ear before he crossed the threshold.

"Stupid boy. See the way you just opened your mouth and your nose and started eating as if I don't feed you in this house.

Behaving like you have no home training." She released his ear and hissed. "If anyone asks you to eat or drink anything again, look at me. You look at my eyes, and I will tell you yes or no. Do you understand me?"

"Yes, Mommy. I understand."

But he did not understand because two weeks later, when they visited a church member, Obinna looked at his mother then turned down a plate of small chops. When they got home, the pinch on his ear was harder. He failed a few more times after that, but finally learned on the day he visited his mother's half sister.

"Obinna, let me bring you puff-puff and Fanta."

He had glanced at his mother and saw the answer clearly. "No thank you, Auntie," he said. "I am not hungry."

"Ah-ah. What do you mean, you are not hungry? Did your mother tell you not to eat in my house?"

"Ah. I didn't o. Obinna, eat. This is your auntie's house. Don't be shy."

Despite what his mother said, Obinna did not change his mind. "No. I'm not hungry."

That evening, as they left his auntie's house and walked to the junction, his mother stroked his head and said, "Good boy. You see, now you have learned."

Obinna had certainly learned. He knew exactly what his mother's eyes communicated, even now in the rowdy market.

He turned to Dunni and dropped her hand. "You . . . you shouldn't have come here." Fear made his voice waver. "Please leave. You have to leave. Right now."

"What?" She frowned. "I don't understand. I came because I thought we could do something. You mentioned that you've never been to the cinemas, so I thought we could go and then get some ice cream after."

Cinemas, ice cream. At this, Obinna wanted to laugh. But humor quickly turned to anger. "I am selling food with my mother in the market, soaked in sweat." His tone was sharp and unkind. "What makes you think I have the liberty to go to the cinemas or buy ice cream?" Then his anger left as swiftly as it had come.

He looked at his shabby T-shirt, his unflattering beige shorts stained with blotches of stew, and his rubber slippers coated with grains of sand and several layers of dust. And then he looked at Dunni, her clean yellow dress that flowed over her knees and exposed her unblemished dark-brown skin. Her leather sandals were spotless and had probably never journeyed to this side of the city until today.

Now Obinna understood why his mother was upset. It wasn't just that a girl had come looking for him. It was that a girl like her had come looking for a boy like him.

"Dunni, you don't belong here." His voice cracked, his chest tightened, but he forced the words out. "And you certainly don't belong with me."

He saw the glimmer of tears in her eyes but turned away before they could fall. He couldn't watch them fall.

He sat beside his mother, took the ladle from her hand, and served. Neither of them said a word. The words would come later, much later.

At home, Obinna and his mother washed the coolers and set them on the kitchen floor to dry. After taking their baths, they ate dinner—*eba* and *oha* soup—in silence.

Obinna had been on edge since returning from the market. Upon stepping inside the house, he'd braced himself for a slap, but it had not come. Now, he waited for a lecture. And still, nothing.

After dinner, he washed the plates, while his mother sat in the living room and slid a toothpick between her teeth. At the will of the power holding company, the electricity came on. The ceiling fan spun and chased the heat away. His mother didn't turn on the small television in the room. She studied the wall and picked her teeth.

Obinna knew her silence was part of his punishment, a tactic to unnerve him further, but he couldn't stand it any longer.

"Mommy." He cleared his throat and stood in front of her. "About this afternoon."

"What about it?"

"Well . . . I . . . I . . ." He lost his courage. "Nothing. Good night." He turned and rushed toward the bedroom.

"I sent you to school to learn, so you can make something of your life. But you are now chasing girls, *abi*?"

He paused and turned around slowly.

"Big boy, you now have a girlfriend."

"Mommy, she is not my girlfriend."

His mother sat upright, placed her elbows on her knees, and

leaned forward. "Then *wetin* concern you, concern rich man *pickin*, eh? Obinna, what business do you have with a girl like that, flaunting her money in my face and driving to the market in a big car to come and see you? What business do you have with her? Answer me!"

He wanted to, but he didn't know what to say.

"What did I tell you before you went to that school?" She stood and tightened the wrapper around her waist. "What did I say to you?"

He sorted through his memory quickly. "You said, 'If you come to this house with fire on your head, you will put it out with your own hands.'"

"Okay. And what do you think that girl is? She is fire, Obinna. Trouble."

"But, Mommy—"

"But what?" She approached him, and he flinched, expecting something that didn't come. "Listen to me. You see this small house I have and this small business I am managing, I have peace. Even though your father abandoned us, despite it all, I have managed to secure my peace of mind. And no one can take that from me. No one can go out to look for trouble, bring it to my doorstep, and say it is my own. No one can bring stress into my life and kill me before my time. No one. Not even you." She hissed and marched into the kitchen.

Obinna never wanted to be an additional problem his mother would have to pray about. But he was now. She mumbled a prayer while futilely arranging kitchen utensils. The words *Jesus* and *deliver* escaped the clanking of pots.

In the middle of the night, Obinna turned on the mattress, careful not to wake his mother on the other end. He looked at the ceiling and whispered a prayer of his own. He hardly ever prayed, but he did that night. He prayed attending church on Sunday morning would prompt his mother to forgive him and forget everything that had happened that day. Then he prayed for Monday morning, for the grace and the willpower to stay away from Dunni.

CHAPTER THIRTEEN

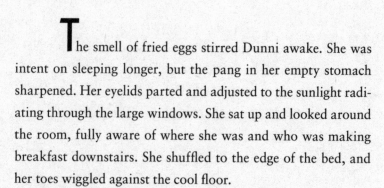

The smell of fried eggs stirred Dunni awake. She was intent on sleeping longer, but the pang in her empty stomach sharpened. Her eyelids parted and adjusted to the sunlight radiating through the large windows. She sat up and looked around the room, fully aware of where she was and who was making breakfast downstairs. She shuffled to the edge of the bed, and her toes wiggled against the cool floor.

The white T-shirt flapped on her thighs as she walked into the bathroom. Atop the counter, a handwritten note rested beside a toothbrush. The message on it was short.

For you.

Dunni squeezed toothpaste onto the toothbrush and studied her reflection in the mirror while working the bristles over her teeth. Her makeup was no longer where it ought to be; red lipstick and bronzer smeared across her face, and one false lash had shifted to her eyebrow. She rinsed her mouth then ripped the false lashes off before splashing water on her face and scrubbing. Colors and glitter flowed down the drain. After drying her face with a towel, she untangled the knots in her hair.

Sunlight came through every angle of the house, as there were more windows than walls. Dunni squinted while walking down the floating steps, then widened her eyes in the hallway. Vibrant abstract art covered the walls and seemed to demand her wits to unravel their complexity. After lingering, she followed the smell of eggs and the clanking of pans.

In the brightly lit kitchen, made brighter by the white countertop and cabinets, Obinna stood at the stove, his back to Dunni. Leaning against the doorframe, she watched him stir whatever sizzled in the frying pan. She was still adjusting to the new version of him—his toned, muscular physique that was apparent in the flimsy T-shirt he wore. The Obinna she'd known had been slim, bonier in some parts than others. It had been one of his insecurities—the way playing soccer and eating pounded yam and *eba* did nothing for his slender build.

"Stop all that nonsense, *na*," she'd said one day when he'd complained about his skinny arms that weren't defined with muscles or bulky with fat like the other boys in their class. "Obi, nothing is wrong with you. I like you just like this." And she'd meant it. She loved the way his stature did not intimidate her or make her feel small. She found it was delicate and still strong, but in a way that gave her room to be strong as well. However, Dunni's taste had changed. She was no longer a teenager with too much spirit and notions of the world, determined to be shielded from nothing. She was a woman who had been strong for too long—forced to take on too much. And Obinna's new frame, with muscles swelling beneath his fawn skin, was the epitome of strength. It gave Dunni a sense of security she hadn't craved as a teenager. She craved it now though. She was so desperate to let go and no longer be strong.

"Hey. You're awake." Obinna faced her and smiled, a slow smile that lifted only one side of his lips.

"Yeah." She stepped into the kitchen, still in his T-shirt; it was long enough that she didn't have to tug on the hem constantly. "What time is it?"

He glanced at the silver watch on his wrist. "Eight fifteen. How did you sleep?"

"Fine." She didn't want to dwell on the awkwardness of the situation—on the fact that she was in his house, in his shirt, and barefoot in his kitchen, eyeing the breakfast he had made. "How about you?" She hoped the flow of conversation would make things bearable.

"Well, I didn't get much sleep." He placed two plates on the counter; each had an omelet and two sausages. "What would you prefer? Coffee, tea, or orange juice?"

"Um . . . orange juice."

He walked to the refrigerator and returned with Dunni's request. "Sit," he said, pulling out a barstool.

When she sat, her hands clasped in her lap, he poured the juice into a tall glass. "Thank you." She sipped, and the citrus flavor hit the fresh coating of mint on her tongue.

"You're welcome." He sat beside her. "You must be hungry."

"Yeah." Dunni eyed the meal in front of her and salivated. Rather than waiting for his go-ahead, she picked up the fork and cut through the omelet.

"Okay." Obinna chuckled while watching the quickness of her mouth. "I guess I underestimated the extent of your hunger."

She nodded and bit through a sausage.

For a few minutes, they ate in silence. They paid more attention to their plates than each other. Though as Dunni grew full, her focus returned. Without the pang in her stomach acting as a distraction, she placed her fork down, a gentle clink against the plate, and looked at Obinna. He stopped chewing and dropped his cutlery as well. He sipped from his steaming cup of coffee and wiped the corners of his lips with a napkin.

"Dunni." For a long while, that was all he said. He didn't look at her but at his hands. "I was ashamed," he confessed. "After what happened with your mother, I didn't know how to continue seeing you. She made me feel like . . . like I was garbage." He pressed his eyes closed and shook his head. "It was the shame I felt. That is what kept me away. I felt like nothing, and I didn't know how to be with you like that."

There was a strain in Dunni's heart as she watched him. She wanted to ask if he still felt that shame, if it had been the motivation for purchasing his luxurious car and his grand house. Was he trying to prove something to her mother?

"I thought that feeling would wear off eventually." He lifted his eyes and met her gaze. "I saw your emails. I read them. I just could not respond. I kept telling myself I would respond in a week and then a month . . . sometime when I felt like myself again. But one year passed and then another and another, and I never felt like myself."

"Even now?"

"Dunni, that day did something to me. I don't think I will ever be the person I was before it happened, and I'm okay with that."

For a moment, they said nothing. Their breaths were deep, slow, matched. Then Dunni broke the coordinated rhythm by inhaling sharply.

"I told you I was in trouble," she said. "In the emails. I told you—more than once—that I was in trouble. Did you think that was a joke—something I said to get you to respond?"

He nodded. "Wasn't it?"

Dunni watched him, her lips sealed. She didn't tell Obinna how that day had also changed her, how it had reconstructed the teenage girl who was too passionate, too outspoken, too stubborn, too hopeful; how it sculpted her and chiseled away all these attributes until she was a docile woman with a broken heart and a repressed voice, whose laughter lacked a certain quality.

"It doesn't matter," she told him instead. "What difference does it make now?"

It wasn't only a question for him. It was a question for herself. *What difference did it make?* His explanation had not erased twelve years of resentment and hurt, and it had probably done nothing for her relationship with Christopher.

"Dunni, I'm sorry." Obinna sighed and ran a hand over his face. "I'm so sorry."

"Don't apologize," she said, flat and weary. "It was an impossible situation."

"Yes. But we had a plan. And I let you down. I'm sorry." He shifted on the stool, and his leg tilted and met hers.

There were many times during their budding relationship when this subtle nod of affection was all they had—knees touching under a crowded lunch table or a classroom desk. It had been their tender beginning, small moments that eventually led to her lying on her back with him over her. That specific memory, Obinna entering her for the first time, caused Dunni's heart to skip. Her hand jerked and knocked over the glass of orange juice.

The pulpy liquid splashed on Obinna's chest, soaked his shirt, and dripped to his gray sweatpants. He jumped up and pressed a napkin to his chest.

"Oh my God. I . . . I'm so sorry."

"It's okay. I guess I'm lucky you didn't ask for tea or coffee." He chuckled lightly, then tossed the drenched napkin on the counter and looked over his clothes. "Let me change out of these. Okay? I'll be down in a minute." He turned toward the door before she could apologize further.

During his absence, Dunni wiped up the spilled juice and cleared the dishes. Ten minutes had gone by, and he still had not returned. She went upstairs in search of him and heard his voice in the bedroom. He sat on the edge of the bed, speaking on the phone while looking through a folder packed with papers. He didn't wear a shirt. Perhaps the call had stopped him from changing.

"Sorry. Give me a minute," he whispered to her.

She nodded and moved toward the bathroom, but as she walked, her stare lingered on something across his back, something that required her to pause and squint.

In need of a closer look, she climbed onto the bed and shuffled on her knees until the old scar on Obinna's left shoulder blade became clearer. She touched it, the texture rough beneath her trembling fingertips. He flinched, and the memory of that day emerged in Dunni's mind. Tears fell from her eyes and hit Obinna's back, and he ended his phone call promptly and sat still.

Dunni didn't know what to say. Frankly, words seemed inconsequential, so she kissed the scar instead. She trailed her pursed lips along the length of it. When the skin flattened and smoothed, she went back to the scar and kissed more intently. She did this again and again, then slipped her arms over his chest and held him. And even though it wasn't enough, she whispered, "I'm sorry." And then she said it in Igbo and then Yoruba as if apologizing in another language expanded the meaning, deepened it, conveyed something English could not. "*Ndo. Ma binu.*"

Frozen, Obinna did not say a word. When the muscles in his back and shoulders relaxed, he lifted Dunni's left hand from his chest. Slowly, he twisted the engagement ring and slid it off her slender finger. The ring clicked on the nightstand, and then Obinna kissed her finger as she had kissed his back, as if she too had a scar.

The weight of the ring replaced with the weight of his lips seemed like exchanging the bad for the good, righting some wrong. Though, Dunni had to ask herself if what was happening was wrong. She was engaged. She had agreed to marry Christopher, but she also remembered the promise she'd made years ago to Obinna, and that, even without the formality of a ring and a bent knee, felt just as solid. More so even.

Obinna's lips stayed on her finger. She inhaled deeply. Anticipation hung in the air, pulsating as if it were alive and hungry. Hadn't it all been leading to this? Every little interaction they'd had since they met two days ago had been like knees touching under a crowded table—subtle affections leading to a pivotal inevitability.

Obinna shifted and faced her. They watched each other intently, and she ran a fingertip along the slopes of his face, using another sense to capture his new appearance—the man and not the boy.

"You look the same," she said. "And at the same time, you don't."

"Is that a bad thing?"

She brushed her thumb over his lip then said, "No. It isn't."

He smiled. "You've changed too. You look mature."

"Old?"

"No." He laughed. "The last time I saw you, you were a girl. That's the image I've carried with me for years. I looked for you on Facebook, so I could get a more current image."

"I'm not on social media."

"Yeah. I figured. The image of you as a teenage girl in a uniform is the only one I've ever had. So, I'm still getting used to seeing you like this."

Frowning, she glanced at her body—her knees bent beneath

her, the white T-shirt scrunched on her thighs. "Don't you like me like this? Don't you like the way I look now?"

"Of course I do. Dunni, you are gorgeous and elegant and sexy—everything I could have ever imagined and so much more." He held her chin and lifted it, aligning their lips. "Seriously, I'm fucking mesmerized. And if I'm being honest, I would really love to kiss you right now."

A tingling sensation warmed her spine. Her eyes grew wide and expectant. She waited, but he didn't inch closer. He watched her; his smoldering eyes asked for permission.

Dunni smiled. "Yes," she said. "Kiss me."

It happened slowly, delayed even with their eagerness. But then it happened. His lips met hers. The contact sent a ripple of heat through her body. Her heart thumped.

Their unsteady lips moved against each other's with uncertainty and caution, trying to remember and recapture the rhythm they'd had years ago. And then gradually, their lips relaxed, and they stopped grasping at the past. They relished the newness they had now, the familiar yet uncharted.

His tongue caressed hers with impeccably gentle strokes. It seemed as if he was communicating something to her. They were communicating with each other, and even without words, there was a shared understanding. The years had passed in a whirlwind; it had changed them, it had stripped them of their former selves, but this had not changed. Their connection and feelings for each other had weathered it all.

Dunni didn't question why these things stayed intact. The answer scared her. Instead, she focused on Obinna. She ran her hand over the sculpt of his chest, felt his muscles—the strength she wanted to give in to—and her last ounce of reserve disappeared. When Obinna gripped the hem of her T-shirt and paused, she nodded, giving him permission.

They undressed each other, flung every article of clothing to the floor. Dunni's back sank into the layers of white linen, and Obinna aligned his body with hers. He gathered her breast in his warm palm and massaged her nipple, teasing her with a pinch-and-release motion. She moaned, aroused and restless. The pressure inside her—the one that had been present for years, the one no man had eased—intensified and ached. She wrapped her arms around his neck, drew his face to hers, and whispered, "Make love to me."

She didn't want the alternative—the fleeting illusion of a connection she had felt with every man after him. Dunni wanted a sensation that hit every layer of her—her body, soul, mind, and even parts unknown to her. It had been twelve years without that feeling, but as Obinna entered her and their eyes connected, that inimitable sensation no other man had ever given her kindled. Fire, flutters, pressure, release, euphoria were an intense tide that erupted and consumed every fraction of her.

Their hips moved rhythmically with a matched speed, equal parts giving and receiving pleasure. Dunni's fingertips skimmed the hard lines of his body, then pressed into his firm backside and felt the flex of muscles as he alternated the pace of his thrusts. He was so damn confident. Dunni compared the boy who had taken her virginity with the man she saw now—one's movement clumsy and unsure, the other's dominant and deliberate.

Just as his lips trailed her neck, he reached for her left hand and interlaced their fingers. The scars on their palms met. Twelve years ago, when they'd split their skin open and clenched their bloody hands, Dunni had felt something inside her uproot and anchor itself to Obinna. It was strange, but it was the only way to describe the connection, a connection that weakened with them apart. But she felt it again now, something of hers taking root inside of him, reestablishing itself with a force that made her breathless.

CHAPTER FOURTEEN

Obinna propped up on his elbow and looked down at Dunni, her hair spread out on the pillow. He smiled, and she couldn't help but do the same.

"Dunni." He sighed, and his smile shrunk. "Stay. Please."

He didn't need to put more words into his request. She knew what he meant. "I can't." She wished he hadn't asked and tainted the moment with the reality of her returning to America. Her flight was in a few hours.

"You can't just leave."

"And I can't just stay." She drew the duvet over her chest, no longer comfortable being naked while having a mood-dampening conversation. "I have a life in Seattle. I can't leave everything on a whim."

"Then I'll come with you."

"What?" She sat upright. "You can't."

"It's been twelve years. You can't just come back into my life and then disappear."

"I'm not disappearing."

"Then what are you doing, huh?"

"It's complicated." She glanced at the engagement ring on the nightstand. The realization of what she'd done hit her now. Even with the elation she felt from being with Obinna, she felt guilty too. Her guilt was like sand in a meal she was enjoying. Regardless, she didn't pacify her guilt by justifying her actions, attributing it to weakness, nor did she utterly condemn what she'd done with Obinna. She couldn't have the pleasure without the guilt, nor the guilt without the pleasure. They existed together. It was impossible to separate the grains of sand from her meal, so she ate them both.

Obinna followed her gaze and frowned. "This man." He cleared his throat. "You mentioned you've been with him for a year."

She nodded.

"How did you meet?"

"Our mothers are friends. They introduced us."

"I see. And do you love him? Do you really love him?"

It was difficult to tell Obinna the same lie she had told everyone else. Her lips couldn't form the words, not now. Not after they'd made love. "No," she answered. "I don't."

"Okay." Obinna studied her with narrowed eyes. "I don't understand. If you don't love him, why the hell are you wearing his ring?"

"Christopher is a good guy. I care for him deeply."

"I'm sure you do, but that can't be enough to sustain a marriage. Why are you willing to commit your life to someone you don't love? Is it because of your mother?"

"She thinks we make a suitable match. She thinks he's good for me."

"She thinks. Dunni, what about you? What do you think? The Dunni that I knew would never—"

"People change, Obi," she snapped. "I've changed." Her voice lowered to a whisper. "I'm not a reckless, loudmouthed teenager anymore. I'm not that person." She looked away, slightly pained by the admission.

"Okay." He cupped her cheek and tilted it so their eyes connected again. "Then stay. Let me get to know the person you are now. *Biko*. These few hours with you are not enough. Let us have more time to talk further, to work through this situation."

"What situation?" It was a ridiculous question, but she asked it anyway, curious to hear his response.

He laughed, then tugged on the duvet she gripped to her chest. "This situation." He held her breast and ran a thumb over a nipple. He watched her reaction—the lazy flutter of her eyelids and the gentle graze of her teeth over her bottom lip. "We have a lot to work through." He lured her to lie down again. "So, stay. *Biko*."

She nodded. Though she questioned if it was because his fingers between her thighs muddled her reasoning or because she wanted to stay, because she couldn't imagine leaving him ever again.

"For a little while," she told him. "I'll stay for a little while."

Dunni woke up and extended a hand to her side, feeling folds of linen instead of Obinna. Her eyes grew wide in search of him. He wasn't in the room, though the faint scent of food that slipped through the slight break in the door indicated he was in the kitchen as he had been that morning. She skimmed off the bed and decided on a shower.

After lathering herself with a body wash that had a spicy masculine fragrance, she toweled off then entered Obinna's closet. Her fingers ran across the suits hung up and organized by color, then stopped at the section designated to T-shirts. She pulled out a V-neck tee and slipped it on before going downstairs.

As she neared the kitchen, she inhaled the hearty blend of tomatoes, *tatashe*, and onions flavored with spices and herbs. It was a familiar smell, one she had only ever associated with Obinna.

He was exactly where he had been in the morning, standing in front of the stove, a wooden spoon in his hand as he stirred the contents in a pot. Being with him still felt unreal. She watched him closely and waited for a glitch—some ripple in the air—that would indicate it was all a mirage. When nothing like that happened, she neared him.

"Hey."

"You're awake." Obinna turned and faced her. "Slept well?" When she nodded, he pressed his lips to her forehead. "I'm making—"

"*Ofada* stew." Dunni looked at the bubbling red stew; the

layer of oil that rose to its surface confirmed it was ready. "It looks and smells . . ." She smacked her lips. "Amazing."

"And in case you were wondering, it's just as good as my mother's."

"Well." She eyed him and smirked. "I'll be the judge of that."

"Eh-heh?" He wrapped an arm around her waist and drew her into his chest. "Are you doubting me?"

"A little."

He tickled her, and she squirmed while laughing. And even when his fingers stopped moving against her sides, she continued to laugh, a real laugh rather than something heavy with pretense. It was the kind of laugh she didn't feel only in her throat. She felt it in her stomach as it fluttered and contracted, and in her toes, as they wiggled against the cool kitchen tiles. Each chuckle eased out of her with the same quality she'd noted and admired in Gigi's laugh the night before. Dunni was happy and slightly detached from the other factors in her life, including the engagement ring still on the nightstand. When Obinna kissed her, she became completely detached. They moved blindly toward the counter, then jerked apart at the sound of a loud chime.

"It's just the doorbell," Obinna said. "Would you mind getting it while I finish up here?"

"Um . . ." Dunni glanced at her attire. "I don't think I'm dressed appropriately."

"It's okay. It's only Gigi."

"Oh." Although confused, Dunni didn't ask why Gigi was at his door. "Sure. I'll get it."

At the foyer, she pulled the door open after ensuring her T-shirt rested flat on her thighs.

"Dunni," Gigi said. "Mm-hmm. I had a feeling you'd be here." She stepped into the house, a knowing smile on her face. "After you left the reception last night and Nicholas followed, I had a strong feeling it was going to lead to this."

Dunni closed the door and lowered her eyes. Guilt and shame resurfaced at the thought of what she had done. She didn't look up, too afraid to see Gigi's judgment.

"I should probably apologize," Gigi said abruptly. "Actually, I definitely should."

"Huh?" Dunni's brows plunged into a deep frown. "Apologize? For what?"

"For what I said last night—at the reception." She ran her fingers along the bag strap that crossed her chest. "The thing about Nick fucking half of Lagos. I only said it to shut Cynthia up, but it obviously upset you."

It had hurt Dunni immensely. The knowledge that Obinna had been with a lot of women—that he was some sort of Lagos playboy—was a lot to handle. But Dunni had tried to ignore that detail while in bed with him. She'd tried to ignore it as she took a shower in his bathroom and wore his shirt and even as she entered the kitchen, prepared to eat what he had cooked. How many had there been? How many had taken part in the ritual of sleeping in his bed, wearing his clothes, and eating his meals?

"How many have there been?" Dunni said to Gigi, no longer willing to ask herself a question she did not have the answer to.

"How many what?"

"Women. How many women has he been with?"

Gigi laughed, tossing her shaved head back. "Honey, how do you suppose I would know that?"

"Okay. How many women have you seen him with?"

"I don't know. I've lost count."

"Fuck." Dunni pressed a hand to her forehead and damned her curiosity.

"Hey. Listen." Gigi squeezed Dunni's shoulders. "I've known Nicholas for three years. He's very closed off. He hardly lets anyone get close to him. All those girls he hooked up with meant nothing. From what I saw last night, this thing between the two of you is more than a fling. For him and I suspect for you too?"

Dunni nodded. "I . . . I . . ." Her voice, strained by emotions, shook. "I've known him since I was seventeen."

"Yeah," Gigi said softly. "He told me."

"The other night when I saw him for the first time in years, I just . . ." Dunni forced the words out despite the tightness in her throat. "I didn't know it would feel that . . . that painful and that good." She expelled a deep breath. "Now, I can't imagine getting on a plane and just leaving him. I don't know how I'm going to do it. In fact, I don't think that I can." Those last words, *I don't think that I can*, were truer than Dunni could express to Gigi.

"Then don't leave him, sweetheart."

"I can't stay here forever. I have responsibilities in America— a job, a fiancé, a . . ." She shook her head. "You must think I'm insane or think very little of me. I'm engaged, and I'm here with another man."

"Judging isn't my thing. Plus, I only met you two days ago. I don't know your life, but I know that sometimes, things aren't always black and white. You're obviously in a complicated situation." Gigi looped her arm through Dunni's and led her toward the kitchen. "Maybe staying with Nicholas for a little while will help you figure things out."

"Yeah. Maybe."

"Hey!" Gigi screamed at Obinna when they entered the kitchen. "Don't be stingy with the meat this time!"

He scooped stew into a small cooler, carefully handling the ladle so nothing poured out as it went from the pot to the container.

"Last time, I swore you only gave me three measly pieces."

"I'm fairly sure I didn't." Obinna snapped the lid on and turned to Gigi. "You just love exaggerating. It must be the actress in you."

"Whatever." She released Dunni's arm, strutted to Obinna, and grabbed the cooler from him. "Since you like to *shakara* and only make this stew once a year, I suppose I should take what I get and be happy."

"Sounds like the sensible thing to do." Obinna smiled, then came to Dunni's side and put an arm around her waist.

"Don't worry. I know how to take a hint. I'm leaving," Gigi said while walking toward the kitchen door. "I'm off to South Africa tomorrow, so I'll see you kids later."

"What are you doing in South Africa?" Dunni asked.

"Filming a movie. Bye. I'll let myself out." She blew a kiss and left; the clack of her heels faded as she neared the front door and then disappeared completely.

"I like her," Dunni said to Obinna.

"Yeah." He walked to a cabinet and pulled out a plate. "It's hard not to."

"Have you ever slept with her?" It seemed like Dunni's mouth was slippery and words were falling out of their own accord. She shouldn't have asked that question but felt strangely entitled to the answer—as if he owed it to her. "Have you slept with Gigi?"

"What?" Obinna paused after opening the pot of white rice.

"She's stunning and confident and interesting."

"Gigi is like my sister. The sister I never wanted but have grown to love." He glanced at Dunni, expecting her to laugh as he did. After noting her straight face, he sighed and reflected the same seriousness. "I met Gigi a few years ago at her first movie premiere. At the after party, she was sitting alone, sulking instead of celebrating. When I asked her why, she said, 'I'm pretty sure this movie is shit and none of my friends are telling me the truth.' So I graciously offered to be honest."

"And what did you tell her?"

"I told her it was one of the worst movies I had ever seen. She was great, but the plot and the script and most of everything was . . . well, shit."

Dunni suppressed a laugh. "Seriously? You said that? And what did she do—punch you?"

"Nope. She said, 'Well, it looks like I need new friends.'" He laughed. "And we've been friends since. We just clicked—in a very platonic way. She's my best friend, so no. I have never slept with Gigi. It's not like that with us—not at all. I promise. Okay?" He waited for Dunni to accept his answer. When she nodded, he turned to the pot and plated the food.

Dunni sat on a barstool, and after placing the plate on the counter and tucking two forks beneath the bed of rice, Obinna sat as well.

They ate in silence. Dunni chewed with her eyes closed and savored the flavors that unearthed memories of their teenage years—of their first meal together and the many they shared after that. She opened her eyes and looked at Obinna. She didn't have to tell him it was delicious. The smile on her face and the large portion of rice she shoved into her mouth conveyed that well enough.

During breakfast, they'd eaten from separate plates. Now, they ate from the same plate as they had years ago. Their forks occasionally clinked together. She scooped up the grains of rice that had fallen from his fork. He sliced the last piece of fried beef with a knife and gave her the bigger half. There was something very intimate about eating like this. It was comforting.

Dunni had tried to re-create the same feeling on the dates she'd gone on in America, but it was always awkward. People valued their personal space over there, and plates were always within the bounds of personal space. Her dates were possessive of their food, never willing to call it *theirs*. "Sure. You can have some of my fries. We can share my salad. Don't finish all of my pasta." With Obinna and always with Obinna, it was theirs.

"That was delicious," Dunni said, wiping the corners of her mouth with a napkin. "Thank you for making that."

"You're welcome." He sipped from a glass of water, then extended the cup to Dunni. "I want you to come away with me," he said, stroking the part of her thigh the large T-shirt didn't conceal. "I've rented a place in Eleko Beach. It's beautiful. Let's go there for a little while—away from everything, just the two of us. So we can figure things out."

It's what Gigi had suggested—that she spend time with Obinna alone to get clarity on her complex situation. "Okay. Sure. But I don't have any of my things here. They're all at my parents' house."

"Then we'll go get them."

"Um . . ." Dunni tensed. "I don't think that's a good idea. I could just take a taxi there and take one back."

"Don't be ridiculous. I'll drive you."

"But my mother might be there."

"So? It isn't like we haven't seen each other since it happened."

"What? You have?"

"Once or twice in passing at events. Of course, we've never said a word to each other."

Dunni shifted on the stool, uneasy at the thought of Obinna anywhere near her mother.

"Relax, Dunni." He squeezed her shoulder. "It was fine. We didn't even acknowledge each other."

"Yeah. But being back there—in that house—won't be like seeing her in passing. You know that, right?"

"It's nothing I can't handle." He stood and picked up the plate. "I'll be fine."

The smile on his face didn't reassure her at all. Nothing could. She suddenly felt sick, her lunch unsettled in her stomach.

He mumbled something about her not worrying, but Dunni did worry. What if her mother was at home? What would Obinna do when he saw her? Though the real question was, What would her mother do once she saw them together after twelve years, after everything she'd done to keep them apart?

CHAPTER FIFTEEN

THEN

On Monday morning, as Obinna entered his classroom, a new reality dawned on him. It was one without Dunni.

He stood in front of the class and looked at the desk they shared. She wasn't there, her knee no longer waiting for the weight of his. To his right, she sat with Molly, the girl with fair skin and flowing auburn hair, courtesy of her white father. Once Molly locked eyes with Obinna, she leaned into Dunni's ear and whispered, no doubt notifying her of his presence.

So Obinna waited; he waited for Dunni to turn and look at him, for their eyes to connect and communicate something other than the tension between them. He waited, stood in front of the classroom, impatient and desperate for a simple acknowledgment.

It did not come.

"Good morning, everyone," Miss Okafor said when she entered the classroom. "Please sit down."

Obinna shuffled to his seat. There was a sharpness in his chest, like something had fragmented and proceeded to prod him with its edges. He slouched into the wooden chair, and his slumped shoulders folded into his chest. Though the thud of a backpack on the desk jolted him upright.

"Obinna," Emeka said with an expansive grin. "How far *na*?"

"Um . . ." Obinna watched Emeka settle beside him. "What are you doing here?"

"Isn't it obvious? I'm your new seatmate." He unzipped his bag and forced out a textbook from the clutter. "Molly wants to sit with Dunni. So . . ." He caught Miss Okafor's glare and mouthed an apology. When the teacher turned to the board, he lowered his tone. "So we sit together now. Which I prefer because Molly talks too much. *Haba*. In fact, are we sure her father is an *Oyinbo* and not a parrot?" He stifled a chuckle with his hand. Once quiet, he noticed Obinna's glum expression. "What's wrong with you?" He followed his gaze, assessed the situation, then nodded. "Okay. Okay. I understand now. You and your girl are having problems. And she didn't want to sit with you. Eh-eh. Makes more sense."

Obinna looked at his clenched hands.

"Cheer up, man," Emeka encouraged. "That girl was too much for you anyway. In fact, she is even too much for me." He muffled another laugh. "We'll find you another girl. A nice girl that won't bite your head off. A nice girl with a nicer *yansh*."

Emeka spoke as if getting another girl required a shopping trip or a visit to an alchemist who fabricated pretty girls from the desires of hormonal teenage boys. There was no storehouse with girls waiting to be claimed or magicians who spun air into teenage dreams. There was no way to replace what Obinna had lost. But did he want to replace it or reclaim it? Wasn't it best to let it go, to let her go? He knew that for his mother, he simply had to.

Obinna tried. For four days, he tried to forget about Dunni. He tried to ignore the sensation of something sharp prodding his insides. At school, he was absentminded, always watching her and waiting for an acknowledgment that never came. At home, he performed his chores sluggishly, motivated only by his mother's nagging. He couldn't grasp why he felt so functionless.

He'd liked girls before. There had been Tolu, who always smelled like baby powder and Tom Tom sweets. Right after her, he'd liked Seun, whose braids were always so neat, her baby hairs slicked down with products that made her forehead shine. He'd liked those girls enough that he'd thought about them at night and watched them as they walked around campus. He'd been too shy to pursue either of them, but it hadn't mattered because in both cases, his feelings had left as quickly as they'd come. When he realized the sudden lack of emotions, he'd searched himself for them like something he'd lost. And then, like something he'd deemed worthless, he'd disregarded his search and carried on.

He couldn't do that with Dunni. His feelings for her were still rooted inside him, more firmly fixed than anything he'd felt for Tolu or Seun. It was a stubborn thing he couldn't ignore, even with his mother's disapproving voice resounding in his head. Obinna couldn't let Dunni go. So as the last bell of the day sounded, he was thankful Emeka was doing the one thing he'd begged him to earlier that day—rush everyone out of the classroom.

"*Oya*. Let's go. Everybody out," he barked, shoving books into bags and nudging bodies toward the door. "Do you want to sleep here? Is this your father's house?"

"Ah-ah. Emeka, when did you become classroom monitor?" Chinedu grumbled. "What's the meaning of all this after-school harassment?"

"Eh-heh." Emeka rolled up his sleeves and showed off his hefty arms. "You want to see harassment?" He took a step toward Chinedu, who quickly slung his bag over his shoulder and rushed out of the classroom. Other students hastened after him.

They listened to Emeka, out of fear. Everyone but Dunni, who purposely moved slower. But Obinna had counted on her defiance.

When their classmates left, Emeka winked at Obinna and walked out. The plan worked. Obinna was alone with Dunni, and Emeka had made it happen. They were friends, and it was a strange turn of events, considering their first encounter. But Emeka was a joker who loved being the center of attention. Sometimes, he got carried away and said the wrong things. And sometimes, he did something unexpectedly kind like lend Molly his only pen or help a friend get his girl back.

Obinna looked at Dunni, who packed her history books into her bag, unaware they were the only two left in the room. She zipped the bag, then looked up just as she flung the strap over her shoulder. Their eyes hadn't met in days. They did now, for a second, before she focused on the door and marched to it.

"Dunni, wait!" He rushed ahead of her, reached the door before she did, then shut it closed.

"Move. Now!"

She was terrifying. If he weren't so desperate to fix things between them, so certain he couldn't go another day without talking to her, he would have cowered.

"Dunni, I'm sorry."

The apology did nothing. The rage in her glare did not flatline. She shoved him and tried to get to the door, and he knew he would lose her if he didn't do more than apologize.

"I was ashamed," he blurted. "I was ashamed of myself. Of my life."

His confession did what his apology could not. Her posture relaxed. The rage in her eyes faded gradually. He went on.

"I never wanted you to see me like that. But then you did, and it was clear in a way it wasn't before."

"What was clear?" she asked, her voice calm and harsh, sweet and bitter, straddled between anger and concern.

"Who you are. And who I am. Without our school uniforms, it became so clear." So painfully clear.

Dunni blew out a breath then released her grip on her bag; it thumped on the floor, and she sat on a desk. "I didn't know all that mattered to you. On your first day, you told the entire class what your mother does for a living. And even with their reaction, you didn't seem ashamed. What changed?"

"Sometimes, I forget how different we are. It's easier when we're at school. But it wasn't easy that day with me sweating under the sun and you being . . . you."

The fact that his mother had gone further to point out their distinction certainly hadn't helped.

"I'm sorry you feel this way, Obi. I wish you didn't."

"I just want to be somebody." He sighed, and his lips shook at the force of his deep breath. "I just want to make something of my life."

"And you will. I know you will." She held out a hand to him, and he took it. "But you should know that doesn't matter to me. No matter who you are and what you have, I will still want you."

And even with the sincerity in her eyes, Obinna was skeptical. "Why?" He had never asked before, but he had wondered during the many times she neared him or grazed his hand with purpose or looked at him as she did now, with so much feeling. *Why me?* Now he voiced his curiosity and braced himself for the truth. "Why do you want me? Why do you like me, Dunni?"

He expected her to list all the reasons, as people do. You're handsome. You're funny. You're smart. You're this and that.

Instead, she shrugged and said, "Honestly, I don't know. I just do."

People didn't give that response. They gave a list, but he

wondered if that was the wrong response. Because what if she'd given a list—handsome, funny, smart? And then one day, he grew old and frail and became more cynical than comical. What if all his defining qualities gradually faded, and she started to cross things off her list? What if the reasons she had to want him, like him, love him, started disappearing until there was nothing at all? What then?

But she hadn't given a list. She had given no reason at all. And Obinna suddenly understood what a perfect response it was.

If Dunni liked him for no reason, then she would never have a reason to stop.

He smiled, relieved. But the feeling didn't last. How could it when her lips were taut and turned down in a frown?

"Dunni, are you okay?"

She shook her head and pulled her hand from his. "You hurt me. At the market. When you said I don't belong with you."

"I'm sorry. I—"

"Listen to me," she interrupted.

He closed his mouth, sealing away his apology and explanation.

"My mother is . . ." She clenched her jaw. "She's difficult. She doesn't even know me, but she tries to control what I wear, my hobbies, what university I go to—everything.

"My father is better. But he has ideas of who he wants me to be as well. They feel like they own me and can shape me into whatever they like. But I don't want to be owned by them. I don't want to belong to them or anyone!" Her voice rose, an element other than volume amplifying it. Maybe it was conviction or frustration. "But." Her voice was small and tender now, a whisper with a hint of vulnerability. "I wouldn't mind belonging to you, Obi. I wouldn't mind being yours. So, when you said that at the market . . ." She sniffed. "It hurt."

"Dunni, I'm so sorry." He took her hand and held it to his chest, hoping the quick rhythm of his heart expressed what he couldn't vocalize. "You are mine." He stepped closer, and their faces aligned. "And I'm yours."

He only now realized this, that his mother and father—who had an automatic claim to him by nature—weren't the only people he could belong to. He could choose to belong to someone else, someone he knew would own him but not control him. It would be his choice, and he chose Dunni as she had chosen him.

"I belong to you too," he whispered as his lips brushed hers.

Dunni shuffled to the edge of the desk and wound her arms around his neck. They watched each other and breathed, releasing all the tension inside them until their bodies relaxed against each other. And then they kissed.

It was the first time Obinna had kissed a girl. It amazed him how touching lips could trigger so many sensations. His entire body hummed and pulsed as the feeling on his lips echoed throughout him. He held Dunni's face and mimicked the movement of her tongue until he mastered the act and kissed deeper, exploring the mouth Emeka swore was built with razors.

It was not, of course. Dunni's mouth was velvet and sweet.

Slowly, their lips stopped moving. They opened their eyes and watched each other, smiling and panting.

And without thinking, Obinna said, "That was my first

kiss." He was seventeen, five months away from eighteen, and he had never kissed a girl. His friends, Emeka included, would have laughed at the admission, and maybe it was laughable. But he didn't care. He wanted her to know.

"Really?" Dunni smiled triumphantly. "I was your first kiss?"

He nodded. "Was I yours?" It was a stupid question. By the way she'd led their kiss before he grasped the technique, he knew the answer.

"No. I've kissed boys before."

He didn't ask how many. He didn't want to know.

"But this was different from the others." She rested her forehead against his. "I liked it better."

He grinned, pleased. "Can I ask you a question?"

"Okay."

"How come you never told me about your mother, about how she is?"

Obinna didn't know much about Dunni's family, only that her parents traveled often, and her older brother attended university in America. Dunni never gave much away.

"There isn't much to say about my mother. We aren't close." She lifted her forehead from his, and her expression turned serious. "While my father travels for business, she travels constantly just for leisure or maybe to get away from me. I'm not sure. But in a lot of ways, I don't really know her."

"You don't know your mother? That's strange."

"Well, she's a strange person. I have never understood her. I don't think I ever will. I don't think she wants me to." Dunni shook her head. "Anyway, that's my mother."

"Thank you for telling me."

They shared a brief kiss, and then she shuffled off the desk.

"I have to go. My father should be here now. Whenever he's in town and free, he likes to pick me up." She grabbed her bag. "Come. I'll introduce you to him."

"Really? Are you sure?"

"I'm sure he would like to meet you."

Obinna realized suddenly that he wouldn't only be meeting Dunni's father, but the man who had funded his scholarship. "I would like to meet him too, so that I can thank him."

Dunni swung the door open, then turned to look at Obinna. "By the way, in case it wasn't obvious, you're my boyfriend now." She smiled. "So tell those *yeye* girls eyeing you to back off."

My boyfriend. Obinna loved that she had confirmed it verbally. Though he was partially confused. "What girls?" he asked as they walked through the door.

"You know who." She elbowed his side, and he laughed. "Abigail, Ini, Lara. Once Molly told everyone we were no longer talking, they just started acting like fools *o*. Do you know how many lives I had to threaten this week?"

"For me?" He found it hard to believe.

"Yes, for you. Apparently, you're a hot commodity." She elbowed him again. "Don't let it go to your head *sha*."

"That's actually impossible." He watched her and fought the urge to laugh. "I didn't know you were so jealous. Threatening girls just to keep me to yourself?"

"Well." She stopped walking and looked at him. "I'm not

entirely sure yet, but I think I'd do anything to keep you to myself."

She wasn't joking. Her serious expression confirmed it. Her admission should have flattered Obinna. Instead, it worried him, because he was sure he would do anything to keep Dunni to himself as well. And maybe, just maybe, that wasn't a good thing.

CHAPTER SIXTEEN

The gate slid open, and Dunni clenched her hands as Obinna drove into her family's estate. She watched him for a reaction, a sign that he was also anxious. His stoic expression gave nothing away.

He parked the car a few feet from the front door and turned to her. "Would you like me to come in with you?"

"What?" The question stunned her. She didn't expect him to be so unbothered. Didn't this place affect him as it did her? She studied his face for the answer and noticed his jaw was stiff, the outline more defined than it had been seconds ago. Her hand rested on the gentle hollow of his cheek. "It's okay," she told him. "Stay in the car."

She said this to protect him. Inside the car, he was safe. Once he stepped out, she feared he would vividly remember the ordeal of that day and lose his composure. She couldn't protect him all those years ago, and even now, this was all she could do. It wasn't enough.

"Give me five minutes. Okay?" Her hand slipped away from his cheek, and he grabbed it quickly.

"Dunni, wait. I . . . I . . ." His grip was unsteady, shaking as he pressed her hand to his chest.

He used to do this when they were younger—align her open palm with his thumping heart, allowing the rhythm to communicate something he didn't know how to express. Back then, it hadn't taken her much to understand, to associate the quickness beneath her palm as emotions—fondness and then love. Now, the movement beneath her hand communicated something else. Fear.

"Five minutes," she told him. "That's it. I'll come back."

"But what if . . ."

He didn't finish the sentence, but she knew what he intended to say. *What if your mother stops you from leaving? What if you change your mind? What if I never see you again?*

Dunni sighed and allowed her forehead to fall against his. As they sat, unmoving, she wondered why things couldn't be easy for them. Why did this have to be the turn their story took? Why did an introduction at a secondary school lead to so many unexpected and painful challenges? They were finally together, but it was far from a happy reunion. Their happiness was measured—a small and unsatisfying dose; it wouldn't be complete until they addressed everything between them. That was why Dunni needed to get away with him—to address these things, to work through the complications, and to make a decision.

"Five minutes," she assured him again, then stepped out of the car.

In the house, she hastened up the steps and then to her room. She grabbed her Louis Vuitton travel bag and shoved clothes and undergarments into it, rushing to get back to Obinna. Five minutes. That was what she promised him.

"Dunni." Iya Agba stood at the door, one hand on her hip. "Where have you been?" she asked.

"I um . . ." Dunni cleared her throat. "I was with a friend last night . . . after the wedding. It was late. I didn't want to wake you, so I called Paul and told him to tell you. Didn't he?"

"He did." She stepped into the room and assessed Dunni's attire—an oversize T-shirt and sweatpants. "What friend were you with?"

"An old friend."

"An old friend is the reason you missed our appointment with the pastor."

"Shoot." Dunni smacked her forehead. "I completely forgot about that. I'm so sorry."

"And that was the only opportunity we had. You're going back home today."

"Actually, I'm not leaving today. I've decided to stay a little longer."

"But what about—"

"I already called home and made necessary arrangements, so I can extend my stay. I spoke to Christopher as well. Everything is sorted."

"Really?" Iya Agba smiled. "Okay. Good. Then I'll book another meeting with the pastor for tomorrow."

"I can't see the pastor. I'm actually leaving right now." She crammed more clothes into the bag. "I'm going to stay with my friend for a little. But I'll be back."

"Dunni, this situation is serious. I had another dream last night. And this one was different. You didn't die, but you . . ." She contemplated, then shook her head. "I'm still trying to understand it."

"Understand what?"

"In the past, when I had those dreams, I could not do anything because it was meant to happen. It was their time. It took me years to accept that. But with you, it is different." She considered her granddaughter. "It isn't your time, Dunni. But you have done something that has . . ." She paused and frowned. "What in God's name did you do?"

Dunni stopped packing. She glanced at the scar on her palm, then quickly fisted her hand. "I . . . I didn't do anything," she said, defensive. "I didn't do anything," she affirmed again.

She might as well have been a child denying she had eaten a cookie even with the crumbs on her lips because her grandmother, so certain of her guilt, grabbed her arm and said: "Dunni, tell me what you did."

"Iya Agba, you have to stop all this. Your dreams are just

dreams. They mean nothing. Okay? You're just being superstitious."

Dunni instantly regretted saying that word—*superstitious*.
Her grandmother hated being called that. It made her feel like a
woman in the forest with cowries in her hair and a calabash in
her hand, chanting nonsense to spirits. It made her feel like she
was something diabolical.

"I'm sorry," Dunni said quickly. "I didn't mean that."

But it was too late. Her grandmother let go of her arm and
pinned her lips in a tight line. "Be careful," she said. "Wherever
you are going and *whoever* you are with. Just be careful." She
turned away and left.

Dunni attempted to go after her and apologize further, but
her mother stepped into the room.

"Where have you been, and where are you going?" she asked,
her voice ice-cold.

Dunni quickly zipped up the travel bag, more eager to leave
with her mother present. She'd promised Obinna five minutes.
It was well over that time limit now. She grabbed the bag off the
bed and marched toward the door, but her mother stood in the
doorway.

"I asked you a question. I would appreciate an answer."

Dunni said nothing.

"I was at Tiwa's wedding reception yesterday. I arrived a little after dinner. I didn't see you. Why is that?" She watched her
daughter with narrowed eyes. "Mrs. Osifo told me you left with
a man."

Dunni's grip on the bag strap tightened.

"Nicholas Arinze. Or Obinna." She arched a defined eyebrow. "You spent the night with him, didn't you? And I presume he's the one in the car?"

Dunni denied nothing.

"You're engaged, and you're running off with another man?"

"He isn't just another man! You know that!" Dunni finally said, fuming. "And I am not running off!"

"Then what are you doing?"

"I just need time, okay? I need time to figure all this out."

"Figure what out?"

"If I want to be with a man I don't love. Or if I want to be with a man I have loved since I was seventeen." She straightened her back and exhaled. "Get out of my way, Mother."

"I can't let you leave with him."

"Haven't you done enough? Haven't you?" Tears came down Dunni's eyes. "There is still a scar on his back. You left a permanent scar on him." Her voice shook. She gasped as she spoke. "Get out of my way. Right now."

"Dunni, you don't understand how I . . ." She lowered her eyes, then lifted them to meet her daughter's. "Don't go." Her voice softened. "Stay. I know I can't stop you but—"

"That's right. You can't." Dunni shoved past her mother and marched through the door and then down the stairs.

Obinna paced by the car. With the five minutes she had promised expired, he had grown restless. He ran to Dunni the instant he saw her and held her wet cheek. "You're crying. What's wrong? What happened?"

"Nothing." She sniffed. "Let's just go."

He led her to the car, then tossed her bag in the boot. As he attempted to enter the driver's seat, he paused. Dunni's mother appeared at the doorway. Obinna met her gaze, then opened his mouth. Dunni braced herself. Thankfully, he said nothing. He climbed into the car, shut the door, and drove off.

CHAPTER SEVENTEEN

THEN

As Obinna neared the Mercedes G-Class, he wiped the moisture on his palms onto his trousers.

"What's wrong?" Dunni asked him. "You're nervous about meeting my father?"

Actually, he was terrified but didn't correct her.

"You're so cute." She ogled him, and Obinna averted his gaze from hers.

"Stop looking at me like that."

"Like what? Like I want to kiss you? Because I do."

"Dunni, don't you dare."

"Come on *na*. Just one quick peck."

Her father was a few feet ahead of them, leaning against his car and looking at his phone.

"Dunni, do you want your father to kill me?"

"Don't you think you're being a little dramatic? No one's

going to kill you over a kiss. Now, close your eyes and stand still. I'll be quick." She stood in front of him. "Please. Come on."

He glanced at her father, then huffed. "Okay. But be quick." He closed his eyes and waited.

A second passed, and then another. Nothing happened. He opened his eyes and saw the smirk on Dunni's face. Then it became obvious. She was taunting him, trying to rattle him further. "You're a troublemaker, you know."

She laughed. "Did you really think I was going to do that? Kiss you in front of my father? Do you want us both to die?" Her lips spread out evenly to form a sweet smile. "Come on." She walked ahead, and he followed. "I'm sure he'll like you. Just relax."

They came face-to-face with her father, and Obinna tried to keep his spine straight and his head high as Dunni introduced them.

"Mr. Damijo, sir, it's a pleasure to meet you," Obinna said, firmly taking the hand extended to him. Even with his attempt at appearing confident, he felt insignificant beside the imposing man, who had an aura of importance. He wore a gray *atiku* and black loafers that shone as if Obinna's mother had doused them with olive oil. A gold cross dangled from a chain around his neck; it was small but noticeable.

"How are your studies?"

"Good, sir. Very good. I want to thank you for this opportunity. I am so grateful."

"Prove your gratitude by working hard."

"Yes. I will, sir. I am."

Dunni stood at Obinna's side and watched the interaction, perhaps even enjoying it.

"I hope a bright boy like yourself has big plans for his future."

"Yes, sir. Absolutely."

"Well, I'll be happy to hear about them—perhaps steer you in the right direction if necessary. Get in." He opened the back door, and Dunni entered the car without a second thought.

Obinna hesitated. "Um . . . I . . ." He cleared his throat. "I usually take public transportation, sir." Every day, Dunni insisted he ride with her and let her driver drop him off. And every day, he declined, reluctant for her to see his home. Though now he feared he wouldn't have the option of declining.

"Don't worry. We can drop you at home," her father insisted. "We aren't in a rush to get anywhere."

In that instant, the tinted window of the passenger door rolled down and stopped below dark eyes. Obinna grew stiff as the eyes, hooded with long lashes, assessed him. His toes curled, and his pinky got caught in a tear in his sock. He couldn't shake it free, so he bore the additional discomfort and wondered if his expression gave anything away.

"Honey." The word was curt and hard like a stone dropping to the ground in one thud. "Let him be on his way. I'm sure you two can finish your discussion another time."

"Nonsense," Mr. Damijo said. "We'll drop him off. Obinna, don't mind my wife. Get in." He waited for Obinna to accept his invitation.

"Come on," Dunni urged, tapping the seat beside her.

"Um . . . okay." Having no other choice, he climbed into the car.

"Hey." Dunni shifted to him, even though he had deliberately put a respectable distance between them. "Ignore my mother," she whispered into his ear. "She's just being herself."

"So, Obinna," Dunni's father said after starting the car. "Where do you live?"

Obinna announced his address and watched Dunni's mother. If she had a reaction, he was oblivious to it, as he saw only the back of her head from where he sat.

The car moved; it left the school grounds, then sped up on the main road, gradually leaving the luxury of paved, clean lanes. Obinna never wanted Dunni to see where he lived, to see how he lived. He'd wanted to maintain the image of himself in his dapper school uniform. And for a month, he had succeeded. But her trip to the market had fragmented that image. Once she saw his home, the image would shatter completely. She would see him for everything he was and everything he was not. What then?

"Obinna," Dunni's father said. "What university do you plan on attending?"

"The University of Lagos, sir."

"Good choice. That is an excellent school."

"Well, I'm happy you feel that way, Daddy. Because I plan on going there too."

Obinna and Dunni had discussed universities only casually, along with their classmates during lunch. All of them planned on attending university overseas. Obinna had been the only one who'd spoken about local universities. The University of Lagos was a good school and a sensible choice. He would go from home rather than live on campus. It would save his mother money. She had already committed to paying the tuition, saying she could afford it with or without a scholarship. But Obinna was unsure if she was being practical or speaking by faith. She did that often—said things as though they were facts. It often left Obinna confused, uncertain of what was truly within his grasp.

Their finances—real or imagined—limited his academic reach, but that wasn't the case for Dunni. Although the thought was depressing, he'd imagined she would attend university abroad. So, her announcement shocked him as it did her parents, who glanced at each other.

"Um . . . Obinna." After a moment, her father continued his line of questioning. "What would you like to study in university?"

"Business, sir."

"Again, a good choice."

The questioning carried on for the duration of the drive. Obinna slowly felt at ease. His back relaxed into the leather seat, and when Dunni extended her hand to him, he took it. They stayed that way for a while, holding hands in the back seat. It was nice, sweet, until the moment Dunni's mother turned around. When she saw their clenched hands, her features grew taut.

Obinna pulled his hand back quickly, feeling like he had done something wrong—touched something he wasn't supposed to. Dunni must not have felt the same. Her hand did not move; it stayed in the space between them, still open, waiting for his hand, waiting for him to be as defiant as she.

But Obinna wasn't like Dunni with all her audacity. He was timid and terrified of her mother.

The car stopped. From the view through the window, it was clear they were no longer in Lekki.

"We're here." Dunni's father, who had been focused on the road, had no idea what was going on. "Obinna, please greet your parents for me."

"Um . . . yes, sir. I will. Thank you for bringing me home." It surprised him that he found his voice, especially with Dunni's mother still watching him. "Have a good evening." He glanced at Dunni, not wanting to linger on her. "Bye." He pushed the door open, and when his feet met the sandy ground, an argument ensued inside the car.

"No. What are you doing? You can't do that," Dunni protested.

"Stay in the car," her mother snapped. "I won't repeat myself."

Dunni obeyed. She folded her arms and mouthed an apology to Obinna.

"Okay." Her mother stepped out of the car. "I would like to greet your parents." She shut the door Obinna had been holding open, and Dunni's face disappeared. "Show me to your house."

"My . . . my . . . my mother might not be there, ma," Obinna stammered.

"Well, let's see." She turned toward the corroded gate that surrounded the two-story flat. "Come on."

He staggered beside her, hesitant and petrified. Even with her heeled shoes on the bumpy ground, she moved with purpose.

They made their way through the gate. Old jerry cans and abandoned wooden furniture lined the grime-coated walls of the beige building. At the far end of the compound, where a stray dog lazed in the sun, several layers of bricks upheld a green water tank. Clothes hung on cable wires flapped against the wind, softly inflating and then deflating. Obinna stopped at his door and retrieved the key from his backpack; he slid it into the lock, then turned the handle and gestured for Dunni's mother to enter. He prayed his mother was not home, because with him was the trouble she had warned him not to bring to her doorstep.

Anxious, he listened for the clanking of pots, the rustling of a broom, or the humming of Christian hymns. The apartment was quiet. Thank God.

"Auntie, my mother is not home. But I will tell her you came."

He would do no such thing.

Dunni's mother didn't say a word. She considered the apartment, her expression blank. She was a difficult woman to read. He couldn't gauge her thoughts, so he followed her darting stare instead and observed the mediocrity of his home through fresh eyes. The small space depicted his lack so blatantly. The brown sofa with a rip in its fabric could not conceal it. The old, tiny television with several broken knobs seemed to scream it. The faded paint on the cracked walls was more telling than anything else. Obinna needed to get her out.

"Auntie, I—"

She held up her hand, and he closed his mouth, too terrified to do anything else.

"Do you know why I'm here?"

Slowly, he bobbed his head. He didn't want to admit it to himself, but he knew. "Yes," he said. "I do."

"Good. Then there's no need for a conversation. I suppose I'll take my leave." She gave the apartment one last glance, then moved toward the door.

"But . . . but I . . ."

She paused and turned to him. "But you what?"

"I'm going to make something of myself," he told her, his confidence breaking through his fear. "I will."

"And I don't doubt that. As my husband said, you are a bright and ambitious young man. I know you will make something of yourself. But my daughter won't be by your side during the years it will take you to get there." She shook her head vigorously. "She won't be there to nurse your ego every time you fail. And she certainly won't be there every time your failures belittle you and you need to shrink her to feel big. I loved a poor and ambitious man once, and it almost killed me. That will not be my daughter. Stay away from her."

She looked at him, not like she had before. This time, strangely, tears glazed her eyes. It was as if a die had been flipped, and its other side—another dimension—revealed.

As she walked through the door, Obinna wondered if Dunni had ever seen this side of her mother.

CHAPTER EIGHTEEN

The one-hour drive from Lekki brought Dunni and Obinna to Eleko Beach, off the coast of Lagos. She'd enjoyed the ride and the silence, which Obinna knew not to disturb with music or questions. After everything that had happened with her grandmother and mother, the silence soothed her. Now, as Obinna parked the car, she exhaled and released the last bit of pent-up tension.

"Where are we?" she asked.

"Jara Resort." He took her hand and pressed his lips to it. "I think you'll like it."

They stepped out of the car, and Dunni rolled her tight shoulders. Her head tilted back as she took in the span of the palm trees. There were so many of them, dispersed around the compound and huddled around the white, two-story beach house they approached. Dunni glanced at Obinna, who carried their bags.

"I like it," she told him.

He returned her smile as they entered the resort. The two workers at the reception desk stood straight the moment they saw Obinna.

"Mr. Arinze, welcome," the man said. "May I take your things?"

"Thank you." He extended the two bags, and the man took them and strode up the stairs.

"When shall the rest of your party be arriving?" the woman behind the desk asked.

"They won't be." Obinna took Dunni's hand. "It's just us."

"Oh. Welcome, ma. Please let me know if you need anything."

"Sure. Thank you," Dunni said.

When she stepped into their room on the second floor, she noticed the balcony that overlooked the beach. She pushed aside the white curtain, slid the glass door open, and stepped out. Aqua-blue water rolled and crashed against the sand. Palm trees that varied in size made the view even more breathtaking. From behind, Obinna wrapped his arms around her stomach.

"Did I say I like it?" Her back relaxed against his chest. "I meant to say I love it."

"Really?"

"Mm-hmm."

He held her waist and turned her around to face him. Smiling, he drew his lips to hers, but she stepped back.

"Obi, I want to. Believe me." A grumble sounded in her throat. "But—"

"But what?"

"I'm engaged."

He frowned. "You don't have to keep reminding me."

"I'm not reminding you to hurt you. I'm only trying to remind you that I'm in a difficult position." Her eyes lowered to the floor. "I feel extremely guilty about what we did earlier. It shouldn't have happened. But I got carried away. I wasn't thinking straight."

"Are you saying you regret it?"

"I'm saying it wasn't fair to Christopher. Or you." She rubbed the bridge of her nose and sighed. "I'm not this person who cheats. But I'm in this strange situation, so I'm trying to figure out what to do. That's why I'm here with you." She squeezed his shoulder tenderly. "But I don't want this to be about sex. We aren't just two people infatuated with each other, are we?"

"Of course not."

"Okay. Then let's talk. We obviously connect physically. Let's connect on another level now. Let me get the chance to know you again. It's been years. I have so many questions. There's so much I want to know. I'm sure there's a lot you want to know also?"

He nodded.

"Then let's not get carried away. Yes?"

"Okay."

"Good. Great." She exhaled, relieved. Then her stare settled on his lips. "Before the platonic bit officially starts, can I just do one thing?"

He squinted and regarded her. "What?"

"Kiss you. Just one small kiss. A peck." She watched him coyly through fluttering lashes.

"And what if that one kiss leads to something else?"

149

"It won't. I won't let it. Seriously."

He contemplated briefly, then gave in. "Okay. Just one small kiss." He closed his eyes and leaned into her.

Dunni, however, did not lean into him.

Seconds passed, and when Obinna opened his eyes—one and then the other—he saw her smirking. Realization hit him, and he laughed.

"Did you really think I was going to kiss you?" She smacked his cheek playfully. "Obinna, you should know better."

"Eh-heh." He spread his arms on the railing, one on either side of her. "So you're still a troublemaker?"

"Only when it concerns you." She bent down and ran under his arm and into the room. "Because you make it so damn easy." She bounced on her toes, anticipating he would try to catch her.

But he entered the room and stood with his hands in his pockets, watching her with a satisfied grin.

"What?" she asked.

"It's just funny."

She stopped moving, her feet flat on the floor. "What is?"

"I thought you had changed—that you were different. And you are. But in a lot of ways, you're still the same person—lively, funny, passionate."

Only with you, she wanted to tell him. *I'm only this person with you.*

"I'm going to make some phone calls and give you a chance to freshen up," he said, then walked to the door.

"Hey," she called after him, and he stopped and faced her.

"The woman at the front desk mentioned something about the rest of your party. What did she mean?"

"For the past two years, I've hosted a mentorship retreat for young people coming out of university, looking to make business connections and such. I was going to host it here this year. I had the space already booked for two days. But I canceled the retreat this morning."

Dunni frowned, then gestured to herself. "For me?"

He nodded. "Yeah."

"How did you know I would stay?"

"I hoped."

A moment of silence passed between them, and Dunni knew this getting-to-know-each-other business was only a formality. When they were younger, she'd liked and later loved Obinna. When her friends asked why, she'd responded, "I don't know. I just do." She'd said the same thing when he had asked. Initially, his personality and appearance had nothing to do with how she felt. But as time passed, they gave her emotions more texture. She spent a lot of time looking at his hooded eyes and had grown to love the shape of them and even the wide base of his nose. She loved his bashfulness. She loved his devotion to his mother and to his studies. Those qualities weren't the base of her feelings, they were more like the garnish. Because with all of it gone, nothing would change. She would still love him and want him as she did now. Because the foundation was already there. The fact that he had canceled his event for her only strengthened her feelings.

CHAPTER NINETEEN

THEN

Ten minutes before the morning bell rang, Obinna rushed through the school's gates. He was the only student who came to school on public transportation. Everyone else arrived in cars—in luxury and prestige with drivers who held the door open for them or parents whom teachers flattered with extensive salutations. Usually, he ignored the dissimilarity between himself and his peers. Today, the parade of cars made it especially difficult. His legs quickened as he attempted to escape it all, but he stumbled and the biology textbook in his hands, the one he had been reading on the bus, fell to the ground. The sheets of paper within the book spilled out, and he groaned, then crouched down.

As he gathered his things, a hand appeared and grabbed his pen. He looked up and saw Dunni. Her long braids, swept over one shoulder, dangled above the ground. Her cocoa-brown skin gleamed as it always did. Whatever moisturizer she used left it glistening all day. When he was near her, he smelled the floral-fruity fragrance of the moisturizer. Sometimes, a light trace of the refreshing scent would stick to his skin—faint enough that he required the full force of his nose to capture it. And when it disappeared completely, he would try to remember the bold and subtle notes and even her distinct scent that added a signature element to the fragrance. Obinna was constantly collecting details, exercising his five senses to make each memory of Dunni more vivid before storing them away. He did this because he feared Dunni wouldn't be his for long.

"Hi." She smiled. "Need some help?"

"Um . . . no. It's okay." Hurriedly, he stuffed the sheets of paper into his textbook and snatched his pen from her. "I have it."

She rose along with him and squinted. "What's wrong?"

"Nothing."

"I've been asking you this question for two weeks, and you've been giving me the same answer—the same lie."

"Lie? I'm not lying."

She rolled her eyes. "Is this about us? About me?"

"What? No."

"Then why have you been acting strange? You've been distant and quieter than usual." She folded her arms. "Seriously. What's this about?"

It was about her mother and her disapproval. Being with Dunni often required Obinna to compartmentalize. While enjoying her company or kissing her, he would attempt to ignore everything her mother had said to him. He hadn't told Dunni about the brief and daunting conversation that occurred in his home two weeks ago. Instead, he had lied—told Dunni her mother had been nice and left after learning his mother wasn't home. He believed lying was the best way to prevent further strain between Dunni and her mother. Though now, his relationship with Dunni seemed strained by the secret he kept.

"Nothing's wrong," he lied again.

She opened her mouth, then closed it. Her eyes wandered to two teachers—one directing the dwindling parade of cars and the other directing students toward the school doors. "Do you want to get out of here?"

"Huh?"

"Do you want to leave?" Her straight lips indicated she was not joking.

"And go where?" Obinna asked.

"On a date."

"A date?" He laughed.

She did not. "We've never been on a date. We have to nurture our relationship beyond campus. Don't you think?"

"Um . . . I suppose."

"My parents are out of the country, so I doubt the school will reach them when they call to report my absence. They'll likely call Paul, but I can handle him. What about you?"

"Well, my mother's phone isn't working right now."

"Perfect. Then let's go." She turned and marched toward the gate.

"Dunni, wait," Obinna whispered while jogging after her. "Stop."

"What?" She paused and faced him.

"We have a biology test tomorrow. Miss Okafor was going to review the past lessons today."

"I can pass that test in my sleep. And so can you. We don't need the review, so let's just go."

"We can't just leave."

"Of course we can. But let's go before Miss Dikeh sees us." She referred to the teacher who had her back to them as she ushered students into the building. "Come on." She took Obinna's hand and nudged him. "Come with me."

The warmth of her palm sweetened the invitation. He gripped her hand, and they ran through the gate and didn't stop until they reached the junction. Between heavy gasps, they laughed. Obinna doubled over, then lifted his head and smiled at Dunni.

"You're going to get me in trouble one day."

"Then I'll get you out." She winked.

He stood upright and huffed. "So? What now?"

"Our first date can begin." She waved down a taxi driving by, and they entered the red Toyota.

"Where to?" the driver asked, his voice deep and gruff.

"Filmhouse Cinemas in Oniru."

"Cinemas?" The driver turned to the back seat and eyed them. There was a buttered loaf of *agege* bread on his lap; crumbs covered the corners of his chapped lips. "*Una* no *dey* go school? No be school uniform *na una* wear so?"

At the scolding, Obinna sank in the seat. Dunni, however, shifted and met the driver's steely stare. "Come *o*," she said, "no be taxi driver *na* you be? *Abi na* you born us?"

"No be small *pikin una* be?" the driver retorted. "Come *dey* do boyfriend and girlfriend, instead of *una* to go school. *Una* don spoil finish."

"You no *dey* shame? Old man like you. See how you *dey* chook mouth for small children matter. Shame no *dey* catch you?"

"Dunni." Obinna tugged her arm, urging her to stop insulting the man who was old enough to be her father. "That's enough. Let's just go. We'll get another taxi or take the bus."

The driver, faced with the threat of losing business, cleared his throat. "Filmhouse Cinemas." He wiped his mouth and turned to the steering wheel. "Them no *dey* show film this early morning, *sha*."

"*Wetin* come concern you for the matter? *Abeg* face front make you drive." Dunni hissed and rolled her eyes. "*Olofofo*."

After grumbling under his breath, the driver entered the road and headed to their destination.

Dunni settled into the seat and exhaled.

Obinna watched her. "I didn't know you could speak pidgin English like that."

"Only when the occasion calls for it."

"Troublemaker," he teased.

"Again, only when the occasion calls for it." She matched his smile and shifted to his side.

"What was that last word you said to him?" Obinna asked. "I think it was Yoruba."

"*Olofofo*," she answered. "It means 'a nosy person, a gossiper.'" While Obinna had whispered his question, Dunni translated loudly, taking the opportunity to insult the driver again.

"Would you teach me some Yoruba?"

"Only if you teach me Igbo."

"Okay."

The duration of the ride involved a brief language lesson. When the car stopped, Dunni paid the driver and hissed before climbing out.

Obinna stared at the immense two-story building with a balcony. It was his first time at the cinemas, so he thought he would appreciate every detail about the experience, even the blue large words that spelled out IMAX atop the building.

He followed Dunni inside, through the sliding doors, and into a massive open space.

"There's no one here," he said.

"That's because no one comes to the cinemas in the morning, but this one always has early viewing times. That's why I chose it." She walked to the woman behind the ticket stand. "Good morning. When does the earliest film start?"

The woman glanced at the computer in front of her. "We have one starting in forty minutes—at ten thirty. And another at eleven."

They decided to see the film at ten thirty. It was an action starring Dwayne Johnson. Obinna had money only for the bus home, so he said nothing as Dunni pulled a silver card from her wallet and swiped it on a machine. The woman behind the counter handed them the tickets and gave them directions to the appropriate theater.

"What do we do before it starts?" Obinna asked as they walked away from the ticket stand. On the walls, there were enormous posters of the latest movies, and he couldn't resist gawking at them.

"We could go to the balcony on the second floor. The view is beautiful from up there, or . . ." Dunni squeezed his hand. "We could go into the theater, and while we wait for the film to start, we could . . ." Her suggestive stare completed the sentence.

"Yes," he blurted. "Let's do that—wait for the film!"

They sat in the middle of the theater. According to Dunni, it was the best viewing spot. When the lights dimmed and the screen lit up with images, Obinna agreed. During the trailers, Dunni left and returned with drinks and a large bucket of popcorn. It was warm and buttery, and Obinna gathered handfuls as he watched the film.

They saw two films. The second was a romantic comedy, which Obinna enjoyed more than the action. Being with Dunni outside of school was strange, but liberating. In a dark theater, lost in another world, theirs shrunk. They answered to no one. For the first time in weeks, Obinna kissed Dunni without reservation, without her mother's disapproval resonating in his head. He felt at ease.

They left the cinemas at two thirty and took a taxi to a location Dunni disclosed only to the driver. When they stepped out of the car and stood in front of a brown-brick building with a Domino's Pizza and a Pinkberry, Obinna's face lit up.

"Which should we have first?" Dunni asked.

He turned to her and grinned widely. "Pizza."

It was a day of firsts—the first time at the cinemas, the first time eating pizza. The crust was warm and fluffy. He loved the way the cheese stretched like okra. Dunni ate two slices while he ate six. It shocked him that he still had room for ice cream.

"This is rich people's ice cream," he told Dunni after licking his spoon.

She laughed. "What do you mean?"

"It's so creamy. And the toppings. I love the toppings." He scooped a mixture of vanilla ice cream, strawberries, and white chocolate chips into his mouth. "I've never had ice cream like this."

"What kind have you had then?"

"The ones that come in the mobile freezer on the bicycle. They aren't like this. They're just ice and sugar and color."

"I've never had those."

"You aren't missing anything. This is much better." He sighed and leaned into the pink plastic chair. He watched Dunni for a while without saying a word, again collecting details of her and storing them away. He smiled. "This has been the best day."

"Really?"

"Absolutely." He extended his hand across the table and took hers. "Thank you."

"You're welcome." Her lips expanded, then shrank almost immediately. "Will you tell me now?"

"Tell you what?"

"Why you've been acting so . . . I don't know. Not like yourself." She leaned into the table and fixed her gaze on him. "What's wrong?"

"Is that why you brought me here? And to the cinemas—to soften me up so you could get an answer?"

"You've seemed tense. I thought a day away from everything would help you relax a little. Did it?"

It had. For hours, he hadn't thought about her mother. He had navigated their relationship without hesitation, and it had felt especially freeing. "It helped," he told her.

"Okay. Good. So tell me. Is it school? Has someone been bothering you? Tell me who it is, and I'll—"

"And you'll what? Beat them up?"

"If it's necessary."

"Dunni." He exhaled. "I don't want you getting into fights for me."

"If not you, then who?"

"No one. Don't get into fights for anyone." He watched her sternly, trying to convey his seriousness. "Besides, no one at school is bothering me."

"Then what is it? And just so you know, I'm tired of asking this question. So for the love of God, just tell me."

"We've been having such a good time. I don't want to ruin our date."

"Having a serious moment won't ruin it. Haven't you seen *The Bachelor*?"

Obinna shook his head. "What's that?"

"It's an American reality show about a man who's searching for a wife, so he goes on dates with a lot of women."

"Okay."

"There's always two parts to every date—the fun part when they go to a carnival or swimming or something. And then the second part when they have dinner and talk about serious things like a childhood trauma, past relationships, or just sad things. Then they cry, they connect, and their relationship grows stronger. It's the formula."

Obinna watched her blankly. "That seems like a terrible show."

"You would think, but it's not. Anyway, the point I'm trying to make is this is the part of our date when we get serious. So, let's do it." She slammed her palm on the table and drew the attention of other customers. "Let's talk, let's cry, let's connect."

Obinna laughed. "Dunni, I'm not going to cry."

"Fine," she groaned. "But at least tell me what's wrong, *na. Biko.*"

Biko. It was the Igbo word for "please." He'd taught it to her during the ride to the cinemas that morning. And that word, his language, spoken by her, penetrated some place in him that was tender, a place an English word couldn't reach or even know to reach.

"Your mother wants me to stay away from you," he told her.

"What?" Dunni's spine straightened. "Did she say that? That day, when she went into your house, did she tell you that?"

Obinna opened his mouth, then closed it. After Dunni had uttered that one word—*biko*—he felt compelled to tell her everything, but he inhaled deeply and cautioned himself. He didn't want Dunni to be upset with her mother. He didn't want to be the reason their relationship got worse rather than better.

"No," he said. "She didn't tell me that. I just . . . um . . . I just had a feeling."

"You just had a feeling?" Dunni cocked her head and studied him. "Are you sure she said nothing? Just tell me the truth."

"No. She said nothing."

"Okay. So, you've been acting strange because you had a feeling?"

"Yeah. I'm sorry."

"It's okay. I just wish you had told me earlier, so we could have talked about it. I could have told you to forget about my mother and focus on us instead—on how we feel about each other. That's all that matters. Nothing else. Okay?"

Slowly, he nodded. "Okay."

For a moment, they didn't say another word. They watched people come in and out of the shop. Obinna was fascinated with each unique order—the flavors, the toppings, and the designs.

"Would you like some more ice cream?" Dunni asked him.

He turned to her and shook his head. "No. I've eaten enough for one day. Thank you. For paying for everything." He tried to ignore that familiar shame of being inadequate. "One day, I'll take you to the cinemas and buy you ice cream. Better yet, I'll take you to Italy, so that we can have some gelato." He expected her to smile, but she didn't.

"Obi, that's sweet but . . ." She paused and thought. "Listen. I'm absolutely confident that you'll be successful. You're so smart and ambitious. But I don't want you to chase success because you think you owe it to me. Chase it for yourself. But not for me—not because you think it will make me want you more."

As she searched his eyes for understanding, he searched hers for sincerity. And even when he saw it blatantly, it wasn't enough to convince him or to lessen that feeling of inadequacy.

"So." Obinna cleared his throat. "On this show. After they've cried and connected. What do they do next?"

Dunni smiled. "They watch fireworks or they slow dance under the stars."

"Interesting. Excuse me for a minute." Obinna stood and walked to the counter. He spoke to the young man on the other end, and as he walked back to the table, the slow song that had been playing on the speakers increased significantly. "May I have this dance?"

Dunni giggled. "Are you serious right now?"

"Absolutely. Come on. Dance with me."

She smirked and took his extended hand.

Patrons looked at them as they swayed, but their eyes stayed on each other.

"I can't believe we're doing this," Dunni said. "Slow dancing in a restaurant."

"I'm sorry it's not under the stars."

"What does it matter as long as I'm with you?" She wrapped her arms around his neck and held him tight. "As long as we're together."

CHAPTER TWENTY

During dinner on the patio, Dunni said little as she sat across from Obinna. The brief phone conversation she'd had with Christopher earlier that evening played in her mind.

"When are you coming home?" he'd asked her.

Dunni stood on the balcony alone, the phone to her ear as she watched the tide roll against the shore. After a moment, she spoke. "In a few days."

The line went quiet.

"Dunni," Christopher said a minute into the silence. "Something seems . . . off." He breathed deeply. "Are you upset? With me? Did I do something wrong?"

At those words, tears she didn't even know were gathering dropped. She had to place a hand over her mouth to stifle a cry. Christopher didn't deserve this. He didn't deserve someone like her, someone who was incapable of loving him despite all his amazing qualities. The problem wasn't him. It was her. In every relationship, it was her—so tied down to her past, she couldn't envision a happy future with any man but her first and only love. Whatever future she figured she would have with Christopher was something she had long ago forced herself to make peace with. It wouldn't be ideal, but it would be something. It would mean moving on with a good man. And Christopher was good. And perhaps without Obinna, without her past, it would have been so easy to love him, to look forward to their future, to wear his ring without that uncomfortable heaviness. But there was Obinna, no longer in her past but in her present.

"Christopher," she said after clearing her throat. "You've done nothing wrong. You're perfect. I'm just . . ." She wiped her wet eyes and huffed. "Listen. I'll be home soon."

She didn't give him an exact day. She didn't indicate if she would be coming home to continue their relationship or to end it. And he asked no further questions, perhaps too afraid of the answer.

After dinner, Obinna and Dunni walked on the beach. Sand crunched beneath their bare feet as they neared the fire pit; it crackled as flames ate through the wood. Embers meandered in the night like fireflies. They sat on a massive bench that encircled the fire. Obinna pulled a blanket over Dunni's legs, and she looked at the string of lights that hung from the palm trees.

"Obi, how much does it cost to rent this whole place?"

"Don't worry about it."

"I'm not worried. I'm just curious. How are you affording all of this? What work do you do?" She'd been meaning to ask him this. He'd mentioned business and the office and clients and conferences, but what exactly did he do for a living?

"When I graduated from university, I couldn't find a job," he said. "I looked for over a year, but nothing. My mother was sick—heart issues. She couldn't work anymore, so I started doing small-small jobs here and there to pay for her medication."

"What kind of jobs?"

"The kind someone with an MBA shouldn't have to do." He ran a hand over his beard stubble. "My mother's illness worsened. At the hospital, the doctor asked for one hundred thousand naira to treat her." He blew out a sharp breath. "A hundred thousand to save her life. I was twenty-four. I worked odd jobs. Where was I supposed to get that kind of money so quickly—in a matter of days?"

"You could have asked me."

"I hadn't spoken to you in years. How could I just reach out suddenly to ask for money? I couldn't."

"Yes, you could have. Obinna, no matter what, I would have done anything for you."

He considered her, then looked away. "I sold some of my things—which weren't worth much. I borrowed money from friends. It wasn't enough. She died."

Dunni placed a hand over his. "I'm so sorry."

He said nothing for a while, and then he cleared his throat. "She was gone, and I was alone. I continued doing odd jobs. A friend from university helped me get work as a server for a catering company that hosted a lot of high-profile events. A lot of successful people attended these events. They spoke about their businesses and investments."

"And you listened to their conversations."

He nodded. "It was like getting a free business seminar. But I had questions, and I knew no one would speak to me as a server."

Dunni arched an eyebrow. "So? What did you do?"

"Well." He laughed. "I would bring my nicest clothes with me, and halfway through my shift, I would change—looking nothing like a server—and join the party."

"Seriously?" Dunni found it hard to believe. The Obinna she remembered was timid, too scared to break the rules, pushed to take risks only because of her. "You just abandoned your job?"

"I had an agreement with my manager. He was studying to get his MBA. I helped him study, and he gave me an hour during my shift to mingle with some of Lagos's most successful people." He looked away, his gaze unfocused as he recounted the details. "I introduced myself as Nicholas and listened to business deals guests had made and new markets I had never heard of. It was incredible. I asked questions while acting like I was one of them."

"Well, damn. That's genius." Dunni nodded her approval. "But didn't anyone notice you were also the server?"

"People never really looked. They took food, drinks, made demands, and carried on. As a server, no one noticed me. But one day, someone did." Obinna pinned his lips closed and suppressed a laugh. "Tiwa Jolade was grabbing a drink off a tray I held and recognized me. I honestly thought she would expose me and have me sacked."

"Well? What did she do?" Dunni nudged, eager for the details.

"She demanded to know what I was up to, so I told her everything. She thought it was bold and very desperate. She invited me to her office."

"And then she gave you money to start a business?" It was the only explanation Dunni could fathom. Tiwa had helped him financially, enabled him to have everything he now had.

"Tiwa didn't give me any money," he said. "Only advice. She told me to buy a piece of land and then to sell it a year later. I needed at least eight million. I had nothing close to that, so she told me to come to her once I had the money."

A cool breeze tousled Dunni's hair. She didn't bother rearranging the wavy tresses, too immersed in Obinna's story. "So? What did you do?"

"I spoke with two friends from university. They agreed to contribute equally. It took us a year to come up with the money, but once we did, we went to Tiwa. She helped us buy a small plot of land in a location she predicted would soon be a hotspot. At twenty-five, I owned a piece of land." He beamed at the accomplishment. "A year later, I sold it for twice what I bought it for."

"That's amazing, Obinna."

"Yeah. Then Tiwa advised me to buy another—to invest. She guided me every step of the way."

"That's how you two became friends?"

He nodded. "She's an incredible person."

Dunni couldn't disagree.

"When I was twenty-eight, I owned two pieces of land in Lekki. Rather than selling them, I built homes, which I rented out. Then I started a development company. That's what I do for a living. That's how I'm able to afford this."

Dunni exhaled, exhausted by the turns the story had taken and relieved at the outcome. "I'm so proud of you. And I know your mother is too."

"It's a shame she didn't live to see it all," he said, a minor quake in his voice.

"Yes." She curled into his side. "It is."

He draped his arm over her shoulder, and for a moment, they watched the fire until he spoke.

"Tell me about America."

Dunni flinched. The mention of America reminded her of reality. This—them hidden away like teenagers who'd skipped class—certainly wasn't it.

"I want to know everything. What happened once you got there? How was Princeton? I bet you were top of your class with plenty of friends, eh?"

He assumed it was like secondary school. He didn't know what it had been like for her. He couldn't possibly imagine. "I don't want to talk about that."

"Why not?"

"I just don't."

"Dunni, you've lived there for years. You came back a new person. You even sound different."

"I don't," she protested defensively, as if he had insulted her.

"You do. You have an accent. It's not too heavy, but it's there. And there's nothing wrong with that. I like it." His fingers ran along the length of her arm. "I just want to know about your life there. I'm curious. I've always been."

"If you were so curious about my life in America, then maybe you should have replied to my emails." She bit her lip the instant the words came out. "I'm sorry. I shouldn't have said that." He had already explained why he stayed away. But she knew it wasn't a good enough excuse, and she'd held that in rather than voice it. Though it seemed like the thought was now hard to suppress.

"It's okay," Obinna said. "Don't worry about it."

But it wasn't okay. Dunni no longer leaned against him, and he no longer stroked her bare arm. They sat apart and watched the fire. There was tension between them, the light atmosphere disturbed by the word *America*.

There was so much she wanted to tell him about living there. But it didn't seem like the sensible thing to do. Not yet. Not until their future was certain. But he was eager. She had to tell him something—a fraction of the truth.

"It was hard," she said. "Difficult. I knew no one. I was all alone and . . ." She forced out words, pushing through the tightness in her throat. "You weren't there. You weren't talking to me, so it made things harder. I was still dealing with what happened that day. I was constantly worrying about you. I was heartbroken. I was trying to fit into this new place where I knew no one. It was the hardest year of my life."

He placed his hand over hers and squeezed. "I'm so sorry."

"I didn't feel like myself there. It was as if pieces of my identity were gradually being stripped away. Even my name."

In Nigeria, her last name was a key that opened and locked any door. People knew it. They respected it. In America, that name carried no weight. It was just an ethnic name her professors could never pronounce correctly, a name broken down in awkward pauses and frustrated huffs until it lost its meaning. She was no one there, and it was both degrading and humbling. It was as if a layer of herself had been peeled off, again and again, until she had to grow new skin—one tougher and capable of dealing with her new insignificance.

"But it got better, right?" Obinna asked.

"It took some time. I struggled academically during my first year. My grades were bad. I was on academic probation, but I pulled through. I adapted."

"Adapted?"

He'd caught that. *Adapted*. In America, it was how she'd survived among classmates, professors, and colleagues who expected something else from people like her. They were waiting to place labels and confirm assumptions, and Dunni had been adamant about never giving them the satisfaction. So she'd adapted, shrunk herself, presented one half of who she was, and kept the other half locked away, safe and collecting dust.

"It seemed like the only way," she told him. "But my grades improved. In my second year, they were better. Third year, they were excellent. Fourth year, I graduated top of my class and got into an excellent master's program. I just completed my Ph.D. in genetics. I work as a research geneticist at a private firm."

His eyes shone with admiration. "Wow. That's very impressive, Dunni. Do you have an area of study?"

"Genome editing."

"That's an interesting and somewhat controversial area. Why did you choose it?"

She shifted against the bench, uneasy. "I'm not really . . . It isn't my . . ." She paused and watched her hands. "My parents thought it would be the best area. They think it's the future of my field, so . . ."

Obinna's eyebrows creased. He studied her and rolled his pursed lips as if gauging the weight of his words. When his lips flattened, he smiled. "I'm sure your parents are very proud of you."

Dunni looked at him. She'd expected to hear a comparison of who she used to be and who she was now—audacious, outspoken, and strong-willed compared to timid, reserved, and compliant. The contrast must have stumped him, but he didn't speak of it, and Dunni was thankful.

"I suppose they are proud. My father brags to his friends a lot, and my mother . . ." She shrugged. "I don't know."

"You don't know if she's proud of you?"

"Well, we aren't close. You know that."

"Yes, but that was years ago. Haven't things changed—improved?"

Dunni searched his face for signs he was joking. When she caught none, she scowled. "I don't understand. Did you think our relationship would improve after what she did to you?"

"That was so long ago. I thought you might have forgiven her."

"Forgiven her?" How could Dunni consider forgiveness when her mother had shown no sign of remorse? Not once. "She doesn't deserve forgiveness, especially since she has never even asked for it." Tears stung her eyes. The breeze dried the moisture before it came down her cheeks.

Obinna drew near to her and closed the space between them. "I know you're hurt, but I need to tell you something. Just listen to me. Okay?"

She bobbed her head. "Okay."

"Do you remember the day your father gave me a ride home from school?"

"Yeah."

"Remember your mother insisted on coming in with me?"

She nodded.

"Okay. While she was inside, she said something I can't forget, even after all these years. She said, 'I loved a poor and ambitious man once, and it almost killed me. That will not be my daughter.' Then she asked me to stay away from you."

Dunni leaned away from Obinna, her head slanted as she observed him. "I don't understand." She tried to rearrange his words, so they made sense. They didn't. "What are you saying?"

"I think your mother might have gone through something. I think she was in a relationship before your father. And I think it was bad. Abusive. Maybe that's why she didn't want me to be with you."

"Because she thought you would hurt me?"

"Yes, but not exactly."

"Then what? What are you talking about?" She pressed her hand to her forehead, rubbing as tension built. "You know what? You're actually giving me a headache right now."

"And you aren't listening to me."

"No, I'm not because you're making no sense." She stood and flung the blanket at him. "She told you one thing that's probably a lie years ago! I have known her my whole life, so stop acting like you know my mother more than I do."

"That isn't what I'm trying to do." He stood as well. He took a step toward her, then receded after noting her exasperated expression. "I'm just trying to understand why she did what she did that day. Maybe understanding will help us both move on and help you have a relationship with her."

"I don't recall telling you I want a relationship with her—not once, so I'm not sure how you got that impression."

"She's your mother—the only one you have. I had mine one day and the next, she was gone forever. There was so much I didn't get to say to her. I don't want that for you. I don't want you hating her because of me."

"My mother is nothing like yours. Yours loved you. Mine is . . ." She pursed her lips, and tears trailed down her cheeks. "You think it ended with what she did to you, but it goes beyond that. You don't know the whole story. You have no idea."

"Then tell me."

"Why? So you can tell me to forgive her in spite of it?" Dunni shook her head. "I'm going to bed. And please. Just give me some space tonight." She turned away and walked toward the beach house.

Dunni had expected many things that night. A conversation that revolved around Obinna defending her mother had not been one.

CHAPTER TWENTY-ONE

THEN

Dunni's large bedroom still amazed Obinna. It was his second time in it, and he still could not hide his astonishment. He sat on the high bed topped with multiple pillows, some decorative.

"Are you comfortable?" she shouted from inside her closet, where she changed out of her school uniform.

"Very," he said, reclining on a pillow. The mattress was plush, yet able to hold his weight. At home, his mattress sagged in certain spots, which he avoided by turning constantly, trying to dodge the sharpness of a spring against his back. That was the mattress he would sleep on that night. He tried to remember that. He tried not to get too comfortable with a brief luxury. He leaped off the bed and walked around the room.

During his first visit, he feared Dunni's parents would show up, but Dunni had assured him they were out of the country.

They were away often—her father on business trips and her mother on holiday. Dunni's elder brother, Jeremiah, schooled in America, so even with the presence of the staff and the occasional visit from her grandmother, Dunni was often alone. When she first begged Obinna to come home with her after school, he had agreed. Paul, her driver, had driven them to the house and then later driven Obinna home. His mother had been livid when he arrived three hours later than usual. He'd made up a lie about school activities. He had lied again that morning—told his mother he would study with friends after school. He felt guilty about lying, but the satisfaction of being with Dunni appeased his guilt slightly and reminded him that he would lie again so they could be together.

Aimlessly, he wandered around the space decorated in pink and white, a very predictable choice for a girl. There were books on her desk—not textbooks, but novels. He picked one up and read the cover.

"*Emma* by Jane Austen." He picked up another. "*Mansfield Park* by Jane Austen." Almost every book was by the same author.

Obinna didn't enjoy reading, only when it applied to school. Dunni read for fun. On Monday mornings, he would ask what she had done during the weekend, and she would answer, with so much pride, "Finished a book." It was strange. Why would anyone spend hours reading when they could watch a film? He dropped the book, and his eyes caught the university catalogs on the desk. He shuffled through them and read the names on the covers out loud.

"Harvard. Stanford. Princeton. Yale. Oxford."

All schools that weren't in Nigeria. What was going on? A month ago, during the car ride with her parents, she had mentioned attending the University of Lagos. And just days ago, they'd sent in their applications. The University of Lagos—that was their plan. They'd discussed it extensively during his first visit to her house. She'd never expressed an interest in other schools, especially ones outside of the country. What had changed? Was she planning on going elsewhere? He felt sick.

"I meant to talk to you about that." Her voice came from behind him.

"What is this?" He turned around, holding the catalogs. "I don't understand. Have you . . . have you . . . applied?"

"Yes. To all but Oxford. I didn't want to. But my parents."

"So what does this mean?" He was afraid to ask, but did anyway. "Are you going?"

"I don't know. I told them I want to stay here and go to UNILAG, but . . ." She shrugged. "I'm still trying to persuade them."

Obinna dropped the catalogs on the table and walked back to the bed. He needed to sit or lie down, whichever would help digest the news better. He sat.

He'd suspected this would happen. That day in the car, when Dunni announced she wanted to attend the University of Lagos, her parents had shared a look, one that communicated something Dunni didn't know or had not yet accepted. Maybe she thought she had a say in the matter. It was clear she didn't. And neither did he. There was nothing he could do. He would have to let her go. And a part of him had known that for a while—since the day her mother regarded him as if he were nothing. He had known the road that brought them together would eventually diverge.

"Obi." Dunni sat beside him. "We'll find a way."

"How?" He looked at her, hoping so desperately she had an answer—a solution.

"I'll try again. I'll convince them to let me stay and go to school here. It will be fine."

He blew out a breath and chewed on his lip. He didn't want to say it, but he had to accept the reality she still denied. "Dunni, they won't let you go to UNILAG—not when Harvard or Yale is an option. Don't you see that? If you get accepted to any of those schools, they'll make you go." He felt stupid for saying *if*. She would gain admission because she was brilliant. "You're going to leave, Dunni. That's the truth."

"How can you say that?" Her voice shrunk and broke. "What . . . what about us?" She reached out and slipped her hand into his.

"What about us?" His gaze dropped to the floor. He couldn't look at her. "We're just boyfriend and girlfriend. People have boyfriends and girlfriends in secondary school all the time. But then they graduate. And they go their separate ways and eventually forget about each other."

"Is that what you think will happen with us?"

He said nothing.

"Really?" She pulled her hand back and stood. "Secondary school sweethearts. That's all you think we are?"

He should have said all the right things. He should have told her how he really felt, but he was too embarrassed.

We are so much more, he wanted to tell her. *I felt it the moment I saw you. We are Obinna and Dunni, a pairing that makes sense like bread and butter or* boli *and groundnut. I think we might be soul mates. But that term scares me. You scare me. You're too good for me—too rich, too smart, too beautiful, too bold, too stubborn, too passionate. I keep praying you won't realize it—that you'll grow so content with me, you'll never go looking for something else, something better. And then I hate myself for being selfish. I hate myself for not being enough, for not having the ability to dream beyond the borders of this country along with you. I hate myself because I'm scared. I'm scared that one day, you'll look at me the way your mother looked at me. I'm scared that you'll see only who I am now and not who I can be. I'm scared I'll never be that person.*

He wanted to say all this to her. Instead, he watched her walk away.

The bathroom door slammed shut, and even though only a block of wood separated them, it felt like they were already an ocean and continent apart.

Obinna stood and picked up his bag from the floor. He flung the strap over his shoulder and walked to the bedroom door. The metal handle chilled his palm. He would turn it, open the door, and leave her house. Leave her. Wasn't it best that way? Their relationship would end eventually. Why prolong it?

He would leave, and that would be it. He would never hold her hand again. He would never kiss her again. Even the simplicity of knees touching would be gone. She would no longer be his. They would graduate, and she would go to America. He would learn to normalize her absence. Then maybe one day, he would forget who they were and who they could have been. The hope, the possibility of a future with her, would reluctantly but eventually disappear. Years later, he would find someone else, someone not as beautiful or smart or charismatic as Dunni, but he would ignore that and love her anyway. They would have what he called "easy love." And he would settle comfortably into it, always holding on loosely because he was never given a reason to hold on tightly, a reason to fight for it. And because of that, he would be a mediocre husband, never truly comprehending what he had—the worth of it. And occasionally, as he existed in his comfortable routine, he would think about his secondary school girlfriend, the one who'd activated something dormant in him. And he would wonder what could have happened if he had fought.

Obinna's bag slid off his shoulder and thumped on the floor. Swiftly, he marched to the bathroom door and knocked.

"Dunni, I didn't mean it." He rushed his words, quickly trying to undo what he had done. "I didn't mean what I said." His silence had been a mistake. His skepticism, a bigger mistake. "I'm sorry. I'm so sorry. We aren't just a secondary school fling. We're . . ." He huffed and pushed the words out. "We're soul mates."

There it was. Soul mates. The words were so heavy. They bore more weight than saying *I love you. Soul mates.* Lately, he'd been trying to understand the term, so he could appropriately apply it to how he felt about Dunni. And after much contemplation, he'd concluded that when God created him, he chipped away at something inside him—broke it off—and placed it inside Dunni. All his missing parts were in her, and vice versa. It was how they complemented and completed each other. It was the reason he'd felt something activate inside him the day he met her—because every part of him was whole.

"I know it sounds crazy," he said. "But I've always known—since the moment we met."

Beyond the closed door, she sniffed.

"Dunni, please. Don't cry." Obinna didn't think the door wasn't locked, but he chose not to open it. He wanted her to come out when she felt ready. "I'm here. Okay? I'm just going to stay right here." He slid to the floor, his back to the closed door. "Whenever you're ready."

Five minutes went by. He thought of giving her more time, but cleared his throat and spoke.

"On the first day of school, you told me something your grandmother always says. Do you remember?"

Dunni didn't respond.

"'The future has already happened. We're just trying to catch up to it.'" He pressed the back of his head against the door and smiled. "Dunni, this is us catching up. I think there's an incredible future waiting for us. This and every step we take is us trying to catch up to it."

Again, she sniffed.

Just as he settled into the silence again, she spoke.

"What . . . what exactly are we catching up to?" Her voice was small, tender, hopeful. "Tell me. Paint a picture for me, so I know what to look forward to."

Obinna sat up straight. "We have a house," he said, his voice upbeat. "It's big but not too big, so you're never too far from me."

"Where is this house—Nigeria, England, America?"

"Here. In Lagos."

"And are we living in sin or are we married?" There was humor in her voice, along with her signature sharpness.

"Married. Definitely married. We got married after we graduated from university. We have a dog. He likes you a lot more than he likes me."

"Mm-hmm." The door creaked, then opened. She looked at him; her eyes were puffy and red. "Seems plausible."

He stood and faced her. He touched the corner of her right eye and caught one last tear on his thumb.

"Tell me more. Children? Do we have any?"

"We do. A girl. She's the first."

Dunni giggled. "Her name. What's her name?"

This detail had escaped him. He didn't have a name for their future daughter. His eyes wandered.

"You don't know our child's name?" She shook her head, then walked to the desk. "Her name is Austen." She grabbed a book and presented it to Obinna. "After Jane Austen, my favorite author."

"What?" He chuckled. "You want to name our daughter after a writer? And isn't Austen a boy's name? If anything, why not Jane?"

"Jane is the practical option. I want the impractical option." Of course she did.

"Besides, I love the sound of it. Don't you?"

"Yes, but what does it mean?"

"Great and magnificent." She smiled proudly, and even her inflamed eyes took nothing from it. "I did my homework."

"You did." He mirrored her smile. "So, we're going to name our daughter after an author."

"The greatest romance author of all time. Come." She walked to the bed and bounced on it. "I'll show you." She sat upright, her back pressed against pillows and her legs spread out. "I'll read you some of it, so you see what I mean."

"Mm-hmm. Okay." He sat on the bed just as she did—back against the pillows and legs spread out—but then he shuffled, reclined, and placed his head on her lap. "So what are you reading?"

"One of my favorites. *Pride and Prejudice*. You'll like it."

Without uttering a word, he listened. Her voice soothed him, and her fingers that stroked his head relaxed him further. She snapped the book closed after two chapters, and he found he was disappointed until she shifted and rested beside him— face-to-face.

"Did you like it?" she asked.

"I did."

"What about the name Austen? Do you approve?"

"Yes. I approve."

He kissed her. It started gently and then it became wild. She moaned. He loved it when she did that. It made him kiss her deeper. When they pulled apart to breathe, they stared at each other, chests pounding, and spoke in sync.

"I love you."

CHAPTER TWENTY-TWO

Dunni sat upright in bed, her phone pressed to her ear while speaking to her friend in Seattle.

"I can't believe you're up this late, Emily. You're never up this late. Why aren't you sleeping?"

It was 8:15 a.m. on Monday in Lagos. With Seattle nine hours behind, it was 11:15 p.m. on Sunday there.

Emily sighed. "The girls have a bake sale at school tomorrow. Just putting finishing touches on some cupcakes."

"Oh shit. I was supposed to help you with that. I totally forgot. Sorry."

"Girl, it's not a big deal. You . . . ugh . . . hold on a minute." Emily grumbled and cursed as utensils clanked to the floor. The clatter ceased, and the phone line went quiet.

"Hello? Em?" Dunni said, her voice pinched with concern. "Everything okay?"

"Yeah." Emily panted. "I had a little mishap, but all four dozen cupcakes are safe . . . or at least salvageable." She laughed. "Anyway, as I was saying, you have never taken a vacation—ever. Not for the five years I've known you. You deserve this."

Five years. Sometimes, it surprised Dunni how much time had passed since she moved into a town house in West Hill and met her neighbor Emily Carr, a wife and mother of two little girls. They'd connected instantly, mostly over their mutual love of chardonnay and *The Bachelor*. The eight-year age difference between them didn't hinder a strong friendship from forming. Over the years, Dunni had grown to rely on Emily and consider her a big sister. And Emily had grown to rely on Dunni, especially during the annual school bake sale.

"Well, I'm sorry I can't be there. You seem a little . . . um . . . stressed."

"I just iced the last cupcake. I'm all good. But . . ." Emily paused and snorted. "You do a much better job with icing than I do."

"It can't be that bad. Send me a picture."

"Okay. You asked for it."

Dunni waited. Within seconds of the request, her phone vibrated. She looked at the screen and squinted at the cupcakes decorated with clumps of white and pink icing. "Well, damn." She giggled. "I can't say you lied."

"Told ya. Anyway . . ." Emily yawned. "I'm beat. I'm gonna check on the girls and head to bed."

"Okay. Good night, and give the girls a kiss for me."

"Sure. And, Dunni." Emily's voice grow stern. "Try, for the love of God, to loosen up and have fun. Seriously."

Dunni rolled her eyes. "Okay. I'll try. Talk later." She ended the call and flipped through a copy of *Pride and Prejudice*. It was her favorite novel, a comforting read that presented her with no surprises. She knew how it began and how it ended, and there was a sort of safety in that.

"Dunni?" Her name came after a knock on the door.

She stopped reading and watched the door open, gradually parting to reveal Obinna.

"Good morning," he said, his tiny voice stripped of confidence.

"Hey." She placed a finger between the pages, marking where she stopped, and closed the book.

"How are you? How did you sleep?" he asked.

She had slept little—only a few hours. And though she wanted to credit her lack of sleep to jet lag, she knew it had more to do with the conversation she'd had with Obinna the previous night. "I slept fine," she lied. "And you?"

"Horribly." He entered the room and closed the door. "I don't think I slept more than three hours. I couldn't stop thinking about last night. You were right. It wasn't my place to say all that. I was out of line, especially since—"

"You have no idea what's been going on with my mom and me."

He nodded. "Yeah. I'm sorry." He sat on the edge of the bed. "Really. I am."

"It's okay." She extended her hand and stroked the corners of his lips that were fixed in a firm, straight line. She preferred them smiling. "I couldn't sleep either."

"Why?"

"Because you annoyed me. And because you weren't here. With me." She felt the gentle tug of a smile beneath her fingertips. "I was looking forward to spending the night with you. I know we agreed not to do anything, but I just wanted you close." His lips expanded to a full smile, and something tense inside her unwound.

"I wanted to spend the night with you too." He shuffled and sat on the mattress, then kissed her bare shoulder where a spaghetti strap hung loosely. "What are you up to?"

"Just reading." She flipped the book open and acted nonchalant, as if his lips on her skin hadn't made her heartbeat race.

"Let me guess. Jane Austen?"

"How'd you know?"

"How could I possibly forget your obsession?" He laughed and peered down at the pages. "Which one is it?"

"*Pride and Prejudice.*"

"Well, don't let me interrupt you." He repositioned himself, sprawling out and placing his head on her legs. "Okay. Read to me."

He suddenly looked sweet and vulnerable, like the boy she had known so long ago. He lifted his eyes and urged her to read, and she did. For thirty minutes, she stroked his shaved head and read to him. And it seemed as if they had never been apart, as if they had a collection of similar moments.

"Your voice is very soothing, you know that?"

"Thank you." She closed the book and placed it on the night-stand.

A minute of silence passed between them. The swishing ocean beyond the sliding glass door made the silence tolerable. She didn't feel the pressure to speak or to do much other than recline on the bed and face him. With her fingertip, she traced the contours of his face that were still new to her, like the rest of his body. She wanted to see all of him, lit by daylight. She wanted to feel the sculpt of his body beneath her palm and memorize this new version of him with every one of her senses. She contained the impulse and pulled back her wandering finger.

"How's your brother?" Obinna asked.

Dunni breathed deeply, still fighting the impulse that put a strain on her heart. "Good. He also lives in Seattle."

"Is he married?"

"Yeah. He got married last year. They're expecting their first child."

"That's great. And which is he? A doctor or a lawyer?"

Dunni laughed. "Surprisingly, neither. He's a sports commentator on a TV station."

"Interesting. He's on television. Your parents must love that."

"Yeah. They really do." She bit her lip while building the nerve to ask a difficult question. "What about your father? Did he ever come back or contact you and your mother?" She held her breath and waited for an answer that involved a happy reunion.

"We never heard from him. He might be dead. He might be

alive." Obinna shrugged. "My mother never got that answer before she died. But I can't live the rest of my life without knowing."

She took his hand and interlocked their fingers.

"A few weeks ago, I hired a private detective to look into it."

"And have you heard anything?"

"Not yet. But I'm trying to be patient." He brought their joined hands to his lips. "Enough about that. How about your grandmother? Is she well?"

It was a polite way of asking if she was still alive. "Yeah. She's doing good."

"I bet you two are still close, huh?"

"Yeah. As close as we can be when I live in another country."

"Does she still have those dreams?"

Dunni stiffened. "She does. But they're just dreams. They mean nothing."

"Just dreams?" Obinna arched an eyebrow. "When we were in school, you believed they were more than that. Now you've changed your mind?"

"Now I've grown up. I don't believe in those sorts of things anymore."

"Those sorts of things?" he asked.

"Superstition—things I can't see or explain. And as I remember, neither did you. Did something change your mind?"

"Yes. This." He lifted his hand and displayed the flesh-colored scar across his palm, the one identical to hers. "The oath we made."

The room was cool, air-conditioned. But Dunni's skin heated and sweat seeped through her pores.

"After we made it, my perspective changed." He sat up. "I changed."

"We were just children. We did something stupid based on the stories we heard and the damn Nollywood movies we watched. It meant nothing."

"It meant everything. Don't act like you didn't feel something." He squinted and searched her eyes. "Dunni, what we did bonded us. We loved each other before, but after the oath, it became more intense. It became . . ." He rubbed his forehead. "Frankly, I don't know how to explain it. All I know is that it changed everything. Can you really deny that?"

"I don't want to talk about this anymore." She tossed the covers aside and rose from the bed. "Please. I feel like this is going to lead to us fighting."

"Fighting? We're just talking."

"And I don't want to talk about it anymore."

"So, is this how it's going to be?" He stood and blew out a breath. "You get upset, decide you don't want to discuss a topic, and just shut down? Is this how it's going to be with us?"

Us. That was the endgame, wasn't it? For them to be an *us.* Her fiancé was in another country, and she was testing the waters with another man. But not just any man. Obinna. She owed it to him—to herself too—to test the waters, to entertain the idea of an *us.*

"No," she told him. "This isn't how it's going to be. I'm sorry. It's just that, this is all still a lot. Can we just ease into things, maybe not talk about everything at once? Doses, Obinna. Please."

"Okay. Yeah." He nodded. "Doses. I understand. Sorry I overwhelmed you."

"Thanks." She turned to the glass door and watched the view of the beach. "It's really beautiful. Don't you think?" She extended her hand to him, waiting for him to take it and join her. When he didn't, she turned and knew, instantly, why he hadn't moved and why his narrowed eyes were fixed on her back.

He had seen the tattoo on her shoulder blade, the one she'd been using her hair and clothes and bed sheets to hide from him. She'd worn a camisole to sleep, not expecting him to show up. But he had, and he'd seen it.

Her nails dug into her moist palms as she waited for his reaction.

"Dunni, your tattoo." He stepped toward her. "What does it say?" By his stunned expression, it was obvious he already knew. It seemed like he wanted only her confirmation. "What does it say?" he asked again.

"Austen," she whispered. "It says *Austen*."

He cocked his head from side to side. "Why?" His eyes watered, his chin trembled. He feared the answer, but he demanded it again. "Why does it say that?"

"To remember," she answered. "Just to remember."

"Remember what?"

"Us. What we could have had."

He shook his head, unconvinced, and Dunni gathered her nerve—all the audacity required to tell him the truth. She arranged the explanation in her head, placing the words side by side so she knew the order of each. She braced herself for his response—his anger, his pain, the guilt he would likely feel. Then she waited for him to ask.

He opened his mouth, shaping words that were interrupted by an abrupt knock at the door.

Dunni exhaled.

"Yes?" Obinna said in a clipped tone. "What is it?"

"Sorry to disturb you, sir." The voice on the other side of the door was delicate; it belonged to a woman. "But you have a guest at the front desk."

"A guest? Who?"

"She says her name is Gigi."

His strained expression fell flat. "Okay. I'm on my way down."

"I'll let her know, sir." Quick footsteps pattered down the hallway.

"Gigi?" Dunni said. "I thought she was going to South Africa."

"So did I." He rubbed his eyes that were suddenly weary. "I'm going down to speak with her—see if everything's okay."

"Yeah. Sure."

He watched her closely, then looked away and left the room.

Dunni had been prepared to tell him the truth. He deserved the truth. Though, a part of her felt he had forfeited his right to it when he ignored her many emails and walked away.

She extended a hand to her back and ran fingers along the name imprinted on her skin, the name they had chosen together. Regardless of what he had done, he deserved the truth.

He had a biological right to it.

CHAPTER TWENTY-THREE

THEN

The lunchroom buzzed, lively with chatter and laughter. Obinna and Dunni sat together, their knees touching under the crowded table. Emeka stood over them and used exaggerated body movements to illustrate how he had captured a bushpig while visiting his grandparents in the village during Christmas break. Usually, Dunni questioned the details of his story, trying to prove he was lying. Today, she said nothing.

She leaned into Obinna and lowered her head on his shoulder. It was strange. They never showed affection openly at school. Everyone knew they were together, but they offered little evidence to support that fact, preferring not to be the center of attention. Though Dunni's head on Obinna's slender shoulder instantly drew the attention of the group at the table. Emeka shut his mouth mid-sentence and smirked.

"So my story is so good, it has you lovebirds snuggling. And I haven't even reached the climax yet." He snorted. "Climax. Pun definitely intended."

"We aren't snuggling," Obinna corrected. "We're just . . ." He looked down at Dunni and waited for her to finish his sentence or simply tell Emeka to shut up. But again, she acted out of character, ignoring Emeka and staring straight at Lara, who sat opposite them. Instantly, it was obvious why Dunni's head was on his shoulder. She was making a point to one specific person.

"Lara," she said. "Can you do me a favor and stop looking at my boyfriend like you want to sink your teeth into him?"

A mixture of gasps and chuckles spread around the table.

"I . . . I wasn't looking at him," Lara stammered. "I was just . . ." She shifted in her seat. "I was just . . . um."

"You were just what?" Dunni lifted her head, picked up her spoon, and leaned into the table. "Look. If you value your eyeballs, I suggest you control them or I will scoop them out with this spoon."

"Okay." Obinna stood and grabbed Dunni's hand. "That's enough. Let's get some air." He pulled her out of the lunchroom, even as she struggled.

They didn't make it to the yard, only to the end of the corridor before Dunni hauled her hand from his grip. "What do you think you're doing?"

"Me?" He groaned. "Dunni, what about you? You can't go around threatening people."

"Did you see the way she was looking at you? What's the meaning of that? Eh? If she has a little crush on you, that's fine. She can write about it in her diary when she gets home. Instead, she's eyeing you while I'm sitting right there. The girl has too much audacity. Maybe I should beat some out of her."

"It doesn't matter what she was doing!" He noted the volume in his voice, the harshness. He didn't want to shout at her, so he released a deep breath before continuing. "She's the second girl you've threatened this week. And I find it hard to believe they have any sort of crush on me."

"Are you saying I'm imagining it?"

"I'm not saying that. I'm just . . ." He pressed his hand to his forehead. As much as he loved Dunni and her personality that was so different from his, sometimes he found it hard to understand her reasoning. Sometimes, he was overwhelmed by her stubbornness and impulsiveness. Those moments were rare, but they always left him reeling. "I don't understand why you act like this sometimes. I don't like it."

As if shame had replaced her anger, she dropped her head. "I was jealous. Sometimes, I get jealous." She lifted her eyes and looked at him. "Don't you?"

"Of course I do. I think about the other boys you kissed before me." He didn't know how many there were or know their names, but it bothered him regardless. "I've noticed how Obed always asks if he can carry your bag and how often Tunde invites you to his house. All these things make me jealous."

"So why haven't you done anything about it?"

"Dunni, this is real life, not one of your historical romance novels. I can't challenge everyone to a duel because they look at you. Besides, have you seen me?" He spread out his arms. "I'm too thin. I don't think I would survive that."

They laughed, the tension between them slowly ebbing.

"Fighting Obed or Tunde doesn't prove that I love you. You know that, right?"

She shrugged.

"Listen." He took her hand. "I can show you I love you in so many other ways."

"Like . . ."

"The way I look at you. The way I treat you. How I speak to you. And how I touch you and—"

"Make love to me?"

He flinched, caught off guard. They hadn't had sex yet, but he had thought of it many times, and it appeared she had too.

"Obi." She wrapped her arms around his neck and drew his face to hers. "I want us to have sex. Do you want that?"

He nodded fervently.

"Great. Then today after school."

"What?" A surge of adrenaline tingled his body. "Today?"

"Yes. We love each other, and I'm ready. But if you aren't, we can—"

"I'm ready," he said hurriedly. "I'm ready, Dunni."

With Dunni's parents out of the country again, they were alone in her house with two maids downstairs, and according to Dunni, they were maids especially good at minding their own business.

Dunni locked her bedroom door and moved to the bed, where Obinna sat, twiddling his thumbs.

"Are you sure about this?" he asked her.

"Yes. Are you?"

He nodded. "Have you done it before?"

"No," she said.

"Okay. So, we're both clueless here." He laughed awkwardly. Sweat dotted his forehead.

"I'm not completely clueless." She pulled her burgundy jacket off and dropped it on the floor. "And I'm sure you aren't either. I know how teenage boys can be. And don't you dare say you aren't one of those boys because you are. You're just polite about it—more reserved." She untucked her white-collar shirt from her skirt. "Which I admire and appreciate. But I need you to be a little less reserved right now." She undid three buttons; her bra peeked through the open flaps of the shirt. "A lot less reserved. Can you do that?"

He exhaled, swallowed saliva to moisten his dry throat, then pushed out the word *yes*.

"Good. Would you like to undress me or shall I continue?"

Her confidence stunned him—left him absolutely speechless. It also intimidated him and turned him on. "Yeah." He stood and cleared his throat. "I can undress you."

With unsteady hands, he released the last three buttons, then rolled the shirt off her shoulders and onto the floor. His stare settled on her breasts, covered by a blue bra.

"Kiss me," she said.

"Where?" There were so many possibilities, so many places his lips could touch.

"Anywhere you like." She met his gaze and smiled. "Don't be shy, Obi. Go ahead."

He lowered his lips to her neck and planted a light kiss, and then another. He applied more pressure, then opened his lips slightly to take her skin into his mouth. She moaned; it confirmed he was doing something right. More confident, he reached for her bra. His attempt at unhooking it was clumsy, but he managed. The blue lace fabric loosened against her chest, and he slipped the straps off her shoulders.

Her breasts were small and full. They were perfect. He stilled, caught between gawking at them and touching them. Before he decided on an action, Dunni pulled off his jacket and then his white shirt. Suddenly, he became self-conscious—more aware of his lean physique without clothes to give him a false bulk. Fat and muscles didn't clad his bones like most boys his age. No matter how much he ate or how much sports he played, he remained the same.

"Obi." Dunni stroked his slumped shoulders that folded inward. "I've told you a hundred times. You're perfect. I love your body. That's the truth." She wrapped her arms around his neck and pressed her bare chest to his.

Obinna felt a rise in his trousers. His insecurities ebbed like smoke, and he kissed her. They grabbed at each other, removing the last of their clothes until they fell on the bed, naked.

"Condom," Dunni murmured. "I have some." She extended

an arm to her nightstand, pulled the drawer open, and rummaged through it. "Here." She handed him a small silver sachet. "Do you know how to put it on?"

Distracted, Obinna's eyes moved over her naked body—her soft curves, her smooth dark skin that seemed to shine as if coated with oil. He touched her backside; his hand rose and fell along with the curve of her ass. He squeezed it, and she giggled.

"Obi, did you hear anything I just said?"

He blinked, then met her gaze. "Huh?"

"Do you know how?"

He looked at the condom in her hand. "Where did you get that from?"

"The store. I bought it. Last week—just in case."

"You just walked into a store and bought condoms?"

"Well, yes. It's not illegal." She directed the silver sachet at him again. "Come on. Do you know how to put it on?"

Thankfully, he did. He'd learned from his neighbor Solo. Or as people in the area called him, Solo the *Bahd* Guy. On the one occasion Obinna's mother had not forced him to attend Wednesday service, he had gone to Solo's flat in search of idle entertainment and had received an impromptu lesson on how to put on a condom. Solo insisted Obinna was no longer a child and needed to learn the mechanics of practicing safe sex. That had been four months ago. Now as Obinna rolled on the latex, he was thankful for Solo's lesson.

"Okay." He looked down at Dunni. "Should we turn off the lights? Maybe light some candles?"

She laughed. "I don't have any candles. And I want the lights on. I want to see you, and I want you to see me."

"But I also want it to be romantic," he said. "It's your first time—our first time. I want it to be memorable."

"Obinna, we don't need all that stuff. It's already romantic and memorable because we love each other. That's all that matters." She ran her fingers along his chest. "Now, please, for the love of God, stop talking and come closer."

CHAPTER TWENTY-FOUR

THEN

Obinna lay on his back and caught his breath. To his right, Dunni released a heavy sigh. They stared at each other and smiled.

It had been awkward at first. When Obinna entered her, she'd winced but encouraged him to continue. Cautiously, he settled deeper inside her, feeling a sensation that resonated through him. They discovered a pace that suited them and moved with their eyes set on each other, further communicating the depths of their emotions.

Now he looked at her and wondered if she'd enjoyed it. "How was it?" he asked. "How was it for you?"

Her smile expanded. "Wonderful." She pressed her lips to his. "Next time will be even better."

"Next time?"

"Yeah. Did you think this was going to be a onetime situation?" She laughed. "No *o*. This is our new after-school activity. Or would you rather do homework?"

Obinna's forehead fell against hers. "No," he said. "I would rather this. With you any day after school. Or every day for the rest of our lives." His gaze was soft and amorous, and then gradually it turned concerned.

Sometimes, what he felt for Dunni frightened him. Though he turned eighteen in just a few weeks, he was too young to feel the way he did. A part of him wished he could pace himself and love Dunni gradually, with measured doses. For a measure of four months, he would have a crush on her. For eight months, he would like her. Then he would care for her deeply over the course of four years. And finally, he would fall madly in love with her once old enough to understand and contain the magnitude of that emotion. Four reasonably measured doses poured into him like chemicals into a test tube. Nothing ever went wrong when things were appropriately measured. But Obinna's feelings for Dunni hadn't undergone that cautious process. Instead, as if by the will of a mad scientist, each emotion had been poured into him all at once, and he feared something would go wrong. If he lost Dunni, if even a drop of grief tainted the mixture of emotions inside him, it would trigger a reaction that would completely shatter him.

"Obi, I love you. You know that. Right?" She squinted and searched his eyes.

"Of course I do." He caressed her cheek; her skin was warm against his fingers. "And I love you too."

"Okay. Well, there's something I need to tell you."

He noticed tears gather at the corners of her eyes, and his heart thumped as nausea twisted in his stomach. "What is it?"

"I've been meaning to tell you. I just didn't know how." She sat up and pulled the blanket over her chest.

"You've been meaning to tell me what?" He sat up as well. "What is it? Tell me, *na*."

"I got accepted into Princeton."

A heaviness fell on Obinna's chest suddenly. He struggled to breathe.

"Obi." She held his face and lifted it so their eyes connected. "Listen to me. I'm not leaving you."

The weight on his chest eased slightly. "So, you're staying?"

She shook her head. "No. I'm going. My parents have already accepted on my behalf. They've given me no other choice. If I stay to attend UNILAG, they won't pay my school fees." Tears streamed down her cheeks. "I tried reasoning with them. I promise I tried. But . . ."

"You're leaving."

"I'm leaving Nigeria, but I'm not leaving you."

"They are one and the same." His breath became short as the invisible weight pushed on his chest again. "You're leaving me." He gasped for air, but nothing filled his lungs.

"Obi, I think you're having a panic attack. You need to calm down. Just breathe."

He couldn't remember how to do something so simple.

"Here." She tilted her forehead against his. "Breathe just like me. Slowly." She took his hand and pressed his palm flat against her chest. "Breathe in, breathe out."

He listened to the sounds of her inhales and exhales and felt the steady rhythm of her heart; it soothed him. He mimicked her breathing until he mastered the technique again.

The idea of Dunni going to America hit him hard. He couldn't imagine not seeing her regularly, not talking to her or touching her. The thought was unbearable.

"I have a plan." She smiled even though it was forced. "I worked it all out."

Drained, Obinna said nothing.

"This is what's going to happen. I'll go to America first, and then you'll join me after."

He watched her vacantly, not bothering to question what was obviously a delusion.

"My parents plan to rent an apartment for me off-campus. We'll live there together."

He was concerned now—really concerned about the extent of her imagination or sanity.

"My father says he'll give me a monthly allowance. I'll send you some, so you can apply for a student visa. Or maybe I'll put it into hiring an immigration lawyer—one that can help you come to America faster. I don't know yet. But we'll look into our options. Either way, within months, you'll be in America. We'll be together." She smiled and watched him, waiting for him to do the same.

He didn't.

There was so much wrong with her plan. For one, it was impractical.

"What if you leave and forget about me?" he asked her.

"How can you say that? I can never, ever forget you."

"You say that now, but things change. People change." His head fell into his hands. "You'll be miles away from me. You'll make friends. Maybe find someone else."

"And will you do the same—forget about me and find someone else?"

He lifted his head to meet her stare. "Of course not. Never."

"Okay. Then let's make a promise to each other—to be with no one else."

"People break promises all the time, Dunni. They break them just as easily as they make them." His father's absence had taught him that. "Words hardly ever count for much."

"Then let's include another element." She slid off the bed and walked to the bathroom; the white sheet around her chest dragged on the floor.

"Dunni, what are you doing? Would you just come back?" He wanted to be near her—engulfed in her warmth and scent, all the small details he needed to memorize.

She returned to the room. One hand secured the sheet on her chest, and the other held a razor blade.

"What's that for?" Obinna asked.

"The other element to our promise."

"A razor?"

"No." She climbed on the bed. "Blood."

His narrowed eyes shifted between her face and the razor. "Dunni, what are you talking about?"

"We're going to take a blood oath."

He'd suspected that answer, but hoped for another. "You can't be serious."

"If our words count for nothing, then our blood will count for everything." She beamed. "It's brilliant, isn't it?"

He'd worried about her sanity a few minutes ago. He worried about it again. "Dunni, are you okay? Seriously. Are you okay in here?" He tapped her temple.

She laughed and pushed his hand away. "I'm perfectly fine. I just—"

"You want us to take a blood oath," he said. "Haven't you heard the horror stories or seen those Nollywood films?"

Young lovers did it often, made a promise to stay together forever and sealed it with their blood. Usually, they would break the promise—grow apart and love and eventually marry someone else. Then the consequences would follow. In the films, the person who broke the promise died. Sometimes, both died. In Obinna's former school, whenever his classmates brought up the topic, the consequences were more sinister than death.

Obinna remembered the rumor that had circulated about the headmaster's daughter. She was a beautiful woman in her twenties who came to campus often to visit her father. One day, during a routine visit, she had suddenly gone mad—talking to her father one minute and then screaming and tearing off her clothes the next. The madness, everyone had said, was the result of a broken blood oath. There were many stories like that, cautionary tales for young lovers who were determined to secure their forever regardless of the cost.

"*Shebi* you know blood is not just liquid," his mother told him one day, just as he dismissed another story about a broken oath. "There is something in it that even science cannot perceive. You might say, 'Oh, this my mother talks too much. She is too superstitious.' But there are things beyond our understanding. We are not even supposed to understand them, only to follow their rules. And when it comes to blood, there is one rule: when you give a drop, know that you will eventually give a gallon. Because whenever you give it, you feed something. Something that is never satisfied. Something that always wants more."

Now Obinna looked at the razor in Dunni's hand and cringed.

"Are you scared?" she asked him.

"I don't believe in any of that blood oath nonsense." And he didn't want to because he tried to walk a straight and narrow path paved with practicality.

"I believe in it," Dunni said. "I think doing this will guarantee we'll be together no matter what. And maybe that's the security we need." She stroked his cheek. "And don't worry. There'll be no consequences because we won't break the oath." She held open her hand. "So? Can we?"

Even though Obinna doubted the myth about blood oaths, he also didn't want to take a chance on something he didn't understand, something he had been warned against doing. He should have told her no, but with the urgency in her eyes, it appeared she needed this to feel more secure. "Okay." He placed his left hand in hers.

"This will only hurt a little . . . or a lot, depending on your tolerance for pain." She pushed the razor into his palm, drawing a trail of blood as the sharpness cut through his skin. After doing the same to herself, she interlaced their fingers and merged their bloody palms. "Okay." She met his gaze. "I swear that no matter where life takes me, I will always find my way back to Obinna. I swear to marry him and no one else. If I break this oath, let fate deal with me as it chooses." She exhaled. "Okay. Say the same thing."

He did. He repeated the same words, their hands still pressed together, their blood intermingling, his becoming hers and hers becoming his.

Obinna closed his eyes, suddenly aware of an extension of his mind—the growth of a sixth sense that made him conscious of an abrupt shift, of things rearranging. He sensed the energy in the air as the fabric of the universe evolved, adjusting to what they had said.

When he opened his eyes and looked at Dunni, he knew they hadn't made a promise only to each other. They had made a promise to the universe, to forces they couldn't see who took record of every word they had said and finalized two endings that would come from them keeping their promise or breaking it.

CHAPTER TWENTY-FIVE

Dunni sat beside Gigi at the edge of the pool, their feet in the water. Wide-brim panama hats shielded them from the sun, at its peak at a little past noon.

"I'm sorry filming for your movie got postponed," Dunni said. She lowered her cat-eye sunglasses and looked at Gigi. Without the tinted frames, Gigi's yellow bikini stood out, a stunning contrast to her deep-umber complexion.

"Yeah. It was really disappointing. I was at home, drowning in self-pity. When I get like that, Nick's the only person who can pull me out of it, so I drove down."

"Did he help?"

"Yeah. Gave me a good old-fashioned pep talk this morning—snapped me right out of it."

"Good."

"Thanks for being so accommodating. I know you and Nick probably wanted to be alone."

"Don't worry about it. It's a big enough place."

"Still." Gigi's lips, coated in a glittery gloss, expanded. "I appreciate it."

Dunni returned the smile and repositioned her glasses on the bridge of her nose. "Obinna said you brought a guy along. A boyfriend?"

"Ew. Big Boy is not my boyfriend."

"Big Boy?" Dunni wasn't sure if the name referred to a body type or a specific body part. She cleared her throat and suppressed a laugh. "Is that his name?"

"Of course not. It's just a nickname. But now that I think about it, I can't even remember his real name." She narrowed her eyes and sipped her mimosa. "Maybe you know it."

"Me? Why would I know it?"

"Nicholas said you know him. Apparently, he's an old friend from secondary school."

Dunni frowned. "Obinna didn't mention it when he came back to our room."

But then again, he'd said little to her. He'd barely made eye contact. They didn't continue the conversation the knock at the door had interrupted. Instead, they divided their time in the bathroom. Dunni took a shower first, then Obinna entered the bathroom as she left. As they walked past each other, he'd frozen under the doorway and fixated on her back, where her white towel dipped below the tattoo. Sensing him watching, she'd turned around and met his pained and perplexed stare.

"Obinna," she'd said, the truth on the tip of her tongue. "I need to—"

"Breakfast should be ready. Feel free to go ahead without me." He'd shut the door without another word.

Dunni shook the tense interaction from her mind and focused, instead, on the mysterious friend from secondary school. "I suppose I had a few, so I'm not entirely sure which you're referring to. You sure you can't remember his name?"

"Umm." Gigi tapped her chin while contemplating. "Emmanuel?" She shook her head. "No, that isn't it. Emenike? Nope. Wait a minute." She snapped her fingers, and her eyes widened. "Emeka. Yes! That's it."

"Emeka? Emeka is Big Boy? And he's here?"

"The one and only, baby!" The loud, overly confident voice came from behind, and Dunni's head spun toward it.

"Emeka?" Her hand came over her gasping mouth. "Oh my God. Is that really you?"

In her mind, there was only one image of the teenage boy with the loud mouth. He was tall and chubby. Now, he was obscenely muscular—a certified bodybuilder. He walked alongside Obinna, both nearing the pool in their swimsuits. It all seemed surreal—the way her past had wrestled into her present. First, with Obinna. Now, with Emeka. The sight of them made her happy and sad as she thought of who they'd been years ago— before graduation, before the disastrous party at her house, before she got on a plane, before she was forced to grow up too fast.

"Dunni, how long has it been?" Emeka said, sitting beside her. "So you just went abroad and forgot about me, *shebi*? Is that how you are?"

She laughed and shoved him. "What about you? You no *sabi* call person?"

"Was that pidgin English?" He tossed his head back and chuckled. "So, America didn't completely suck the Nigerian out of you."

"It still wasn't sharp though," Obinna said. He stood above them, his hands in his pockets. "She's lost a bit of the rhythm."

"Oh, please." Dunni rolled her eyes. "*Na* because I *dey* pity *una*. If I say make I speak am well-well, *e* go burst *una* brain for here."

All four of them broke out in laughter.

Clearing his throat, Emeka slipped into the water and freed up his spot for Obinna.

"I still can't believe you're here. And with Gigi." Dunni eyed the pair suggestively.

"Yes, my beautiful, talented sweetheart." Emeka swam to Gigi and positioned himself between her legs. He watched her adoringly, even as she looked away. "Do you see how much she likes to *shakara*? She acts like she doesn't want me around, but then she invites me here."

"Don't flatter yourself," Gigi said in a dry monotone. "It was a long drive. I didn't want to get bored, and you were available."

"I don't believe that at all." He pressed his lips to her knee and then to her inner thigh.

The corners of Gigi's lips quivered as she fought a smile.

"Let's just stop all this running around, eh?" Emeka went on. "Be my girlfriend."

The flicker of a smile left Gigi's lips. With a brow arched, she glared at Emeka; the look was bound to send a shiver through him. "I've told you a hundred times. It's not happening. You just aren't good enough for me."

Stunned, Dunni's eyebrows shot up. She expected Emeka to storm off. The statement would have left any man's ego bruised and battered. Instead, he nodded.

"Okay," he said calmly. "And why aren't I good enough for you?"

"I need a man who doesn't stand behind his father's shadow and achievements." She leaned into him, her lips inches from his. "Hop off your daddy's back, and then we'll see."

Emeka grinned, a silent agreement, and closed the inches between their lips with a kiss.

A moan escaped Gigi as the kiss deepened.

Dunni and Obinna shared a look that conveyed their discomfort. Their eyes stayed on each other and softened as they smiled. The tension of earlier left in an instant, and she shifted closer to him just as his arm came around her shoulders.

"They're an interesting couple," he said, laughing.

"Very." Dunni looked at the unusual pair. "So." She cleared her throat, calling for their attention. "How did you guys meet?"

Gigi drew back and exhaled. "At a party," she said. "Nicholas threw a New Year's Eve party last year."

"Oh." Dunni looked between Emeka and Obinna. "Did you two stay in touch after we graduated?"

"No," Emeka answered. "I went to the University of Toronto—the Harvard of Canada." He beamed with pride. "After, I lived in Thailand for a while. I came back to Lagos two years ago and ran into Obinna at an event, and we reconnected." His dark eyes, as mischievous as they'd been twelve years ago, darted between Obinna and Dunni. "So, what's going on with you two? When I first ran into Obinna, he told me you were in America. He said you guys no longer spoke to each other. Yet here you are—together."

"We ran into each other recently—met at a friend's wedding," Obinna said. "We're just catching up, reconnecting."

"Oh? Reconnecting? Okay *o*." A smug smile tilted one corner of Emeka's mouth.

Dunni remembered that expression—suggestive and taunting. It was his signature. Years later, and he was still the same joker, looking for trouble.

"What do you want to say?" she asked him. "Go on. Spit it out before it eats your insides."

Everyone laughed.

"No, it's just . . ." He swam away from Gigi, toward the center of the pool. "You both are wasting your time."

"Wasting our time. How so?"

"With this reconnecting nonsense. There's no need for it." He dipped his head into the water and popped out. "Just marry already *na*. *Wetin*? You are meant for each other. I knew that even in secondary school. I thought you guys knew it too. What happened?"

Dunni thought on the question and calculated the many events that had pushed Obinna and her apart. Then she watched Emeka with tenderness, as if delivering unpleasant news to a hopeful child. "Too much," she told him. "Too damn much."

CHAPTER TWENTY-SIX

The white linens that draped the cabana flapped gently in the wind. Dunni leaned into Obinna as they watched the swaying waters tinted with the indigo and reddish hues of twilight.

After dinner with Emeka and Gigi, Obinna had led Dunni to the beach. Glass lanterns that paved a path to the cabana guided their steps. Inside, they relaxed on a bed and sipped champagne that had chilled in an ice bucket.

"So," Obinna said. "Tell me more about your life in Seattle. Do you like your job? Do you have close friends?"

"I like my field. You know I've always loved science."

He nodded. "I remember."

"I have a few close friends. Emily is my next-door neighbor. I've known her for what seems like a lifetime. She's incredible. Then there's Mira, but she's currently teaching in Dubai. I met her at university. She's equally incredible. And then there's Anna. She's—"

"Incredible?" Obinna finished with a smile.

"Yeah." Dunni laughed. "Pretty much."

"Good friends and a good job. It sounds like your life in Seattle is great."

She shrugged. "I suppose."

"Have you ever thought of coming back home—to Lagos?"

"No." It had never crossed her mind. As much as Dunni missed Lagos, the thought of returning to start a life there had never been an option. To her, it seemed like returning to the ruins of an imagined future and trying to build something unremarkable atop it. "I have a life in Seattle."

"We could have a life here. Together. Just like we always planned. Look." He sighed, and his tone turned serious. "I'm sorry about how I reacted this morning after seeing the tattoo."

"You don't have to apologize. You were shocked. I understand."

"No. It wasn't just that. The truth is, I felt guilty."

"For what?" she asked.

"For not giving you the life we planned, the life I promised we would have. I'm sorry, Dunni." He took her hand and squeezed it. "But here we are. After everything, we're together, and we can still have that life." His grip tightened; his hold was just as desperate as the look in his eyes. "Emeka was right. Us trying to reconnect is a waste of time."

"What are you saying?"

"I'm saying, what's stopping us from starting our lives together right now?" He placed his glass of champagne aside and sat upright. "Dunni, I love you. I never stopped loving you. I couldn't. And I didn't want to because I always knew you were it. Twelve years without you didn't shake that certainty from my mind—from my heart. Did it for you?"

"No. It didn't."

And for a long time, she'd hated herself for being unable to hate him, for still praying for him, for still worrying about him, for still wanting and needing him, and for still believing in them, in a childhood wish.

When Dunni was a teenager, something beyond her physical body—beyond skin, blood, muscles, and bones—something hidden beneath layers of her confirmed her feelings for Obinna were neither fleeting nor trivial. And even with that certainty, Dunni had tried to rationalize her emotions—to pick them apart and reduce them to cells she could place under a microscope to study. She wanted to understand her feelings for him, especially why they had developed so quickly. But science couldn't provide an explanation. So, she'd imagined an otherworldly entity who cultivated emotions in an orchard, plucked them once ripe, and planted them in lovers, already full and bursting with life. And those emotions never withered, having an immortal quality.

"I love you, Obinna. I always have. Nothing has changed that." She placed her hand over his chest and felt his heart's reaction to her confession. It was as frantic as hers. "You're it. I have always known." Air gushed out of her, a release so satisfying her body drooped.

"Dunni, marry me."

She gasped before finding her voice. "What?"

"Let's begin our lives together. No more wasting time." He stroked her cheek. "Be my wife. This is inevitable. We are inevitable."

Dunni's life was complicated. Her relationship with Obinna, even more complicated. But the answer to his proposal, regardless of all the complications, was simple. It was yes. She should have said it. Instead, she shook her head.

"I can't. You know I can't. Not until I sort things out with Christopher."

Obinna's lips turned down in a frown, but he interlaced their fingers and nodded. "Okay. I understand."

They walked back to the beach house, glancing at each other and smiling, a proposal between them and an answer, even though it hadn't been voiced. They entered the lobby, and the fair-skinned woman behind the front desk shifted her attention from the computer.

"Good evening. Can I help you with anything?" She squinted, tilted her head, and studied Obinna. "Nicholas?"

Obinna smiled at her. "Alex."

"Hey." She stepped away from the desk and approached him. "Oh my God." She giggled, unnaturally soft for a grown woman who should have some bass in her voice.

"What are you doing here?"

"I work here part-time. It's temporary." Another giggle, followed by a hair flip. "What about you? What are you doing here? And who's she?"

"This is my—"

"Entertainment for the night?" Alex said. "She's cute. Really cute. Want me to join you guys upstairs?"

"What?" Dunni blurted, her eyes bulging.

"Um . . . Alex, no," Obinna quickly explained. "It's not—"

"Come on. For old times' sake." She pouted and caressed his arm. "Don't you remember all the fun we used to have? I've missed you, Nick."

Dunni was stunned. Minutes ago, she had been so close to saying yes and making the biggest decision she had made on her own in years.

After leaving Nigeria and losing contact with Obinna, she had made one last life-changing decision before switching to autopilot and allowing her parents to dictate her life. It had been easier that way, less for her to think or worry about. They had suggested her career path, where she would live after graduating, her area of research, and of course, her husband. Their guidance created a stability Dunni relied on, one she needed in her life. Now she wondered if being with Obinna would involve substituting that stability for chaos. She looked at Alex, another person who confirmed his reputation as a playboy, and the answer struck her, painful and undeniable. She released Obinna's hand and rushed up the stairs.

CHAPTER TWENTY-SEVEN

Dunni tossed clothes into her travel bag. The brief phone conversation she had minutes ago increased her angst and urgency. She needed to leave the resort immediately. Obinna knocked on the other side of the locked bedroom door, as he'd been doing for five minutes.

After rushing into the room, Dunni had locked the door, desperate for some space to think. But then her phone vibrated on the nightstand. Iya Agba's name appeared on the screen, but when Dunni answered, she heard Christopher's voice. Now she moved faster, grabbing her belongings and stashing them into the travel bag.

"Dunni," Obinna called to her. The edge in his voice proved he'd run out of patience. "Enough of this. Open the door."

Once she'd zipped the bag closed, she turned the lock.

"What in God's name is going on with you?" He huffed and

marched into the room. "Locking the door and just ignoring me." He paused when he saw the packed bag. His mouth fell open, but words didn't come out.

"I'm going home . . . well, back to my parents' house."

"What do you mean, you're going home? Where is this coming from?"

"Christopher is in Lagos. At my parents' place. He got in this afternoon. To surprise me." Or to remind her that she had a fiancé. "He's been trying to reach me, but . . ." She pressed her fingers to her forehead and tried to ease the gathering tension. "I have to go."

"To end things with him. Right?"

"I don't know."

"What do you mean, you don't know?" He shut the door and neared her. "Dunni, what's going on? On the beach, we talked about us and—"

"Us?" Suddenly, the word had a different texture and taste; it was something she wanted to spit out rather than savor. "There is no us."

Obinna leaned back and shook his head. "I don't understand. Is this because of Alex? I know she was rude, and I've spoken to her. It won't happen again. If it will make you more comfortable, I can speak to the manager and ask that someone else take her shift while we're here. But please don't punish me for how she acted."

"I'm not trying to punish you." She groaned, frustrated and exhausted. "I'm just trying to be cautious and rational."

"Cautious? Rational? About what?"

"You, Obi. How many more women are going to pop up, claiming they had a past with you? I can't keep dealing with that crap. There's no room for that kind of madness in my life."

"So, that's what this is about? You're angry at the relationships I had in the past? Didn't you date anyone while we were apart?"

"Yes. Two guys before Christopher. That's it. What about you? How many women have you been with?"

"Dunni." He blew out a deep breath. "They meant nothing. They were just a way to fill the void you left."

"I could have filled that void perfectly, don't you think? But you stayed away. If you wanted, you could have found me. I still have my old email address. I check it occasionally."

"I was—"

"Yes, I know." She held up a hand, silencing him. "You already explained why you stayed away, but I've been thinking, and I don't accept it. Your explanation isn't a good enough reason."

He didn't speak, and her eyes darted as she considered what he'd said earlier.

"We are inevitable." Her narrowed eyes settled on him. "You said that on the beach. What did you mean by that?"

"Um . . . that we belong together. I've always been certain of that."

"And what exactly is your certainty based on?"

He opened his mouth to answer, then closed it as he mused.

"Obinna, is your certainty in us based on instincts, a gut feeling, or that stupid oath we made? You believe it connected us. Is that why you sat on your ass, ignored every email I ever sent, slept with one woman after another, because you believed the oath would work its magic and bring us together again? Is that why you made no effort to reach out to me?"

"What?" His eyebrows shot up in surprise. "No. Of course not."

"Then what was it? Why did you just leave me? What's the true reason?" She waited for the answer, but it didn't come.

She picked up the travel bag and her cell phone. As if prompted by her eagerness to leave, the device vibrated with an incoming text message. Paul was thirty minutes away. Dunni moved to the door, then paused and looked at Obinna, hoping he would say something, offer an explanation that would delay her departure. Instead, he stood silent and unmoving. Tears gleamed in his eyes, but did not fall. She exhaled, opened the door, and walked out of the room.

CHAPTER TWENTY-EIGHT

THEN

Obinna had gotten better at lying to his mother. He no longer felt guilty. When he first started lying about attending after-school activities—the clubs and tutoring sessions he claimed would help his university applications—he'd felt guilty. Back then, he would force the words out and struggle to hold his mother's intimidating gaze. Now, four weeks after the blood oath, he lied with so much ease and did so guilt-free, driven only by the need to be with Dunni.

Something had changed in him. After their bloody palms merged, he'd gone home a different person. That night, while in bed, he'd felt odd—hungry even though he had eaten dinner and was full, thirsty even though his throat was not dry, weak even though he felt charged for the first time in his life. He had spent hours turning. Then, as he lay on his back and watched the ceiling fan spin slowly, he figured it out. He had grown dependent on something. It wasn't food. It wasn't water. It wasn't rest. It was Dunni.

He watched the ceiling fan turn; cool air dried the sweat on his face as he examined himself and recognized the loss of self-control and caution and sensibility. Everything he felt for Dunni had amplified significantly, because all the factors that once kept him in check were gone.

Now, as they stepped into her house, he glanced at her and wanted to ask if the change was one-sided. Did she feel it too? What exactly happened when their hands touched, when they said those words, when they made that promise to each other?

"You've been quiet," she said. "Is everything okay?"

"Yes. I'm fine."

"You sure?"

He nodded.

"Okay." She dropped her bag at the base of the grand staircase.

"Aren't we going upstairs—to your room?"

"No. We aren't having sex today."

They usually did whenever he came to her house, even when they made plans to study or watch a film. They had gotten better at it. Dunni moaned a lot more. He loved watching her face whenever that happened. It made him feel good. He had grown confident with touching her, knowing all her preferences. He had even grown more comfortable in her house. The maids knew him. Though they said nothing to him—only smiled and went on with their business. Dunni had threatened them to do just that and say nothing to her parents. Obinna didn't question her tactics. Just as he had to lie, she had to make threats.

"I want you to meet someone."

"Meet who? Are your parents here?" His shoulders squared as he stiffened.

"No. Not my parents. Besides, you've already met them."

Obinna exhaled. "Okay. Then who?"

"My grandmother."

"I thought she was in Port Harcourt for your auntie's *omugwo*."

"She's only visiting. She's going back in a week, and I want you to meet her before she leaves."

Obinna scratched his sweaty neck. Meeting Dunni's mother had not gone well. Would meeting her grandmother be equally disastrous? "I don't know about this."

"Are you scared?"

He didn't deny it.

"I've already told her about you. She wants to meet you."

"What exactly did you tell her?"

"Just come." She grabbed his hand and pulled him toward the kitchen while he dragged his feet.

A petite woman stood by the stove, her back to them as she stirred the contents in a pot. The air smelled savory and sweet. Obinna detected a whiff of fried plantains. His mouth watered, then dried the instant the woman turned and faced him. She looked between the two of them and a discreet smile touched the corners of her lips.

"Good afternoon, Iya Agba," Dunni greeted.

"My dear, how are you? How was school?"

"Good, thank you."

Obinna wanted his first impression to be strong, but when he opened his mouth to speak, words did not come out. Dunni nudged him with her elbow, but it didn't resolve his sudden speechlessness.

"You must be Obinna." The elderly woman had a tender yet firm voice. She strolled toward him, and a soft peppermint scent emanated off her *iro* and *buba*. Her smile expanded, and the lines on her face creased. "I have heard a lot about you."

He cleared his throat and pushed out what he hoped would be a dignified response. "I . . . I have heard a lot about you too, ma. It is nice to meet you."

"Mm-hmm." She extended her hand and held his chin, the grip gentle. "My granddaughter says she is going to marry you one day."

"What?" His eyes widened. He wanted to turn to Dunni, but the hold on his chin restricted him.

"You seem surprised. Is this news to you?"

"No, ma." Heat rose to his neck. "We . . . we've talked about it."

"Talked?"

"Concluded, ma," he corrected quickly. "I just didn't know we were telling people, especially our grandmothers." He bit his tongue. He shouldn't have mentioned that last part. "No offense, ma."

She laughed softly and released his chin. "I made beans and fried plantains. I hope you both are hungry?"

Dunni answered with a cheerful yes and nudged Obinna to do the same.

"Yes, ma. Very."

"So. What has my granddaughter told you about me?" She returned to the stove and stirred the pot of beans.

"Um . . ." He didn't know how to answer, and the obscure words Dunni mouthed didn't push him in the right direction. "She said you were, um . . . interesting."

"Interesting?" She stopped moving the wooden spoon in the pot and turned to him. "Mm. I like being interesting."

As she turned off the heat, Obinna realized Dunni had gotten her personality from her grandmother. They had the same energy too. This fact put him at ease.

"So, when is this wedding to my granddaughter?"

Obinna wondered if she was patronizing them or truly supporting their relationship, which faced the threat of distance. Dunni still planned to attend Princeton. In a few months, she would leave. He tried not to think about how he would feed his need once she was gone. He would address that when the time came.

"After we graduate from university," he answered.

"We want to finish school first," Dunni added. "Then we can really start our lives together."

Her grandmother said nothing. She looked at them, her lips tightly pressed together as she smiled. Again, Obinna considered her motive.

"You both sit." She gestured to the wooden stools beside the white counter. "I'll dish the food."

"Let me help you, ma," he offered.

She held up her hand, stopping him from approaching the stove. "No need. I can manage."

Obinna and Dunni sat side by side, their knees touching beneath the counter. Her grandmother hummed as she dished beans and plantains onto a plate. She placed the food in front of Obinna, then returned to the stove. It didn't occur to either of them to wait for another serving. Dunni pulled two forks from a drawer, handed one to Obinna, and they ate. When her grandmother turned to them with another plate, she paused, and her smile flattened.

"Iya," Dunni said. "Are you okay?"

"Yes. Of course." She cleared her throat. "I suppose this is mine then." She sat on a stool opposite the pair and considered them while pushing a fork through a plantain.

"This is delicious, ma," Obinna said.

She held his stare and searched his eyes, and then her smile slowly returned. "Call me Iya Agba," she told him. "Or Grandma. Whichever you prefer."

Obinna nodded. "Yes, ma. Iya Agba."

They ate quietly, and as Dunni rose to fill their plate with more food, a maid, one Dunni called her favorite, rushed into the kitchen.

"Best?" Dunni said. "Why are you running? What is it?"

"Your mother." The maid panted. "She is here."

"What do you mean, she's here? She's in Amsterdam for another week."

Best shook her head. "She's outside. A car service just dropped her off."

"Shit," Dunni mumbled under her breath.

"What do you want me to do? Delay her? Prevent her from entering the kitchen?"

"Aha-aha," Dunni's grandmother said. "So, she is home. What is the problem?"

Obinna and Dunni shared a look that translated their mutual concern.

"Oh. Okay. I see." She nodded knowingly. "Well, don't worry. I'm here. But frankly, if she is so worried about you, she should try staying in this house and taking care of you like a proper mother." She hissed and scooped a combination of beans and plantain into her mouth.

Obinna's heart raced. Within seconds, sweat drenched his shirt. He hopped off the stool and picked up his bag. "Is there a back door?" he asked, frantically looking around the kitchen.

"Obinna, don't be ridiculous. My daughter-in-law won't kill you for being here."

He wasn't so certain about that. The last time he saw Dunni's mother, she had given him a clear warning, one he had dismissed. He feared the repercussions of his defiance. Even with the support of Dunni's grandmother, he searched the room for an escape route. And then he heard the click and clack of heels approaching, the sound like hailstone hitting glass. It stopped.

Obinna held his breath.

"What is this?" The voice was like a razor and pepper and

ice. It cut, it burned, it caused Obinna to freeze like a thief caught in the act.

"Welcome back, Mom," Dunni said with very little warmth. "You remember Obinna, right?"

"I do." She arched an eyebrow and measured him, as she had the first time they met. "What is he doing here? With you. In my house."

"He is eating," Dunni's grandmother answered. "And he is welcome here."

The room fell silent as the two women, who were likely always at odds, glared at each other.

After a moment, Dunni's mother focused on Obinna. "Get. Out."

"Yes, ma," he said. "I apologize for intruding."

"You're not intruding. He's not intruding, Mom. I invited him. I wanted him here. You can't just throw him out. We weren't even doing anything. We were just eating. That's it!" Tears filled Dunni's eyes. "Why are you being like this?"

"Dunni, it's okay," Obinna said, his voice calm. "I have to go anyway." He looked at her grandmother. "Iya Agba, thank you so much. It was a pleasure meeting you." He managed a smile that concealed his embarrassment poorly, then walked toward the kitchen door.

"Obinna."

He stopped moving and turned to face Dunni's mother.

"The next time I see you in this house or with my daughter, I won't take it so lightly."

The first time she had warned him to stay away from Dunni,

it had been private. He had been ashamed, but at least the four walls of his house kept his shame a secret. Today, his shame had been public, right in front of the girl he loved.

He wondered if this moment would alter Dunni's perception of him. Would this be the moment she realized he wasn't good enough for her? Was it only a matter of time before Dunni looked at him the way her mother looked at him?

CHAPTER TWENTY-NINE

Dunni stepped into her parents' house at a little past eleven at night. Paul walked ahead of her, carrying her travel bag.

"No need to take it up," she told him. "I'll do it myself."

He stopped short of climbing the stairs. "Are you sure?"

"It's late. Go home. And thank you for coming to get me so quickly."

"No problem, ma. Good night." He placed the bag on the floor and walked through the front door.

Dunni wanted to go to bed, curl under the safety of sheets, and block out the world. But up the stairs, in a room she had claimed as hers, her fiancé lay in bed, waiting for her. With Christopher no longer a continent away, Dunni's guilt seemed more real; it gained a new dimension—sharp ends that prodded her insides. Over the past few days, she had gone from a wedding reception to her ex-boyfriend's home and then to a beach resort. One reason prompted each decision and action. She loved Obinna. That was the sole reason, but it was so enormous it made everything else shrink and lose its significance. Standing in the foyer, amid the silence and the darkness, she recalled how truly significant Christopher was. He was her fiancé, and he was a good person.

"You're back."

Dunni's head snapped up, toward her grandmother, who descended the stairs. "Iya, you shouldn't walk in the dark." She rushed to the elderly woman, took her arm, and guided her to the landing. "Why aren't you sleeping? Were you waiting for me?"

"I was only coming down for a glass of water." She eyed her granddaughter and hissed. "Why would I be waiting for you to come home? You've made it clear that you can take care of yourself, so why should an old, superstitious woman like myself be bothered?"

Dunni sighed, recalling their last conversation. "Iya, I'm sorry *na*. Really. I didn't mean what I said. I was just under a little stress."

"Mm-hmm." She flicked on a light in the corridor and walked toward the kitchen.

It was not an invitation, but Dunni followed her grandmother, knowing the tension was gone, even without her verbally accepting the apology.

"So." Iya Agba opened the refrigerator; the light from it beamed on the white tiles and brightened the dim room. "You were with your friend." She grabbed a water jug and shut the refrigerator. The room grew darker, lit only by the distant light in the corridor.

"Yes. My friend." Dunni's voice turned rigid. She hoped the stiffness would keep her emotions from breaking through.

"Eh-heh." Iya Agba sat on a stool at the counter, across from Dunni. She poured water into a cup and sipped. "Is that what Obinna is now? A friend?"

At the mention of his name, Dunni sighed. "Did my mother tell you?"

"No." She took another sip of water. "He drove you to this house that day. But I knew even before then."

"How?"

"You didn't come home on the night of Tiwa's wedding. I knew you were with him. Who else could it be? I just hoped you would tell me on your own."

"Oh." Dunni diverted her eyes to some dark, inconspicuous part of the kitchen. She couldn't bear to look at her grandmother. "I'm sorry I didn't tell you, Iya."

"I'm just confused. All those years ago, I thought he changed his mind about being with you. That's what you told me."

"It's what I thought."

"Okay. So, were you mistaken? Did something happen? Is that why he stayed away?"

"Iya, I don't know. I really don't know."

"What do you mean, you don't know? You've been with him for days. Didn't you ask him questions? Didn't you demand an explanation from him?"

"I did. We talked. I asked him and . . ." She rubbed her forehead. "I don't know."

A moment of silence passed between them.

"You still love him," Iya Agba said abruptly. "Don't you?"

Dunni nodded. "So much. It's like nothing changed." She chewed her lip and fought back a sob.

"And he still loves you?"

"That's what he told me."

"Okay. So, when are you going to stop wasting Christopher's time and tell him you cannot marry him?"

Dunni flinched at her grandmother's words. "What?"

"Are you saying it has never crossed your mind? Because it has crossed mine many times."

"Many times? Iya, where is this even coming from? You've never had a problem with Christopher."

"My problem is not with him."

"Okay. Then who is it with?"

"No one. I just know that Christopher is not meant for you."

"Since when?" Curious, Dunni leaned into the counter and studied the parts of her grandmother's face visible in the dim room.

"Do you remember when you brought Obinna here, so I could meet him?"

Dunni nodded. She recalled telling her grandmother about him. For an hour, she'd gone on about how she felt and about the future they had planned. Between chuckles, her grandmother had said, "I want to meet this boy."

"That day, when I met him, I thought nothing of the

relationship. I thought it was just young love, guaranteed to fade. So I patronized the two of you." She closed her eyes, as if evoking the memory. "I made beans and fried plantains. I still remember. I placed a plate in front of Obinna—the food was for him." She opened her eyes, a slight pinch between her brows. "But when I came to the counter with your plate, you both were sharing his food."

"Okay." Dunni shrugged. "Back then, we always ate together. So what?"

"There was just something about it. I cannot explain it, but when I saw you both doing that, I just knew."

"You just knew what?"

"That you two were supposed to be together. I know you might call me superstitious again, but that is all I can tell you. I knew because I felt it. There is no other explanation. I just felt it. Can you try to understand that?"

Dunni didn't have to try. She understood that intangible feeling of just knowing without an explanation, without proof, without reason. Just knowing, as she had years ago and even now. Even with the pain and confusion and anger and resentment and her fiancé upstairs, she knew.

"Have you told him?" Iya Agba asked.

"Told him what?"

"That you were pregnant?"

Dunni pressed her eyes closed at the sound of those words. "I couldn't," she said, looking at her grandmother. "I couldn't do it."

"You were with him for three days. Why didn't you tell him?"

"It's not a particularly easy thing to say. I wanted to tell him this morning. He saw my tattoo. It was the perfect opportunity, but we were interrupted. And even if we weren't, I don't know that I could have done it." Tears gathered at the rims of her eyes, then spilled down. "I don't know how I would have gotten the words out."

With her thumb, Iya Agba wiped the tears on Dunni's cheeks. "It's okay. I understand."

"I don't know what I'm going to do."

"You are going to end this engagement with Christopher and tell Obinna everything—the complete truth."

Someone cleared their throat abruptly, an obvious demand for attention. Dunni's mother stood under the doorframe. She walked into the kitchen; her silk burgundy robe caught the silver gleam of the moon that came through the windows.

"Iya, can I please speak with my daughter privately?"

Iya Agba took a sip from her glass. Her eyes, above the rim, shifted between her granddaughter and her daughter-in-law. "Why not?" She managed a fake smile, then slid off the stool. "Good night, dear. We will talk later." She kissed Dunni's cheek and left the kitchen.

The atmosphere changed immediately; it grew taut with tension.

"So. What is it? What do you want to talk about?" Dunni asked, her voice weary.

"I was at the door, listening to your grandmother steer you in the wrong direction."

Dunni sighed. She had the words, but not the energy. Too much had already happened that day. She hopped off the chair. "I'm going to bed."

"You still love him."

Dunni froze short of the door and faced her mother.

"You still love each other."

"You mean after everything you did? Yes."

"You may not believe it, but everything I did back then was for you—to protect you."

"To protect me?" She scoffed. "From what? What were you protecting me from exactly—a teenage boy who took the bus to school rather than a car, who lived in a poor part of the city, who didn't have the things we did? How was he a threat to me?"

"You don't understand."

"Then help me understand. Because it's been years, and I'm still baffled." She wanted an explanation. She needed one. "What kind of person treats someone—a child, for that matter—the way you treated him? For what? Because he had less than you? Because you thought you were better than him?"

Her mother opened her mouth, and her lips moved against soundless words. Her breathing quickened. She rubbed her eyes that suddenly seemed exhausted. "It doesn't matter the reason. I did what I thought was best. But that is all in the past. He's in your past, Dunni. You have to move on. You're engaged to Christopher, for Christ's sake. You have to let Obinna go for good."

"Do you think it's that easy? Do you think I haven't tried to forget him? I've been trying to move on for years. I don't know how. I can't." Dunni huffed. "You can't possibly understand that."

"I do." Her mother bit her lip, as if regretting the admission. Though she continued speaking, even with the tremor in her voice. "I know what it is to love someone like that, to feel that kind of love—the way it digs inside you and plants itself deep, where you didn't even know something could reach. And then you can't shake it off—you can never shake it off. It just stays there, growing, festering, consuming you. I know."

Dunni took steps forward to ensure those words had come from her mother's mouth. "Are you talking about Daddy?" She found it hard to believe because she knew that sort of love didn't exist between her parents. They had something different.

"No. Not your father. Someone else."

Someone else. Instantly, Dunni remembered what Obinna had said at the fire pit. She studied her mother. "Who?"

"It doesn't matter." She held the cord on her robe and twisted it around a finger. "He doesn't matter anymore."

"But you loved him."

"Yes. And people call that kind of love epic." She rolled her eyes. "What they don't tell you is how dangerous it can also be, how it can prevent you from thinking rationally."

Obinna had been right. Dunni's mother had experienced something terrible at the hands of someone she loved. What could it have been? Dunni wanted the entire story, but there were boundaries between her and her mother, ones that prohibited intimacy; they'd been established so long ago, and she didn't know how to navigate them.

"It's okay to love someone rationally," her mother told her. "Without all the passion, without giving all of yourself to them."

"Is that how you love Daddy?"

"It is. And I think that's how you love Christopher. And that's okay. That kind of love can be good too. In some ways, it's even stronger. It's sensible and reliable and constant and safe. That is what you have with Christopher. You trust him. He has always been there for you. You can't say the same about Obinna."

There it was. Dunni's fears echoed. And by her mother, of all people.

"Regardless of what I did, he chose to leave you. He could have contacted you but didn't. How many emails did you send him? How many did he respond to? None. Because he is unreliable."

Dunni wanted to defend Obinna. With everything in her, she wanted to defend him, but how could she? Her mother was right.

"Dunni, not everyone needs a whirlwind romance. In my experience, it does more damage than good."

After taking a shower, Dunni lifted the covers and slipped beneath them. Christopher's body heat greeted her.

"Hey." He peered at her through squinted eyes. "There you are. Where've you been?"

"Um . . . I was just hanging out with friends from secondary school." And in some ways, that was the truth. And in some ways, it was not. "I can't believe you're here—in Lagos."

"I missed you," he said, shifting closer to her. "I needed to see you. On the phone you sounded off. I needed to make sure we were okay." He paused. "Are we?"

"Yeah. Of course." Gosh, she wished that were true. "I shouldn't have extended my stay. Actually, I shouldn't have come to Nigeria at all. I shouldn't have left you."

"I wish you hadn't either, baby. I love you."

She was supposed to respond now, but the words never came organically; she had to guide them out of her mouth with a metaphorical flashlight and compass and trail of breadcrumbs. "I love you too."

This time, a new understanding accompanied those words. Maybe she loved Christopher the way her parents loved each other. It was nothing close to what she felt for Obinna. It was sensible, reliable, and safe.

And perhaps it was best.

CHAPTER THIRTY

THEN

The next day at school, Dunni apologized to Obinna repeatedly, then complained about her mother, listing all the ways she was an inadequate parent and human being. Obinna pretended to listen. But really, he was calculating and trying to work out what he could subtract from his life and add in its place, so he could be enough for Dunni. He mapped out plans that would lead to wealth. He thought of shortcuts that would take him to his destination within months rather than years. He thought of the area boys in his neighborhood who loitered in unfinished buildings and whistled for recruits. He thought of answering their call and accompanying them on a few jobs, giving up his morals so he could pocket something—anything, no matter how small. He did this for months, staring into space, his eyes constantly darting.

Dunni joked about his absentmindedness rather than acknowledge the change in him—the fact that his knee had stopped finding hers under the table, that he smiled rarely, and didn't laugh at all, even when she said something worth a chuckle. Dunni didn't want to acknowledge this change. Maybe she feared it. She'd started to talk too much—too fast, too eager—never allowing a moment of silence to pass. Maybe she knew that without her constant chatter, they would have to confront everything between them—her mother and of course, America. So Dunni talked, and Obinna pretended to listen while calculating. Always calculating.

They existed like this in the months leading up to graduation. And then on that day, as they stood on opposite ends of a crowded room with their families and diplomas in their hands, they spotted each other and for the first time in months, acknowledged a truth they could no longer ignore. Secondary school was over. Obinna had gotten accepted into three universities. He would attend the University of Lagos in September, and Dunni would attend Princeton University.

"I can't believe it's all over," Emeka said. He flung his hands in the air and cheered. "Thank God! I can't wait to get out of this country—to get some freedom."

"Yeah. Freedom," Obinna muttered inattentively while watching his mother and auntie walk toward the refreshment table.

"You don't sound too happy, *sha*? *Wetin?*"

"Nothing." He blinked sharply and turned away from his family. "It's nothing."

"Really?" Emeka watched Obinna skeptically but didn't probe. "Okay. Well, it looks like I have to go." He waved his hand above the crowd, signaling to his father, who held a phone to his ear. He looked like the sort of stern man who didn't have a moment to spare. "I'll see you at Dunni's graduation party tomorrow."

"I don't think I'm going to make it."

"Ah-ah. You can't make it to your girlfriend's party. Why? Are you two fighting again? Should I come and mediate?" He snorted. "Or should I play the therapist. Which one?"

"Neither. We're fine."

"Okay. So, you're coming to Dunni's party then?"

"Of course he is. Where else would he be?" Dunni came behind them and threw her arms around their shoulders.

Obinna's eyes widened, attentive as he scanned the room for his mother and hers. Neither was looking at them. He sighed, but he was only half-relieved. Dunni was too close to him. He rolled his shoulder, gradually shifting her arm off.

"He said he isn't coming to the party," Emeka explained, as he took small steps away from them. "But you deal with that. I have to go." He turned and rushed toward his father.

"What's he talking about?" She still wore her black graduation robe; the opening in the middle revealed her white, knee-length dress. "What does he mean, you're not coming?"

"Do you really think that's smart—coming to your house after what happened last time? Your mother told me she never wants to see me there again." The memory of that day revived his shame. He looked at his polished dress shoes. They belonged to his father, but with three layers of socks, they fit Obinna perfectly.

"Forget about her. It's my party. My father said I can invite anyone I want. And I want you there. Everyone from our class is coming. It won't be the same without you. I'll be miserable." Her hand brushed his. The subtle movement warmed his skin and softened his resolve. "We only have a short time together before . . ." She bit her lip. "You know. Let's make the most of the time we have. Forget about my mother. She won't try what she did last time."

"I just don't think—"

"Please." Her hand brushed his again. "For me. Because you love me."

That was it for his resolve—it disappeared. "Okay," he told her. "I'll come."

Obinna paced back and forth on the street, reconsidering his decision to attend Dunni's party. Instead of crossing the threshold of the gate, he listened to the sounds coming from inside the compound—music, laughter, and bodies splashing in the pool. Still considering his attendance, he ran a hand over his shirt to ensure there were no wrinkles. The blue polo shirt and black jeans were some of his nicest clothes. Would his classmates consider them stylish? Or would they detect the cheap quality with one glance? Obinna couldn't stand further humiliation, especially since he hadn't recovered from his last two encounters with Dunni's mother. He had to leave. He turned and took a few steps down the street, then someone shouted his name. The orotund voice belonged to only one person. Emeka.

Reluctantly, while fighting the temptation to run, Obinna turned and watched Emeka step out of a black SUV. He shut the car door and laughed.

"Are you confused? The party is this way!"

Obinna looked over Emeka, from his red T-shirt to his blue jeans and impeccably white basketball shoes. His insides twisted; his insecurity rose to his throat like vomit.

"Where you *dey* go?"

"Um . . . I . . . nowhere." The window to escape had closed. He huffed and jogged back to the gate.

"But you were just . . ." Emeka shook his head. "Forget it. Let's just go inside. I'm ready to unwind. I deserve it, you know. See how I slaved all year to get good marks."

"You slaved? For good marks?" Obinna sorted. "You *sabi* lie *sha*!"

They both laughed, and Obinna didn't realize when he crossed the threshold of the gate and stepped into the compound.

He'd been inside a few times already, but this time was different. Various noises replaced the quietness that usually greeted him and Dunni, who were left to their own devices in an empty house. Usually, there were two or three maids going about their duties. Now there were servers in uniforms, holding trays with finger food and drinks; some catered to the small group in front of the house while others moved to the backyard.

"Oh yes!" Emeka rubbed his jutted stomach. "They have sliders."

"What are those?"

"You know, mini hamburgers."

Obinna didn't know. He had never heard of a slider, and he had never tried a hamburger, but he didn't admit to it. "Oh. Okay. Those."

"Let's get some and see what else they have." Emeka approached a server and grabbed a slider. He chewed with a grin, then turned to their classmates, who leaned against the large pillars beside the front door. "I know you guys have been bored, but don't worry. The life of the party has arrived. The enjoyment can now commence."

"And who exactly is the life of the party? You?" Simi snickered. She stood with her boyfriend and three other boys, and they all chuckled. "*Abeg*, Obinna, come get your boy. Come help him carry his big-ass ego. His shoulders must be killing him."

"Have you seen his shoulders?" Obinna asked. "In fact, have you seen his whole physique? He was built to carry that ego. It's a load he is equipped to carry."

"*Abeg* tell them," Emeka said, puffing out his chest. "Who no know, go know."

The knot in Obinna's stomach loosened as everyone laughed. Maybe he had overreacted earlier, attempting an escape when he should have been here with his friends and Dunni. He had to find her.

"Here." Emeka snatched two tall glasses off a tray a server held and handed one to Obinna. "These are so good."

Obinna sipped from the straw, and as the cold, sweet drink filled his mouth, he moaned.

"Okay," Simi said, smiling. "I guess Obinna likes piña coladas."

He nodded and licked his lips. "Anyway, I'm going to find Dunni. I'll see you guys later." He took a step toward the pathway that led to the backyard, then a shrill, familiar voice called out his name. He flinched, and the glass in his hand met the concrete and broke apart in large shards. Obinna contemplated picking up the shattered pieces or turning to face Dunni's mother. Noting his shaking hands, he decided on the latter.

She stood where he had seconds ago, beside his friends. Her glare debased him as usual, stripped away the last piece of self-worth he had. He'd lost some of it the first day he met her. He'd lost more of it that day in front of Dunni. Now, in front of his classmates, he lost the rest.

She gathered her long dress in one hand and walked toward him. "How many times have I told you to stay away from my daughter? Hmm? And I believe I also told you never to set foot on my property again, but here you are."

Something cold ran down Obinna's spine. His eyes shifted to his friends, who watched the scene unfold.

"Boys like you never listen," she continued. "You have nothing. And you expect a girl like my daughter to give you everything—even more than she has to give. Get out!"

Obinna wanted to run, but his legs did not move. They were heavy; they didn't obey the signal his brain sent.

"Come on, Auntie," Emeka said from where he stood. "There's no need for all this *na*. We're all just having fun." He smiled and tried to convey his signature playfulness, but his unsteady voice didn't hold humor.

"Why are you still standing there?" Dunni's mother paid no

attention to Emeka. Her voice increased, even as it shook with emotion. "Get off my property, or I will throw you out!"

Transfixed by fear, Obinna could not move. He breathed deeply and tried to loosen his stiff muscles. His toes wiggled. *Thank God*. He picked up his feet, ready to take a step, but her fingers rammed into his chest. He lost his balance and fell. His back met both the hardness of the ground and the sharpness of the glass he had dropped earlier.

"What's going on?" The angst-ridden voice was Dunni's. She stood among the crowd that had come from the backyard, some wearing bathing suits.

All eyes were on Obinna. No one moved. Perhaps it was shock, the same shock that kept him from moving earlier. When Dunni finally shook off her stupor, she attempted to run to him, but Paul held her back.

"Do not let her near him," her mother instructed the driver.

Paul frowned as Dunni squirmed in his arms. Clearly, he was uncomfortable with the situation. "Madam, is this really necessary? Let me just take him home."

"If you move or let her go, you will no longer have a job here."

At that point, Emeka lost his cool. "This is so fucked up." He rushed to Obinna and kneeled on the ground. "Let's get the hell out of here." Gently, he wrapped an arm around his friend and lifted him.

Dunni screamed the instant Obinna stood, the instant she saw the piece of glass wedged in his back and the blood that drenched his shirt. "He's hurt! Don't you see that? Paul, let me go!" She fought hard against him, but it was pointless. "He needs help!"

"It's okay," Emeka said. "I've got this. I'll take him to the hospital. He'll be okay." He glared at Dunni's mother, whose eyes were suddenly softer.

Her brows crinkled as she looked between Obinna and the blood on the ground. She assessed the scene as if she hadn't been present for it, as if she had stepped out of her body and was only now returning.

"Come on," Emeka said. "Let's go." He walked through the gate with Obinna's weight on him. "What the hell is wrong with that woman?"

Even with the throbbing ache that made him slump, Obinna turned his head and looked at Dunni and then at their classmates, who had witnessed the most degrading moment of his life.

CHAPTER THIRTY-ONE

THEN

Aknock at the front door made Obinna's eyes break open. He rested on the sofa in the living room, his stomach flat on the cushion. He'd been sleeping this way for a week, since he received the stitches on his back. Still in pain, he couldn't bear any other position. The knock sounded again. He groaned and called his mother, then realized she had left a while ago to attend evening service at church. Her absence was a relief. She hadn't left his side since the incident.

That day, she arrived at the hospital after Emeka called her. When she entered the room, she'd screamed, "Jesus!" The wrapper around her waist was loose, and she didn't care to tighten it as she ran to the bed. "What happened?"

Obinna had told Emeka to lie when she asked, but he didn't. He told her everything, and his mother's concern quickly turned to rage.

"Didn't I tell you to stay away from that girl? Eh, Obinna? Didn't I tell you to leave her alone? Do you see yourself now? Do you see yourself? You are in a hospital." Then abruptly, she directed her anger to Dunni's mother. "Does that woman think she can just treat you like this? Does she believe there are no repercussions—that she can just get away with this? Okay. We shall see."

She had gone to the police station to report the incident, but nothing was done. Nothing could be done when a food vendor made claims against one of the most affluent families in Lagos. His mother gave up her quest for justice and tended to him instead. She cried too, late at night when she believed he was asleep. She also prayed. Though she no longer reverenced God, but questioned him. She asked why her life was so difficult, why her husband had left, and why her son had been victimized. After the series of questions, she would grow silent, as if waiting for answers. When nothing came, she would cry again. And sometimes, so would Obinna.

The knock at the door repeated, and slowly, he pushed himself off the sofa and stood. He walked to the door with his back straight, trying not to bend so the soreness from the injury wouldn't intensify.

"Who is it?"

"Obi?" The voice was soft but audible even through the wooden door. "It's me."

His heartbeat sped up. He had not seen Dunni or spoken to her in days. That new need in him was starved. He'd been feeding it with images of her, the most vivid ones he could conjure.

Sometimes, he said her name—whispered it gently, so the sylla-bles caressed his lips as if they were made of substance. But those were temporary solutions; they'd kept him going like the air he inhaled and trapped in his chest until it dissolved and he needed to take another breath. They weren't enough, but the sound of her voice gave him air. He had surplus suddenly and had to breathe rapidly to keep up. He pulled the door open, and before he could think twice about his nosy neighbors, who would likely report the scene to his mother, he drew Dunni into his arms. The pain at his back, the strain on his stitches, did not faze him.

"I'm sorry, Obi. I'm so sorry. I . . . I . . ." Sobs interrupted her speech.

"It's okay." He rested his forehead against hers, and they stayed that way for a moment, looking at each other. "Come in." He took her hand and led her inside.

She focused on him rather than the condition of his home—the worn sofa, the unbalanced center table, the busted television.

"Dunni, what are you doing here? It's late. Why aren't you at home?"

"I had to see you." She rubbed her wet cheeks. "I'm sorry it took me so long to come. It's been impossible for me to leave the house. My mother told Paul not to drive me anywhere."

"Then how did you get here?"

"I snuck out and took a taxi. I had to come see you. I spoke to Emeka. He told me you're okay. But I had to see for myself." She stroked his jawline and tears came down her eyes again. "I am sorry for what happened to you and that I couldn't do any-thing. I should have . . ."

"Listen to me." He held her face between his hands. "It wasn't your fault. I don't blame you for anything."

"Well, I blame myself. I should have done something. I should have—"

He covered her lips with his, a gentle kiss that deepened even as more tears came down her cheeks.

"Obi." She pulled away sharply. "I'm leaving."

"Stay a little longer, *na*. My mother isn't home. She won't be back for a while."

"No. That isn't what I mean." She sighed. "I'm going to America. Next week."

"What?" It made no sense. They had two more months together. He would get better, and they would find ways to see each other. Emeka had even volunteered his house for them to meet. "What are you talking about?"

"My mother convinced my father to send me there earlier than planned. They arranged an internship for me with a friend of theirs who works at a research clinic. I tried my best, Obi. I did everything I could to convince them to let me stay longer but . . ." Her shoulders slumped. "I'm going. In a few days."

Dunni was leaving him. As that painful reality struck Obinna, he thought of all the ways he could react—shout, break something, cry, rant. But his outburst would change nothing. She would leave him in a matter of days.

He took her hand and weighed it in his. That detail mattered to him. It would help in the days to come when he needed to conjure a vivid memory. He closed his eyes while memorizing the smoothness of her palm. That detail was also important.

"Obinna. Are you okay?"

He opened his eyes and focused on the buttons on her pink dress; he undid each gradually. She watched him without uttering a word. He took off all her clothes, and when she was naked, he cupped one breast and massaged her nipple. His attention shifted to her expressive face. Her eyelids flapped slowly. Her teeth sank in her lip, biting and grinding against the flushed, plump skin. He trailed the soft curves that took his hand from her waist to her hip and then to her ass. He kissed her, and his mind worked to capture the sensation of her mouth and the taste of it.

Dunni pulled his shirt off. Her fingers ran over his chest, then extended to his back. He flinched when she traced the raw wound. Her eyes welled up again.

"Focus on us right now," he told her. "Just us. Don't think about anything else. Okay?"

She nodded, and her fingers slipped to his pants. She pulled them down, then tugged on his underwear.

They were naked in his mother's living room. Obinna didn't think of what would happen if she were to walk in. He didn't think of what his nosy neighbors would tell her when she returned. He disregarded the consequences, lowered Dunni onto the sofa, and made love to her. They made love to each other, their gaze breaking only in the brief moments when they blinked—when they glimpsed darkness and then opened their eyes and saw each other.

How could he be so close to her—be beside her and inside her—and still want to be closer? It wasn't enough. He wanted to dive into Dunni, swim in her depths, bury himself and coat himself with layers of her. And at that moment, he realized he didn't only love her. There was something else he couldn't express. Maybe there was no singular word for it. But that emotion, whatever it was, was vast. It demanded too much of him—his willpower, his sensibility, his pride. And although he had to give up pieces of himself to contain its immensity, he considered it a small price because Dunni was worth everything. And he was not worth much.

But one day, he would be. Before then, he would have to give up more, including their plans. He would have to give up America, their future, and their promise. He would do it, so he could build something extraordinary from his mediocrity. So he could be a man worthy of her—a man she could love not for a season but always. He was not that man yet and feared she would soon realize it. Before that happened, before she mirrored the same disdain as her mother, Obinna would have to give Dunni up.

She buttoned her dress, and he pulled up his boxers. "I got you something." She picked her bag up from the floor and dug inside it. "Here." She extended a phone to him. "I set it up with a number and credit. A lot of credit. You even have Internet. You can check your emails easier. And I can call you while I'm there. You can call me too."

"I can't accept this."

"Why not?"

"Dunni, how am I supposed to explain a phone to my mother—one this expensive?"

"Lie. Tell her anything you want. Just take it." She grabbed his hand and placed the phone in his palm. Though his fingers didn't curl around it. "Obi, we have to stay in constant contact while I'm over there, or I will lose my mind."

"Okay. I'll take it." He gripped the device and forced a smile. "Don't worry. We'll stay in touch." His voice quivered as he forced the lie out. "We'll talk every time we can."

"Yeah. And once my father gives me my first allowance, we'll start the application process. I've already started looking into the requirements."

"Okay." Unsure of what else to say, he watched his feet.

"Are you all right?" she asked. "I mean, I know you aren't . . . but . . ."

"I'm going to miss you." He placed a hand over hers. "So much."

"I'm going to miss you too, but we'll be together soon." Her eyes wandered to his bare back, to the spot he'd told her to ignore minutes ago.

"My mother will be home soon." He stood and searched the room for his shirt. He saw it under the chair, and as he bent to grab it, Dunni's fingertips stroked the injury. His spine straightened, then relaxed when her pursed lips met his damaged skin.

"I love you." She moved to stand in front of him. "I wish I could really explain it to you—dissect that word, *love*, like one of those frogs in biology class so you could see, really see, what's inside, so you could understand." She exhaled. "But I can't. And you don't know. You will never really know." A small, luke-warm smile lifted the corners of her lips. "But I do, Obi. Just take my word for it. Okay?"

He swallowed, pushed down the lump in his throat, and nodded. "I will. Will you do something for me too?"

"Anything."

"Love me. Even when I'm not there." He wanted to add, *Even when it seems like I've walked away and forgotten you. I haven't. I never will.* But he gave her only those words, and they seemed like just enough.

At the door, she swung her purse and looked at him. "This isn't goodbye. You know that, right?"

"Of course." Aching to change the subject, he examined the Samsung phone in his hand. "It has a camera."

"Yeah. A good one."

He worked his thumb against the screen and opened the camera application. "Smile," he said, holding the phone up.

"Like this?" She made a funny face; her eyes crossed, and her tongue hung limp at the side of her mouth.

"You play too much, you know?" He chuckled. "Seriously. Smile. I don't have any pictures of you, whereas you have countless of me."

She was always taking pictures of him on her phone, even when he wasn't ready for one. Now that he had a phone, he needed pictures. Once she left, they would serve better than memories. They still wouldn't be enough, but he would force his mind and body to adapt—to survive on snapshots until they saw each other again. And they would see each other again. Someday. When Obinna was more than he was now. He would find her. Or maybe the universe, a witness to the oath they had made, would rearrange the order of their lives so they could meet.

Dunni smiled and posed. Obinna took several pictures and laughed, relishing one more moment before everything changed. And even as his heart thumped frantically, as if rebelling against his decision, he felt at peace, assured that he and Dunni were inevitable.

Perhaps it was written in the stars. Perhaps they had written it in blood.

But it was written—irreversible like carving letters into stone.

CHAPTER THIRTY-TWO

Dunni had never said goodbye to Obinna—an official goodbye that implied a conclusion, a period. There had always been an ellipsis in her goodbyes—words omitted with the hope she would say them when they met again.

She didn't want to leave Lagos with an ellipsis. She wanted the period. She needed it, so every shred of hope she had in him and in them could die.

Three days after leaving the resort, she entered Obinna's compound. It was midafternoon. The sun hit the parts of her skin her white T-shirt didn't cover. She slid her sunglasses from her eyes and onto the crown of her head, then peered at the front door as it broke open and he stepped out.

If her heart could stop misbehaving every time she saw him, it would be great. If her feelings could disappear at her command, it would be even better. But neither of those things was possible. He walked forward, and every bit of her reacted to his closeness.

"Hi," he said.

"Hi."

It always started with this simple word, like dipping toes into water before diving in.

"I've been texting," he said. "And calling you. Nonstop."

"Yeah." She'd received a series of text messages from him the day after leaving the resort. He'd wanted to talk. She hadn't responded. "How did you even get my number?"

"Does it matter?"

Her straight face proved it did.

"Tiwa," he answered. "I asked her for it. Begged her actually."

"Oh." Dunni looked at her white sneakers and mentally rehearsed what she had to say. After assembling all the words and gathering her nerve, she sighed and lifted her eyes. "I'm leaving. Tomorrow. I'm going back to Seattle with Christopher. I came to say goodbye." Her fingers curled; her nails dug into her palms. "Goodbye, Obinna."

There it was. Those words. If seventeen-year-old Dunni had said them, would it have changed anything—made her less hopeful and less in love? *Goodbye.* She said it now, both vocally and silently, and wished for a sign the saga between her and Obinna had finally come to an end.

"So, just like that?" he asked.

"What else is there?"

"Us. There's us, Dunni."

"Years ago, yes. But not anymore. We have to let go of the past. We aren't children anymore."

"And you think what we had, what we felt for each other was nothing—some kind of *yeye* childhood fling?" He laughed, the sound dry and void of humor. "Do you seriously believe that?"

No. She didn't. But what did it matter? Would acknowledging the intensity and magnitude of their feelings cause all the chips to fall in place or rearrange the order of their lives so they were together? Would it erase the years they spent apart or the pain that festered during that time? No. It wouldn't change a thing. She loved him, but so what? What did it matter? Obinna had left her. He had built a life without her, and she still did not understand why. But again, what did it matter?

"I should go."

"Dunni, wait!" he shouted, his voice strained and anxious. "I'll tell you the truth. Okay? I'll tell you the real reason I stayed away."

She stopped short of the gate, intrigued by what he had to say. Maybe it would help her somehow—solidify her goodbye. She turned and faced him.

"I needed time and space to make something of myself. I needed time to get all of this." He gestured to his surroundings. "This house, my cars, my business, my success, everything I have. I did it for you."

"For me?" She looked at everything within the compound. "I didn't ask for any of this."

"But you would have. One day. You would have. And if I

couldn't provide it, you would have looked at me the way your mother looked at me, you would have seen me as she saw me."

"Really? Is that how little you thought of me?"

"No. It's how little I thought of myself." After a long sigh, his shoulders slumped. "I always knew I wasn't good enough for you, and your mother confirmed it again and again. That day at your house, our classmates confirmed it too. They looked at me like I was nothing, so I did this to prove that I'm enough. I did it for you."

Again, Dunni wanted to repeat that she hadn't asked for any of it. Instead, she said nothing.

"I kept thinking that when I had enough money, enough properties, enough cars, enough everything, I would reach out to you. I just needed a little more time, but I was going to reach out to you. I swear.

"I just needed to do this first. And I had to do it alone. Without you. So when you finally saw me, it would be as a man good enough for you, not a boy in tattered clothes selling food in the market."

Dunni didn't take her eyes off him. She looked him over, then nodded as a realization dawned on her. "You are just like your father."

"My father?" He spat out the words, disgusted.

"Yeah. You left the person you love, the person you made a promise to, because of money—to chase wealth. You are just like him." She didn't care if those words struck something still bruised and tender inside him. Anger prevented her from considering the impact of her words.

"I am nothing like my father."

"For years, I didn't hear a word from you. You just left. I was alone! And I was pregnant!" The unintentional confession stunned her. But it stunned him more.

She saw the moment the words hit his ears and how his emotions altered from shock to confusion to disbelief and then to grief. It was all in the way his thick, expressive brows rose and fell and wrinkled over his crestfallen eyes.

"You were pregnant?"

Dunni had not meant to tell him. What was the point when she intended to walk away from him forever? But she'd been emotional and had forgotten to monitor her words. It was an irreversible mistake.

"I found out three months after I got to America," she explained. "A little after I started school." The memory wasn't easy to revisit; it had been the hardest time of her life. "I tried to tell you. I called. You never answered. Then your number stopped going through. So I sent you emails. You never responded."

"All those times, in the emails, when you said you were in trouble, that was why?"

She nodded. "In one email, I told you I was pregnant—wrote it in bold letters in the subject line. But it bounced back."

"I deleted the account. I thought it would be easier that way."

"Oh. Well, I didn't know that. I just kept sending them, hoping for the best. And then after, I couldn't anymore."

"After? After what?" He watched her mouth, waiting for an answer as his chest rose and dropped. "What happened?"

Reflexively, Dunni's hand reached back to her shoulder blade.

Her fingers slid over the letters etched into her skin, a name precious to them both.

"Austen," he whispered. "A girl." Tears ran down his cheeks. "What happened?"

Dunni's eyelids fluttered, pushing back the gathering moisture. "Obinna, I—"

"You lost her. Didn't you?"

Her fingers fell away from the tattoo. The tears she'd been holding back trailed down her face as she watched him fold over. He sobbed; the hoarse, broken sound was heartrending. She opened her mouth to say the right thing, to tell him the truth, but stopped herself.

"We are so fucking tragic, Obinna." She sniffed and wiped her eyes. "It shouldn't be like this. It shouldn't be this hard, this painful. But it is. It always has been, so let's just stop. Let's just cut our losses." She regarded him with pity and regret and anger and love. "Goodbye."

She hurried through the gate, then entered her car. The air conditioner chilled her warm, damp skin. She gripped the steering wheel, prepared to leave, and then she felt it.

The part of her that had anchored itself to Obinna tugged; it pulled her mind and heart to him.

She remembered this feeling—the pressure and the tension. Years ago, when she left his house, she'd felt it. Though the hope of seeing him again had eased the discomfort. But this time was different. The goodbye had finalized things—replaced the ellipsis with a period.

PART II

CHAPTER THIRTY-THREE

Seattle

Emily opened a bottle of chardonnay and filled Dunni's glass to the rim.

"Oh my God." Dunni laughed. "Em, are you trying to get me wasted?"

"Of course not." She placed an elaborate cheese board on the white counter. "I know you can hold your alcohol, so drink up."

Emily's farmhouse-style kitchen with its apron-front sink, rustic cabinets, and wooden ceiling beams had a warm, homey ambiance that perfectly matched Emily's hospitality. She was a great host, a much better one than Dunni, whose version of a cheese board consisted of slices of sharp cheddar and Ritz crackers. On Monday nights, when Emily crossed the street to watch *The Bachelor*, Dunni ordered takeout. Sunday afternoons at Emily's were typically more elaborate. Currently, there was a chicken in the oven and lemon mushroom orzo on the stove.

Emily sat on the stool across from Dunni and smiled, her white skin warm with a soft flush of pink. "I'm just trying to help you unwind and relax a little."

"I am relaxed."

"Not really. You've been a little off since you got back from Nigeria."

"No, I haven't." Dunni gently lifted the full glass to her lips and sipped.

"You've been back for a week, and I've been watching you. Something is off. What's going on?"

Emily had a keen sense, capable of detecting the most obscure BS. It was less of a natural talent and more of an acquired skill. Five years ago, after welcoming Dunni to the neighborhood with a scented soy candle, she explained that in her past life—before a husband and two kids—she had been a cop. She worked as a photographer now, which seemed like her true calling. Though occasionally, skills from her past profession surfaced.

"So do you want to tell me what's going on?" She placed her elbows on the counter and watched Dunni. Brunette tresses that fell from her loose topknot dangled in her face, but her inquiring, invasive stare remained steady.

Dunni shuffled on the wooden barstool. "Stop looking at me like that."

"If you want me to stop, you know what to do."

Dunni sighed, certain she had no choice. Emily's persistence would otherwise drive her insane. "What do you want to know?"

"I would prefer everything."

After a sip of wine, Dunni exhaled. "His name is Obinna."

She started from the beginning, their first encounter at school. It was a long story, but they had time. Emily's husband was at a sports bar, watching a game, and the kids were watching a movie upstairs. So Dunni told her everything, omitting the oath—the one peculiar detail she preferred to keep private. Wine helped Emily digest the information. It was certainly more than she had expected. When Dunni stopped speaking, Emily huffed and said one word.

"Fuck." It was her first word in twenty minutes.

"I feel terrible for what I did to Christopher," Dunni said. "He didn't deserve it."

"No, he didn't. But I also know you didn't intentionally mean to hurt him. This is a complicated situation. What you and Obinna have seems intense."

That was an understatement.

"What are you going to do?"

"I'm going to tell Christopher the truth."

Emily gasped. "Seriously?"

"Yeah. I wanted to tell him in Nigeria but lost my nerve. I won't again."

"And what if he breaks off the engagement?"

"I'll understand."

"Hmm." Emily leaned back and observed Dunni. "I was right," she said. "You seem off—different."

"Different? How?"

"I don't know. I can't exactly put my finger on it." She smiled. "But I like it."

⁓

Later that day, Dunni sat in bed with a book, prepared to read a chapter before going to sleep. Though her mind wandered to the conversation from earlier. Emily had been right. Something was different. Dunni was different.

For a week, since returning from Lagos, she'd tried to reestablish herself in her routine. It was a pointless effort. As if she'd grown inches while away, she no longer fit her life in Seattle. At work, she performed her duties while harboring a discontent she had trained herself to ignore for years. No longer able to dismiss her unhappiness, she spoke to her manager about joining a new research team, one focused on work that interested her. For the first time in so long, Dunni was aware of her will and her voice. She'd lost it. No, she had given it up willingly, because it had been easier.

Twelve years ago, shortly after discovering she was pregnant, Dunni made the hardest decision of her life. Standing by her choice and living with it had required so much of her. Mentally and emotionally exhausted, she lost the motivation to do anything, even to navigate her life. She relented control to her parents, who took it gladly. They directed, and she followed. But when her plane landed in Lagos, the path they'd paved for her opposed another. And slowly, her motivation returned. It had felt like regaining the use of a sense, being able to taste again—not only discerning sweet and bitter but so many other flavors.

Dunni chose to step out of line and onto another path, one

that didn't lead her to only Obinna but to herself, the girl she used to be. And maybe that was the real reunion.

Life and all its harsh lessons had reconstructed the teenage girl who was too passionate, too outspoken, too stubborn, too hopeful. It resculpted her, chiseled away all these attributes until she was a docile woman with a broken heart and a repressed voice, whose laughter lacked a certain quality.

Dunni had been looking in mirrors for years, but she hadn't been seeing herself. Maybe it was because those pieces of her, carved and discarded by a merciless sculptor, had been in Nigeria with a boy who also had her heart. And maybe she had taken that path not only to see him again, but to reclaim everything in his possession. And even now, she knew she didn't have everything. Maybe she never would. But she had something.

She closed the book and placed it on the nightstand. Wanting to exercise this newly returned motivation like a muscle, to ensure it grew strong and she never returned to a woman on autopilot, she twisted the engagement ring off her finger.

CHAPTER THIRTY-FOUR

Christopher's apartment didn't have a homey atmosphere. The open-concept space resembled an office rather than a home. Dunni didn't like the lack of colors and curtains. The windows were too large, even with the view of downtown Seattle. For two minutes, she sat on the gray couch, mustering the boldness needed to tell him the truth. Yesterday with Emily, she'd been so confident about being honest. Now, the reality unsettled her. Regardless, she rose and approached him.

He stood behind the kitchen counter while looking through his phone. He was a tall man with a bald head that made his thick, groomed beard stand out especially. He had handsome features, with skin the same deep brown as Dunni's.

"Are you hungry?" he asked. "I could order some dinner. What do you feel like?"

"Christopher." Her heart raced. Sweat dampened her skin. "Can we talk?"

"Maybe sushi?" His eyes stayed on the phone screen, scanning the options. "What about tacos? You love fish tacos. Or we could try something else if you prefer."

He knew. He knew what was coming. Maybe he'd noticed the lack of a ring on her finger. Or maybe he'd noticed a difference since they returned from Lagos—the forced conversations she tried to carry, the way she pulled back when he touched her, the stiffness of her lips when he kissed her.

"Christopher, there's something—"

"Why do you always call me that?" He dropped his phone and looked at her.

"Call you what? Your name?"

"Yeah."

"Um . . ." She cocked her head. "What else am I supposed to call you?"

"Baby. Babe. Darling. Honey. Hell, even Chris. But you call me by my full name. It's so damn formal. I'm your fiancé, not your colleague."

Her eyes wandered as she considered the detail he'd pointed out. "I never noticed."

"Really?" He sounded skeptical and peeved.

"Of course not. I wasn't doing it on purpose. I just . . ." What could she say? He'd called her every term of endearment known. Why hadn't it occurred to her to do the same or simply abbreviate his name?

"What do you call him?"

Dunni frowned. "What?"

"The man you were with in Lagos. What do you call him?"

Her stomach lurched. She tugged on her cashmere sweater, wishing the fabric were lightweight so air could pass through it and cool her hot skin.

"I know, Dunni." He pressed both hands on the counter and watched her sternly. "You told me you were extending your stay, for reasons you never explained. You sounded off on the phone. And when I arrived in Lagos, you weren't even at your parents'. I figured it out. I'm not an idiot."

"I was going to tell you," she blurted. "I was . . . I thought . . . I didn't." She closed her mouth. An explanation was pointless. "I am so, so sorry."

"Who is he? This guy that you spent days with, who the hell is he?"

"It doesn't matter. It's over."

He looked at her finger. "Then why aren't you wearing your ring? Are you leaving me to be with him?"

"No. I'm not."

"Then where is your ring, Dunni?"

She dug a hand into her pocket and pulled out the silver engagement ring. She placed it on the counter, between them. "I'm not leaving you to be with him. But I also can't marry you. Everything is different now." She blinked back tears. "I'm different. I'm so sorry."

"But it was a mistake, wasn't it—something you had to get

out of your system before we got married?" He walked to the other end of the counter where she stood. "People make mistakes. I can forgive that." He picked up the ring and held it out to her. "Here. Just put it on. We'll work through whatever this is and get back on track."

Dunni considered him and tried to understand his reaction. "I don't get it," she said. "After what I did, why are you willing to make this work, especially so soon?"

"Because I love you, Dunni."

She deliberated for a moment, then shook her head. "No, you don't."

Whatever Christopher felt was not love, not real love. His eyes always gave it away. He felt something for Dunni, but it was the watered-down love her mother had described—sensible and safe. It was the sort that didn't require the use of every muscle in his heart because it was frail rather than something vigorous and larger than life. For a while, after listening to her mother, Dunni believed that sort of emotion would be enough to sustain her marriage. But she'd been wrong. That kind of love could never satisfy her.

"How can you say I don't love you?" Christopher asked. "I'm standing here, willing to give you another chance. Isn't that proof enough?"

"I think you're giving me another chance because you're scared of losing the safety and reliability of our relationship. To be honest, I am too." She pressed her lips into a weak smile. "In a lot of ways, we're a good match. You don't ask a lot from me, and I don't ask a lot from you. We just exist. And it's comfortable and safe. But you deserve more than that. You deserve to be really happy. To be really in love. Don't you think so?"

His downcast eyes shifted around the spacious apartment, then stilled on her. "Dunni, I care about you. I really do."

"And I care about you too. Very, very much. You're an amazing person." She sniffed and wiped her teary eyes. "But we don't love each other—not really."

"You never gave me a chance to."

She nodded, unable to disagree. "I know."

"If you hadn't been so guarded, so unreachable half the time we were together, I could have. I could have loved you."

And if there weren't pieces of herself a continent away, she could have loved him too.

He dropped the ring on the countertop, and it rolled on its round edges, then rested flat.

CHAPTER THIRTY-FIVE

San Francisco

The opulence of the Fairmont hotel lobby made Dunni less regretful about being in San Francisco rather than in Seattle on a Friday night. She tugged on the hem of her dress. The black fabric met her knees, then shrunk to its original position on her thighs. Her only major regret was not trying on the dress before throwing it in her travel bag. For the rest of the night, she would have to hide her discomfort.

In a slow stride, she approached Tiwa, who sat on one of the curved settees in the lobby. Dunni was in San Francisco because Tiwa had invited her out of pity.

"You should come to take your mind off the breakup," she'd said on the phone a few days ago. "Consider it therapy."

Dunni had been at work, her fingers moving against computer keys, her attention split between her duties and her friend. "I'm fine. Seriously. The breakup was for the best."

She had been telling everyone that, everyone but her mother, whose calls she avoided.

"Just take the weekend off. Come to San Francisco. It's my sister's birthday. Come celebrate with us. It will be good for you."

"Which sister?"

"Hannah. We're making an entire weekend out of it. It's gonna be great."

"Well, I would love to come, but I can't just leave everything and go to San Francisco for the weekend. I have responsibilities."

"Okay." Tiwa blew out a breath. "I didn't want to do this, but you owe me one."

"Owe you?" Dunni chuckled. "How?"

"You think I don't know what you did? You think I don't know how you just vanished from my wedding reception?"

Dunni had cursed under her breath, then worked up the nerve to ask an uncomfortable question. "Do you know who I left with?"

"I heard. But that is only my business when you decide it is. Until then, you gotta make amends for leaving my wedding. And no need for excuses or apologies. I won't accept either. You know what you have to do."

Now Dunni reached the brown settee and forced a smile. "Hey."

"Hey." Tiwa sprung up. She wore a strapless leather dress with a chocolate hue that matched her complexion flawlessly. "I'm so happy you're here."

"Thanks for inviting me." Dunni hugged her, then pulled

back and cleared her throat. "I mean, guilt-tripping me into coming."

"Desperate times." Tiwa smirked. "You look great, by the way."

"Thanks. And you look incredible. As always." She scanned the lobby, then frowned. "Where's everyone else?"

"They haven't come down yet. I wanted to speak with you before we head out." Tiwa sat and tapped the cushion beside her.

"Okay." Dunni settled down and angled her body toward her friend. Concern and curiosity made her anxious and attentive. She edged closer and studied Tiwa's strained expression. "What's going on?"

"Well, I'm in a very uncomfortable situation right now." She twisted her wedding ring. "But I feel like I should tell you what's going on, so you're prepared."

"Prepared for what?"

"Nicholas. I mentioned to him I was coming to San Francisco, and you'd be coming too. The next thing I know, he bought a ticket. I couldn't possibly stop him."

"Wait a minute." Dunni sucked in a deep breath and let it go slowly. "Are you saying he's here?"

Tiwa nodded.

"You could have told me."

"You wouldn't have come if I had."

No, she wouldn't have, because Nigeria was supposed to be their last encounter—their goodbye. She'd made peace with that or was trying to, even though sometimes it seemed impossible. Obinna had left an echo of himself inside her, one even the busyness of her schedule couldn't stifle. It was always there. Even now, when she tried to be resolute in her decision to walk away.

"Hey." Tiwa placed a hand over Dunni's. "I don't know what happened in Lagos. And I don't even know what happened back in secondary school. I wish you would trust me enough to tell me, but whenever you're ready. All I know is that Nicholas says he loves you. And that isn't a word he takes lightly." She searched Dunni's eyes, her face tight with concentration. "Do you love him?"

"I do," she admitted, then bit her tongue, punishing it for its inability to lie about that fact.

"Then talk to him. He's here because of you." Tiwa looked above Dunni's head; her eyes communicated with someone.

Dunni didn't have to turn around. She knew Obinna was behind her. The pressure and tension she'd felt for two weeks—since saying goodbye to him in Nigeria—eased.

"He's here," Tiwa said. "Should I go ahead? Give you both time to talk?"

Dunni nodded.

"Okay. Well, call me if you need anything." She stood, then walked toward the elevator.

Obinna appeared in front of Dunni. Their eyes connected. Her heart leaped. The corners of his lips curved upward in a tepid smile. They watched each other in a hotel lobby, slowly crowding with guests. Neither of them said a word. When he sat beside her, she clenched her shaky hands.

"What are you doing here?" Tiwa had answered that question, but Dunni wanted to hear from him. She wanted his truth, not one filtered through a third party.

"I came for you," he answered. "I've been calling and texting you since you left. Nothing goes through."

"I blocked your number."

He nodded. "I figured. How have you been?"

"Miserable. But managing." She didn't feel like lying. "What about you?"

"Miserable. Hardly managing."

She huffed and slouched into the sofa. He did the same. Their heads tilted against the wooden frame of the chair. Guests shuffled across the lobby. Bellhops transported luggage. Chatter and laughter ensued from two elderly women who sat opposite them on another chair.

"Do you remember that day we ran out of biology class and hid in the recreation room?" Obinna asked.

"Of course." Dunni grinned. It was one of her fondest memories. At that stage in their relationship, they were in the delicate space between friendship and romance. "You were so scared." She pressed her lips together and held back a laugh. "You thought we would get caught."

"Yeah. But we didn't. We stayed in that room until the next class and talked. Do you remember what we spoke about?" Obinna slanted his head just as she did, and their eyes met. "I said I wanted an easy love. And you said you wanted the opposite—something worth fighting for. You said if a couple doesn't fight through obstacles, how do they know their love is worth anything? Do you remember?"

She did. Clearly. Now she wondered if that had been her first mistake, believing hardship measured the degree of love.

"We aren't tragic, Dunni." His thick brows knitted in a deep frown. "You said we were tragic. We aren't. Our relationship just requires a lot more effort than others, a lot more fight. And us constantly fighting, jumping over these hurdles, is how we know it's worth anything." He held her hand. "I'm sorry. I'm so sorry I didn't fight for you back then—that I let you go to chase something so stupid. I'm so sorry that I wasn't there for you when you were . . ." He winced, unable to complete the sentence, to say that word. *Pregnant.* "You were right. I am just like my father."

Dunni didn't see the same image of Obinna she'd seen in Nigeria, the one her anger and resentment painted. "No, you're not. You're nothing like your father. You're here. You came back."

Their fingers interlocked, palm pressed against palm, and then Obinna sat up and looked at Dunni's left hand. "Where's your ring?"

"Didn't Tiwa tell you?"

"Tell me what?"

"Well." She sat upright. "I broke off my engagement."

He bit his lip, fighting a smile. "Really? When?"

"On Monday. Christopher is a wonderful man, but I couldn't go through with it." She saw the question in Obinna's elated eyes. "I didn't do it for you," she said. "I did it for myself. I was tired of people dictating my life. I'd let it happen for too long. I couldn't let it happen anymore."

He released the grip on his lip and smiled, proud. "That's good, Dunni."

"Yeah." She relaxed on the chair again, her head on the wooden frame and her gaze on the ornate ceiling.

"Do you ever wonder," Obinna said, also tilting his head back, "what would have happened if I stuck to the plan we made? Do you ever wonder where we would be now?"

"Yeah." Every day for twelve years. But she didn't tell him about the duration, about the sleepless nights where she tossed, disturbed by the many scenarios her what-ifs created.

"I regret it, you know." The bass left his voice, and he spoke faintly. "I regret not sticking to the plan. Things could have been so different."

"We were just kids, Obi. And sometimes I forget how young we were. No matter what, we were bound to make mistakes at some point. Maybe, in the long run, our plan wouldn't have worked. Or maybe it would have. Who knows?"

What if he had stuck to their plan? What if he'd come to America, and they lived together in her apartment? What if her pregnancy put a strain on their relationship and the pressures of school put an additional strain on them? What if they studied every day, even on the weekends when they were supposed to visit American landmarks? What if making love became tedious, something they scheduled between classes and assignments and study sessions? What if they each made friends who pulled them in different directions, toward different interests and experiences? What if they slowly grew bitter and their love lost its luster, and their past and present became a tragic before and after? What if?

"We can't dwell on what might have been," she told him. "It's pointless. You're here now. And so am I."

It was a small step toward the future they'd been chasing since the day they met. Maybe now, with their maturity, their experiences, and their independence, they were equipped to handle their relationship. Maybe now was the perfect time for them.

Finally.

CHAPTER THIRTY-SIX

There were different stages of love that ranged from the sensible version Dunni's mother had described to the version Dunni felt for Obinna. As she relished the feeling of him inside her, she wondered if there was another stage. Had she reached the limit, the peak of that emotion? Or was there more? If there was, she wanted it. Even if it meant breaking off pieces of herself to contain it. Even if the magnitude threatened to split her skin open. She was ravenous and reckless and obsessed. She was aware of all the rightness and wrongness of what she felt, and even then, didn't want to give either up because they complemented each other somehow. The right and the wrong felt good. It felt true.

She and Obinna moved against each other; their tempo and motion alternated, creating sensations that intensified. Dunni wrapped her legs around his waist and pulled him farther into her. Sweat slicked his chest as he thrust. He cupped her breast, then brushed her nipple with his thumb. Their moans filled the hotel room, the sound increasing as they climaxed.

He kissed her, then rolled over on his back. "That was . . ." He expelled a raspy breath. "Amazing."

Dunni curled against his side. "Yeah. It was." She pressed her face to his chest and inhaled the musky scent on his skin.

They fell silent as their breathing leveled. Even the quiet moments between them didn't feel quiet. There were no words, but another form of communication transpired between them, through glances and touches and even beyond that.

"I want to ask you something." Obinna stared down at her, a slight pinch between his brows. "But I don't want you to get angry."

"Why do you assume I'd get angry?"

"Well, you know how body used to pepper you. You always get worked up. You're always looking for any reason to beat someone."

She snorted. "Okay. You're exaggerating."

One of his eyebrows shot up. "But am I? When was the last time you got into a fight?"

"I'm a grown woman. I don't get into fights. I use my words."

"As I recall, they were just as dangerous. Remember how you used to lash Emeka?" He shook his head. "Poor boy. He can't even catch a break because now, Gigi is tormenting him."

"Yeah, but I think he kinda likes it."

"You might be right."

They shook with laughter.

"Okay." Dunni settled down, getting back on track. "What do you want to ask me?"

"Well." He turned on his side and faced her. "Why is it that you've completely dismissed what we did that day?" He held her left hand and interlaced their fingers, aligning the scars on their palms. "You act like it meant nothing."

Dunni shuffled upright and gathered the white sheets to her chest.

"You're angry."

"I'm not angry." She only wished he hadn't brought up this topic. It was a needle that popped the lightheartedness of the atmosphere. She stood and walked to the bathroom. A robe hung on a hook behind the door, and she pulled it off and wore it. When she returned to the room, Obinna sat on the edge of the bed in his briefs.

"You keep ignoring it," he mumbled. "Why?"

"Because it's easier."

For years, she had a firm grip on her denial. She looked at the scar on her palm every day and convinced herself it was nothing. She discredited her grandmother's gift as well, because she couldn't possibly deny one without denying the other. Living in America strengthened her denial. Returning to Nigeria weakened it. And even then, she fought to hold on to it—to believe there was nothing strange between her and Obinna. But there was. And it terrified her to think that strangeness was the reason they loved each other so much.

"I don't want to believe we're together because of the oath," she explained to him. "I don't want to believe it's the reason I've loved you for twelve years."

"Is that what you think?"

She shrugged. "The way I love you. The way we love each other seems sometimes . . . unnatural. Obsessive. Wrong. Why do you think that is?"

"Dunni, we've always loved each other."

"Yes, but from that day, everything I felt for you just sort of escalated. And sometimes, I'm not sure if how I feel is because of what we did. We have this connection. But how do we know it's real?"

"Dunni." He extended a hand to her. "Come here."

She took it and sat on the bed with him.

"We loved each other very much before the oath. What we did only fed what already existed between us. That's it."

It was more complicated than that. They'd said things that day, words that had a significant impact.

I swear that no matter where life takes me, I will always find my way back to Obinna. I swear to marry him and no one else.

She recalled the words and winced.

Did that oath dictate their emotions and their actions, stripping them of their choice and pulling them together at all cost?

"Obi, I don't want to be with you because I don't have a choice, because of something we did when we were stupid kids. I want to be with you because I choose to be."

"And you are. You broke things off with Christopher, and you chose to be here with me." He held her face and kissed her. "You chose me. Nothing else matters."

But it did matter. Dunni didn't trust what she felt for Obinna. How could she have a life with him while questioning everything between them? As she pondered this, another thought pushed into her mind.

How can I have a life with Obinna when I haven't told him the complete truth about being pregnant?

❧

The curtains were pulled back, and starlight and streetlight shone through the large window. The movement on the opposite end of the mattress had caused Dunni's eyes to flutter open. She squinted at the figure on the edge of the bed.

"Obi?" She extended a hand and ran it along his spine. "What are you doing?"

"Nothing. Go back to sleep." There was a quake in his voice, one he tried to hide by clearing his throat.

"What's wrong?" She shuffled on the bed and repositioned herself beside him.

"It's nothing." He held his phone and fixated on an email.

"Obviously, it's something. What is it? Just tell me."

He sighed. "The private investigator. The one I hired to find my father."

"Yeah?"

"He just sent me an email. He found him. He found my father."

Dunni could express neither shock nor relief. Not when there was a major factor to consider. She gripped Obinna's free hand. "Is he alive?"

He nodded. "Yes. He lives here—in America. And you won't believe this." He chuckled under his breath. "He lives in Santa Clara."

"That's like an hour away from here."

"Yeah. He has a wife. He has children. Three."

"I'm so sorry." She didn't know what else to say, how to ease the pain he certainly felt.

"I have to go."

"Go where? To see him?"

"Yes. I'm going in the morning."

"Don't you think that's a little abrupt? Maybe you should take some time to process this."

"I don't need time to process anything." The bass in his voice deepened. "He's living the fucking American Dream—working as a bank manager, living in a two-car-garage house, married with children. After what he did!" He stood and walked to the window, his gaze on the expanse of dusk and streetlights. "I have to go and see him." His voice lost its tension and softened. "I can't do it alone."

Dunni stood and walked to him. She pressed her cheek on his back and wrapped her arms around him. "You don't have to."

CHAPTER THIRTY-SEVEN

In the back seat of the Cadillac, Dunni held Obinna's hand. The chauffeur drove through a suburb of identical beige houses. She watched Obinna attentively, waiting for him to change his mind. Though only seconds from their destination, that didn't seem likely.

He had said little since they left the hotel. The hired car service had picked them up a little past ten in the morning. It was past eleven now. Dunni had a flight back to Seattle in a few hours, but she pushed that aside and focused on Obinna, who looked through the window absentmindedly.

"Are you okay?" It was a stupid question, but she asked it regardless, hoping to get a word out of him.

Rather than speaking, he nodded. The tightness in his jaw was more telling than his curt head bob.

The car stopped, and she scanned his blank expression. "Are you sure about this?"

Again, he nodded without a sound. He opened the door and stepped onto the pavement. Dunni clenched his hand as they walked on the stone pathway.

At the door, his breath grew quick and shallow. The doorbell button lit up with a warm glow when his finger pressed into it.

They waited for an answer.

When the lock turned, Dunni peered at him and tried to pinpoint his emotions. Surely, he felt many things, and she wanted to know what they were. She wanted an equal portion of his burden, sliced in the middle and divided like the piece of goat meat at the bottom of his lunch flask. She wanted to help him, but with his reserved disposition, all she could do was stand beside him and hope it would be enough.

A middle-aged, blond-haired woman opened the door and looked from Dunni to Obinna. Her eyes narrowed as they stayed on him; there was a glint of recognition in them and then confusion. "I'm sorry." She laughed gently. "This is going to sound crazy, but you look . . ." She paused and cocked her head. "You look just like my husband."

Obinna and Dunni glanced at each other.

"I'm sorry." The woman laughed again, shaking off her stunned haze. "Can I help you?"

The question went unanswered by Obinna, whose stare was far off and unfocused.

"Yes," Dunni said, quickly filling the silence. "We're here to see someone. Kelechi Arinze."

The woman smiled warmly, as if she'd expected that answer. "Yes. He's my husband."

"And he's my father." It was the first sentence Obinna had uttered since getting in the car.

The blunt response shocked Dunni as it did the woman standing beneath the doorframe. A deep blush warmed her ivory skin just as her eyes expanded.

"Is he here?" Obinna asked.

"Um . . . yeah," she murmured. "He is. Come in." She stepped aside and gestured for them to enter.

The house was modest, with a casual and comfortable décor. Though it was the lack of a distinct décor—uncoordinated colors and furniture—that gave it that specific casualness and comfort.

"He's in the backyard," the woman said, directing them to a taupe sofa. "Gardening. He enjoys gardening—growing things. Most men don't, but he does. Gardening really isn't my thing. Books. I like books—reading. I'm Clara, by the way. Did I already mention that?" She bit her lip. "Sorry. I'm rambling. I . . . I'll let him know you're here." She left the room in a haste.

Obinna inspected the space—the flat-screen television, the pile of magazines on the coffee table, the bookshelf against the wall. When footsteps sounded, he fixed his eyes on the doorway, and Dunni did the same.

They waited. The footsteps stopped somewhere in the corridor. Seconds went by. They each watched the doorway expectantly while clinging to the other's hand, and then Obinna's breath ceased abruptly. He stared at the man who stood before them. His father.

Their physical attributes were identical, their stature—height and build—similar. Their eyes didn't fall away from each other, the sternness in their gazes unwavering even as seconds passed. Then an unexpected wave of emotion broke the tension. Obinna's father lost hold of whatever facade he held on to. Perhaps the shame of coming face-to-face with the son he abandoned became too much and caused the middle-aged man to sob.

Clara appeared behind him and rubbed his back. "Here, honey." She directed him to a cushioned armchair. "There you go. It's okay." She soothed him as if he were a child rather than a grown man who had deserted his family, left them to fend for themselves while he chased greener pastures and apparently found them.

The sternness in Obinna's eyes did not fade. It stayed intact, even gaining another element as it reflected his disgust. Dunni expected his features to soften, to reveal the pain of abandonment and betrayal. But that wasn't the case. She realized then that Obinna had not come for a heart-to-heart. He'd come with his anger and resentment, ready to unleash them.

"Obinna." Kelechi wiped his eyes and looked at his son. "I can't believe I'm looking at you."

"This must be incredibly emotional for you both." Clara patted her husband's back. "After being apart for so long. What a reunion, right?"

"So, he told you about me."

"Yes. Before we got married. He said things between your mother and him didn't work out. And he eventually lost contact with you."

"Really? Is that what he told you?" Obinna released a humorless laugh that shook his shoulders. "Wow. You really are a crafty bastard, aren't you?"

Whatever naive lightheartedness Clara had brought into the conversation vanished as she looked between Obinna and her husband, whose head hung low as any guilty man's would. The smile on her face flattened as she drew her hands from him and stood. "Um . . . maybe I should give you both some privacy."

"No. Please. Stay." Obinna gestured for her to retake her seat on the arm of the chair. "I want you to know the kind of man you're married to."

"Obinna, I—"

"I suggest you be quiet," he interrupted his father. "Because there is nothing you can say to justify what you did. Absolutely nothing!"

Dunni flinched at the spike in his voice.

"You packed your bags and left. You promised to come back for us. You promised to provide for us. I didn't believe you. I saw right through you." He scoffed. "But she didn't. She waited for you. She prayed for you. When she thought I wasn't listening, she cried for you." He pressed his hand over his mouth and exhaled. "Every day, she struggled to keep me fed, clothed, and in school. She didn't let herself dwell on your absence—she couldn't. She was too busy trying to survive. She died, trying to survive. And you lived." He looked around the house. "Like this."

Kelechi dropped his head in his hands and sobbed again. Though this time, his wife didn't reach out to comfort him. She stood above him, her brows set in a deep scowl.

"You remarried. You had children. You built a new life and forgot about us. Tell me why. I want to know why."

Kelechi looked at his son, then at the carpeted floor. He opened his mouth, trying to catch words like a frog caught flies. "I . . . I was . . . I thought . . . I . . ." Nothing. There was no explanation, no justification.

"Well." Obinna stood, and so did Dunni. "Have a nice life."

They walked down the corridor and then out of the house. The midday humidity hit them before they entered the air-conditioned car.

The chauffeur worked his finger against the screen on the dashboard, entering details into the GPS.

Obinna's stare was vacant, even as tears gathered in his eyes. "I keep thinking," he whispered, "maybe she would still be alive if he'd been there to help her. If she hadn't been working so hard, if she hadn't been stressed, maybe she would still be alive." His face fell into his palm, and he cried.

Dunni had never seen Obinna cry. The sight triggered an emotion she hadn't felt since she was a reckless teenager. It was anger, but the kind she couldn't pacify by being rational. It was the kind that needed to be expressed, unleashed. Without consideration, she stepped out of the car and marched inside the house.

Kelechi sat in the same spot. His wife still stood over him.

"You know why you left?" Dunni asked him. "It's because you were and still are a selfish, heartless coward!"

Kelechi stood, and she approached him.

"What kind of man abandons his family? They were your

responsibility, and you just left them. Did you even worry about them? Did you wonder if they ate? If they had a roof over their heads? If they were okay?" She pushed back the tears that blurred her vision. "Obinna and his mother used to sell food in the market. They really struggled. They had nothing! And you! You could have helped. You could have, but you didn't."

Clara shifted to the wall and said nothing to defend her husband.

"Please. Stop," Kelechi pleaded. His voice wobbled. "Just go. There is nothing I can do now. What has happened has happened."

"'What has happened has happened?'" The callous, dismissive words enraged Dunni further. "You know what? Go fuck yourself!"

"Dunni, that's enough." Obinna came behind her and held her waist. "Let's go. He isn't worth it."

She fought against his hold, determined to say more. "That's right! You're not worth shit! Obinna is a better man than you'll ever be. He has a successful business. Did you know that?" She felt the need to brag about all the things his son had accomplished without him. Even as Obinna carried her out of the house, she shouted and named everything he'd acquired, only shutting up once she was inside the car.

Obinna asked the chauffeur to give them some privacy, and he stepped outside.

"Dunni, I need you to calm down," he said when they were alone. "Breathe."

"Why did you do that, *na*?" Anger and agitation made her

jittery. "Who sent you to come and carry me out? I wasn't done talking to him yet."

"Trust me, you said enough. A lot." A small smile lifted the corners of his lips. "You're something else, you know that?"

"I'm not sure if that's an insult or a compliment."

"It's definitely a compliment." He pulled her into his arms. Against his embrace, her body stopped shaking. "Are you okay?"

She nodded. "Are you?"

"Yes, and no. But I'm better than I would have been if you hadn't been here. Thank you for coming."

"Of course."

He ran his hand over her hair and flattened the strands that had gone astray during the scuffle to get her out of the house. "I guess you really are a grown woman capable of using her words." He chuckled. "You're no longer that teenage girl—the fighter— always looking for a reason to teach someone a lesson."

"Here's the thing you never realized." She sat up and looked at him. "I wasn't a fighter until I met you. I never insulted Emeka until he insulted you. I never had anyone to defend, to protect, to fight for until you." She shrugged. "I did all those things because I was protective. I still am."

His gaze explored hers, and then he nodded and smiled. "Thank you."

"Sure. And just so you know, if it ever comes to it, I go slap *agbero* for your case. In fact, I go slap police for your case."

"Wait a minute." Obinna cocked his head and pondered. "Aren't those the lyrics to a song?"

"No." She rolled her lips into her mouth and suppressed a laugh.

"Yes, they are." He snapped his fingers. "'Case' by Teni. But you think you're slick, don't you?"

"I am slick. You're just a *tatafo*."

They burst into laughter. It was strange that minutes ago, they'd both been crying—him and then her—and now they were laughing.

~

At Laurel Court, the restaurant within the Fairmont, Dunni ate while glancing at her phone. It was a little past four in the afternoon. Her flight was in three hours. She wanted Obinna to come to Seattle with her, but she hadn't asked yet. They'd returned from Santa Clara two hours ago, and he was still processing the confrontation with his father.

"I get scared sometimes," he admitted after taking a sip of his wine.

"Scared about what?"

"Being like him. He was never a good father, even when he was still with us. What if I'm like him?" He ran a hand over his tired eyes. "He had no business being a father. Maybe I don't either. Maybe children aren't something I should consider."

Dunni flinched as if the words had materialized and punched her.

Realizing what he'd said, his eyes grew wide and apologetic. "I'm so sorry. I shouldn't have said that. That was extremely insensitive of me." He reached for her hand across the table, but she didn't extend it. "I'm sorry, Dunni."

"Is that how you really feel? Or is this something you're feeling in the moment, after everything that's happened today?"

He chewed on his lip. "I don't know."

Her head bobbed. "Okay." She looked at her phone again. This time, she didn't hide her travel plans. "I have a flight in less than three hours. I should pack and head to the airport."

"What? You're leaving? Is this because of what I just said? Are you upset with me?"

She was unsure, but she knew the moment he said those words, everything changed. "I have a presentation at work on Monday—a very important one. I have to get home and prep."

"Then I'll come with you."

Minutes ago, she'd wanted the same thing, but not anymore. "You can't."

"Why not?"

"Because you'll only distract me, and I need to focus."

"Dunni, I came to America for you." He pushed back his chair, prepared to stand. "If you're going home, I'm coming with you."

"Look." Resolve toughened her voice. "It's been a very emotional weekend. A lot has happened. Let's just take a breath—a moment to ourselves, to think of what's next for us."

"To think of what's next? What are you talking about? You're no longer engaged. We're going to be together, of course."

"How? I have a life in Seattle, and you have a life in Lagos. What do we do about that?"

He didn't have an answer.

"Exactly. Let's just take a moment to think all this through. We aren't teenagers anymore. We're adults with responsibilities, so let's not get carried away." She picked up her purse from the table and stood. "I'll call you on Monday after work, after we've had time to think, and we'll take it from there."

"Okay. If that's what you want, then okay." He stood and shoved his hands into his pockets. "I'll escort you to the airport."

"No need," she told him. "You've had a long day. Enjoy the rest of your meal and get some rest." She leaned forward and pressed her lips to his cheek. "I'll text when I get home."

"Okay."

She walked away from him, grateful he hadn't fought her suggestion.

Dunni needed time and space to think. There was a lot to consider before deciding on her future with Obinna.

CHAPTER THIRTY-EIGHT

Blood trickled through the cut on Dunni's thumb. She dropped the knife on the chopping board, ripped off a piece of paper towel, and wrapped it around her severed skin, wincing then cursing under her breath. She glanced at the onions and tomatoes on the kitchen counter, then at the closed drawer that contained takeout menus.

It was a little past six on Monday evening, and at exactly eight, Emily would be at the door with a bottle of wine they would drink while watching *The Bachelor*. With Dunni's mind occupied, making a simple yam porridge seemed nearly impossible. Ordering dinner from one of the takeout menus would check one thing off her list. It would also give her a few minutes, before the sound of Emily's high-pitched laughter, to focus solely on Obinna and come to terms with the decision she had made.

During the day, work and then appointments took most of

her attention. Whenever Obinna had entered her mind, she pushed him out to accommodate other priorities.

Now, alone in the kitchen, before her life demanded more of her, she placed him at the center of her mind. Yesterday, he'd sent her a song by Chiké and Simi called "Running to You." Then he sent a text message.

I heard this song and thought of you. Thank you for always fighting for me.

Dunni couldn't stop listening to the song, humming the melody, and blinking back the tears that automatically gathered at the chorus. She loved him so much. So much that she doubted it.

Years ago, she'd said something to him. She remembered the moment and the exact words. With the frustration of trying to express her emotion and fearing he wouldn't understand, she'd said, "I wish I could really explain it to you—dissect that word, *love*, like one of those frogs in biology class so you could see, really see, what's inside, so you could understand."

She wished the same thing now. She wished she could lay her emotion under a microscope, slice it open, and examine everything within it to see the parts that were real and the parts fabricated by the promise they'd made, a consequence of blood and binding words. Dunni struggled with trusting her emotions, but Obinna did not. He was confident, so certain of what he felt and where it came from.

A soft knock drew her attention to the door. She removed the bloodstained paper towel from around her thumb and tossed it in the garbage. The knock sounded again as she ran warm water over the bruised skin.

"You're early, Emily." Over an hour early. Dunni rubbed her hands on her sweatpants as she walked to the entryway. "Eight o'clock means eight o'clock." She opened the door, prepared to scold her friend further, but froze. Her hand stiffened around the knob, and she blinked slowly and deliberately, trying to clear what she hoped was a hallucination. "Obinna?"

"Hey." He stepped inside with a smile and a bouquet of roses.

"What . . . what are you doing here?"

"I came to see you, of course. I think we've given each other enough space."

"How did you know where I live?"

"Tiwa. I told her I wanted to send you flowers. Though, I didn't tell her I wanted to deliver them personally." He leaned forward to kiss her, but she stepped back.

"You can't be here." Her eyes shifted between him and the stairs. "You need to leave."

He placed the roses on the entryway table and frowned. "Why?"

"This isn't a good time. I'll call you later. And we'll—"

"Mom!"

Dunni's attempt at persuading Obinna out of her home stopped instantly. She pressed her eyes closed, only able to whisper one word. "Please." She looked at him. "Just go."

But he didn't. He stepped farther inside and looked up the stairs expectantly.

"Mom, can I go to Jen and Beth's?" It took a moment, but footsteps rushed down the stairs. The young girl paused when she saw Obinna. "Oh." She looked at Dunni. "I didn't know someone was here."

The adults said nothing.

"Um . . . hi." She cleared her throat and extended a hand to Obinna. "I don't think we've met before. I'm Austen."

Obinna whispered the name and took the hand, holding it but not shaking it. "Austen," he said again.

"Yeah. Nice to meet you." After pulling her hand back, she turned to Dunni. "Mom, I know Jen and Beth are coming over with Auntie Emily soon, but can I go over to theirs anyway? They need to show me something. Please. I already did all my homework."

Things were unraveling in a way and at a pace Dunni had never imagined. Whatever control she had been grasping slipped through her fingers with the fluidity of water. This wasn't how she wanted him to find out. All she could do now was permit Austen to leave, so she and Obinna could be alone.

"Yeah. Go ahead."

"Cool. See you soon." Austen rushed out, and the door clicked closed.

"What's going on?" Obinna's stunned gaze settled on Dunni. "Who is she?"

"My daughter."

"Your daughter." He cocked his head. "How old is she?"

"Maybe you should sit down."

"I don't need to sit down." His voice gained a coarse quality. "Just answer the question. How old is she?"

"Eleven. She's eleven."

He was trying to piece the truth together, but he already knew. He knew the moment he saw her, the moment she said her name. But he wanted confirmation from Dunni.

"Tell me," he said. "Say it."

Tears filled her eyes.

"Say it, Dunni!"

"She's yours. She's your daughter." The confession drew an immense amount of air from her, leaving her breathless and gasping as tears dripped down her eyes.

Obinna hunched slightly, as if bearing the weight of the massive revelation.

"Let me explain."

"You told me you lost the pregnancy."

"I didn't tell you that. You assumed."

"And you didn't think to correct me? You let me believe you lost her! Are you insane?" His chest rose and fell rapidly. "Who does that?"

"I wanted to tell you. I wanted to tell you in Nigeria, but . . ." She grunted. "I couldn't."

"You couldn't? Seriously? We were together for days. You could have told me at any time. I had a right to know."

"Yeah. And that is exactly why I sent you email after email, telling you I was pregnant. But you weren't there, so I raised her on my own."

She didn't want to bring up the past, but it always came back to that. If only he'd read the emails and responded. If only he hadn't shut her out. *If only.*

"In Nigeria, I wanted to tell you, but I wasn't sure about the kind of man you were—if you were reliable and capable of being a father. Your reputation as a playboy didn't help matters." A throbbing headache developed beneath her temples. "If I had told you, you would have insisted on meeting her. And I couldn't just bring you into her life without being certain of your intentions. I had to be certain first—for her. She's my priority."

The storm in Obinna's eyes calmed.

"Then things seemed promising in San Francisco," Dunni went on. "I wanted to tell you about her and ask you to come back to Seattle with me to meet her."

"Then, why didn't you?"

"You said you didn't want to be a father. And Austen deserves a father who wants her."

"I want her," he blurted. "Of course I do."

"But that isn't what you said in San Francisco."

"For God's sake. I didn't mean what I said. After what happened that day, I was emotional. I wasn't thinking straight." He groaned and walked into the living room. The teal curtains were drawn, concealing the view of the backyard. He sat on the tufted cream sofa and watched his clenched hands. "She looks like you. So much."

"All I see is you when I look at her." She sat beside him. "I'm sorry you had to find out like this. I was going to tell you, but needed to work through some things first."

"No, I'm sorry. I could have prevented all of this. If I'd just read the goddamn emails." He shook his head regretfully.

"Because of my stupidity, you went through everything alone." He turned to her. "What was it like? How did you cope?"

The memory of the hardest period in her life brought a fresh set of tears to her eyes. "When I learned I was pregnant, I decided to keep it—her, Austen. School began. I was already dealing with so much, and I had something extra on my plate. I wore baggy clothes to hide my belly. But I couldn't hide it for long, and everyone knew. I was the pregnant freshman. It was so difficult."

"I'm sorry." He held her hand and squeezed it gently.

The round teal ottoman in the center of the room held Dunni's focus. Austen had picked it five years ago while they shopped for pieces for the town house. As they ambled between the furniture displays at a store, her small finger had pointed to it. "This one, Mommy!" Her sharp voice had drawn the attention of nearly everyone in the store, and they laughed. "I want this one! Pick this one!" That memory diluted the ones Dunni recounted to Obinna; the happiness made reliving that hardship bearable.

"I didn't go home for Christmas break," she continued, "because I didn't want my parents to find out. I had Austen in March. I had exams coming up. I was stressed. I was alone. I was depressed. She was so small. I didn't know what to do with a baby, but I couldn't tell my family. So I hired a nanny. She helped a lot. But my final grades were terrible."

Recalling the memories exhausted her and added pressure to her splitting headache.

"When it was summer break, I gave an excuse why I couldn't

come home—I was with friends, I was doing an internship. My parents didn't question it, and it was such a relief. Without the stress of school, things got better. I started bonding with Austen."

"And your parents never found out?"

"One day, when Austen was about five months, there was a knock on my apartment door. When I answered it, there they were—my parents and my grandmother. That's how they found out. A surprise visit."

"Shit," he murmured.

"Yeah. They were beyond livid. My mother and my grandmother knew it was yours, but they didn't tell my father."

"Why not?"

"I told my grandmother you wanted nothing to do with me, so she believed there was no point telling him since you were out of my life. And my mother." Dunni shrugged. "Well, you know how she felt about you. It was easier to pretend you hadn't fathered her grandchild."

Obinna nodded.

"Anyway, when the dust settled, my father increased my allowance so we would have more than enough, and my grandmother moved to America to help me raise Austen. She lived with us until I got my master's degree."

"And your mother? Did she help you raise her?"

"Austen does not exist to my mother. She doesn't speak of her. Whenever she and my father come to visit, she is so cold to her." Dunni looked at the ottoman, allowing the good memory to dilute the bad again. "You think I hate her because of what she did to you, but it's because of how she treats Austen."

Obinna wiped his wet eyes. "I'm sorry, Dunni. I'm so sorry you had to go through all of that. I'm sorry I wasn't there, but I am now. And I'll devote my entire life to making up for what I did and the time I lost. I will be a good father to Austen. And a good husband to you. I swear it."

She looked at their joined hands, and gently, as if pulling a Jenga piece from a stack, drew hers from his. "I want you to be a father to Austen. She deserves that. And I don't want to keep you from her—I never have."

His shifting eyes examined her body language that conveyed something she hadn't voiced yet. "Dunni, what is it?"

"I've been thinking about us. And the oath. And . . ."

"And what?"

"Obi, deciding to keep Austen was the last big decision I made. After that, I just got occupied with raising a child, so I let my parents decide everything because it was easier. I've spent years being a puppet, and I never want to be one again." She stood, her hands trembling. "That's why I can't be with you."

"What?" He rose as well. "What are you talking about?"

"How I feel about you—I don't know what part is real. I don't know what part is me wanting to be with you or the oath pulling us together."

"And what if it's both? Is that so bad?"

"I want it to be all me. I want it to be my choice. Do you understand?"

He studied her like a puzzle he was trying to piece together.

"No. I don't understand you at all, Dunni. Why are you sabotaging your happiness?"

"That isn't what I'm doing. Of course I want to be happy. But I can't spend the rest of my life with you, questioning what I feel and everything between us, wondering if we're together because of the oath. I can't live like that."

He mumbled something in Igbo, then groaned. "Why are you doing this? Eh? We're finally together. For once, nothing is keeping us apart. We can be a family. We love each other. We have a child, for God's sake."

"You're Austen's father. Nothing changes that. You can still be a part of her life even though we aren't together."

"Father?" The small voice came from the break in the front door. Austen's face appeared through the opening. "My father?" She looked at her mother, whose hands were over her mouth. "What's going on, Mom? Who is he?"

"Austen, sweetheart." Dunni tried to keep her voice steady, free of emotion so that her daughter would stay calm. "Why don't you come inside? Okay? Come in so we can talk."

"No." She shook her head. "You told me he was dead. You lied. You lied to me!" She spun around and ran outside.

"Austen! Wait!" Dunni raced through the door. Her bare feet met the moist lawn and then the hard pavement. The cool evening air hit her face with force as she ran faster and tried to catch up with her daughter, who was steps ahead of her. "Austen!" It was the last word that came out of her mouth before the squeak of car tires, trying to stop and then failing.

The impact was grave. The thump of a body hitting the

ground sounded like a hand against a drum. All the air left Dunni. Her heart stopped. Blood spilled into the cracks on the concrete pavement. Everything lost vividness—the streets, the lights, the houses aligned in coordination. Sounds faded. The breeze muted. She couldn't perceive anything.

Only her daughter's unmoving body on the ground.

CHAPTER THIRTY-NINE

The cup of tea Emily had placed in Dunni's hands turned cold. The scent of peppermint and the wisp of steam emanating through the sipping hole faded. Even with the dryness in her sore throat, Dunni did not bother to alleviate her discomfort; she was hardly aware of it.

Single-minded, her thoughts worked in one direction.

Her daughter.

It had been hours since doctors took her into an operating room. In the waiting area, Emily sat to Dunni's right and Tiwa to her left. Obinna paced, as he'd been doing since arriving at the hospital. Dunni's brother, Jeremiah, stopped talking on the phone and crouched in front of her.

"Mom was in London," he whispered. "She's caught a flight and is on her way. She should be here tomorrow. Dad and Iya Agba are also on their way. They should be here tomorrow too."

Dunni didn't give any indication she'd heard what her brother said. Her blank stare stayed on the floor as it had when Obinna explained he'd called Tiwa and as it had when Emily explained she'd called Jeremiah. The presence of friends and family made no difference to her. Her mind processed nothing beyond her grief and shock.

"Dunni."

At the mention of her name, her head snapped up, her focus on the only person she wanted to hear from.

"Christopher." The paramedics had brought Austen to the hospital where he worked. He hadn't led her operation, but he'd assisted. Dunni placed the cup of tea on the table and rushed to him. "How did it go? How is she?"

Obinna stood near her, inquiring with anxious eyes, like everyone else.

"She suffered severe trauma, causing internal bleeding around her heart and lungs. But the surgery went well. She's stable. But she isn't awake yet."

Dunni's heart, already unsettled, thumped faster. She needed to see Austen's eyes—wide open and filled with their signature vivacity. Only that would ease her angst. "When's she going to wake up? How much longer?"

"I don't know. That's up to her."

"Can I see her?"

"Of course. This way." Christopher took a step forward, then paused when Obinna followed. "Just the parent."

"He's her father." Dunni didn't think twice about her words.

"What?" Tiwa and Jeremiah exclaimed at once.

Emily, already privy to the news, watched the scene quietly.

"Did I hear you right?" Tiwa asked. "Nicholas? Nicholas is Austen's father? Since when?"

"Likely always," Emily murmured.

"Who is this guy? What the hell is going on?" Jeremiah's glare settled heavily on Obinna.

"Maybe now isn't the best time to discuss this?" Emily murmured again, though loud enough that everyone heard.

"I'll show you to her room." Christopher directed Dunni down the hallway and stopped at a door. "Here." He watched Obinna enter the room and frowned. "You told me you two weren't in touch."

"We weren't," Dunni said. "We connected recently."

"In Nigeria? Was he who you were with?"

She nodded.

"I see."

"I'm sorry."

He deliberated silently, then shook his head. "Don't be. You were right. We weren't in love. And we both deserve to be. We deserve to be happy." He took her hand and squeezed it tenderly. "I hope he's good to Austen. She deserves a good father."

And for the past several months, Christopher had been that to her. When they started dating, the fact that Dunni was a mother hadn't fazed him. Four months into their relationship, after he had met Austen, he would plan trips to the zoo and museums and parks, always ensuring she felt included. When his schedule allowed it, he would pick up Austen from school and watch her weekend soccer games, always cheering the loudest even when her team was losing.

Dunni blinked back tears. "Thank you, Christopher. For everything."

He nodded his head toward the open door. "Go on. Go see her."

Dunni let him go and stepped into the room. With a trembling hand over her mouth, she gaped at her daughter on the hospital bed, connected to tubes and needles.

"She's going to be okay," Obinna said.

Dunni's sneakers squeaked against the floor as she shuffled to the bed. Obinna stood at the opposite end. With caution, he wrapped his fingers around Austen's limp hand.

"She's going to be okay," he said again. A whimper disrupted the steadiness in his voice. "She's going to be okay." He was trying to convince himself, but was failing.

Dunni's tear-filled eyes connected with his, and she pushed aside her panic. "Yeah. She's going to be just fine."

And it seemed ironic, how the hopeless consoled the hopeless.

CHAPTER FORTY

Sunlight slipped through the seams of Dunni's closed eyes. She lifted her head off the bed her daughter rested on and squinted, adjusting to the brightness that filled the room. Unaware of the time, she sat up in her chair and scanned the room for a clock, but saw her grandmother sitting in the corner.

"Iya Agba." She rubbed her eyes. "When did you get here?"

"Not too long ago, dear. Your parents are speaking with Christopher." She stood and pulled her chair along with her, situating herself beside her granddaughter.

"What time is it?" Dunni asked.

"It's a little past noon. How are you doing?"

"Terrible. I feel like my whole world is shattering."

"I know, but you have to stay strong. For her. Have faith that everything will be fine."

"I'm trying." Dunni smoothed the blanket on Austen's legs. "I'm really trying."

"Obinna is here," Iya Agba said. "I suppose you told him?"

"Yeah."

"That's good."

Silence extended between them, and Dunni felt a sudden pressure to confess something.

"You were right," she said. "Back in Nigeria, you said I did something. You were right."

Her grandmother's expression tightened. "Adedunni, what did you do? Tell me."

"Back in secondary school, Obinna and I . . ." She caught her lip between her teeth and bit down on it. "We took a blood oath."

Iya Agba pressed her eyes closed and rubbed the space between her brows.

"It was my idea. I loved him. I didn't want to lose him."

"And you thought that was the way?" Even with her low tone, a sharpness accompanied every word. "How could you have done something so senseless? You were old enough to know better, old enough to know that these things hardly ever turn out well."

"I just wanted us to be together. Everything seemed to be against us, and I wanted us to end up together."

"Then you should have left that up to yourselves—not to things you do not understand. That is the problem with you children. You take things too lightly." She hissed. "You don't know that when you make a promise like that, it doesn't just stand between the two of you. You invite something else, a third party to bear witness, to take record, to wait and collect."

"To collect what?" Dunni asked.

"What it is promised."

Dunni looked at her daughter and recalled what she and Obinna had recited.

If I break this oath, let fate deal with me as it chooses.

Usually, people were specific. In every case she'd heard of, people chose between two extreme alternatives—death or madness. But she and Obinna had chosen neither. They'd left it up to fate or whatever force they'd evoked to choose their consequence. And it had.

"Iya, yesterday, when Obinna came to my house, I told him I couldn't be with him. And I meant it. Verbally, I broke the oath. And minutes later, Austen got into an accident. We left it up to fate to decide our consequence, and it did." A sob rumbled in her throat, then broke free.

"My love, listen to me." Iya Agba wiped her granddaughter's eyes. "That is not how it works. You cannot break the oath verbally."

"What do you mean?" Dunni sniffed.

"You break it by action only. If you or Obinna had married someone else, you would have broken it and triggered a consequence."

Dunni rubbed her eyes and glanced at her daughter. "So Austen—"

"Was just an accident. This was not your fault. Do you understand me?"

Slowly, Dunni nodded.

"If you had married Christopher, you would have broken the oath. And you were very close to doing that, which explains all the dreams I've been having and why I haven't had one since you broke off the engagement."

"So if I marry Obinna I'll be fine? He becomes my only option?"

"Is there another man you love and want to be with?" Iya Agba cocked her head, waiting for the answer.

"No. But that isn't the point."

"Then what is?"

"How do I trust what I feel for him? How do I know it's real? How do I know it isn't because of what we did?"

"My dear, the oath does not cause two people to love each other. It only takes the emotions that exist and intensifies them." She lifted her granddaughter's chin, allowing their eyes to connect. "Tell me. When did you and Obinna make this oath? Had you just shared your first kiss?"

"No." Dunni looked away from her grandmother and cleared her throat. "We had just made love. For the first time." She shrunk in the chair, as if she expected a smack.

"Relax. I won't beat you for having premarital sex as a teenager." Iya Agba glanced at Austen. "Trust me. I have already gotten past that."

It was a relief.

"Tell me how you felt after your first time? Do you remember?"

She did. Some nights, she conjured the scene in her mind and it lulled her to sleep. "I felt loved and in love." She frowned, frustrated with the word *love*. It was the only word capable of describing how she felt, and yet it was one-dimensional and singular and didn't encompass everything. "I felt . . . beyond love. Does that make sense?"

Iya Agba smiled. "It does."

"It's why I wanted to take the oath. I couldn't imagine losing him."

"The oath only heightened what you felt in that moment. It didn't create it. It already existed. You have to trust that, Dunni. Trust what you feel for him."

"What if I can't?"

"Then you have to decide what you want to do." Iya Agba folded her arms over her *buba* and leaned into the chair. "There are consequences, yes. But you can still make a choice."

CHAPTER FORTY-ONE

Emily once described her relationship with God as transactional. While her mother went through severe cancer treatment, Emily had reclaimed her Christian religion, going to church weekly rather than annually, praying in depth rather than the one-liner at the dining table, and reading her Bible rather than glancing at the short verse the Bible app automatically displayed on her screen. She did this for months—gave her time and devotion in exchange for a miracle. Dunni had found it odd and insincere. She didn't want to be one of those people who boxed up their faith, stored it away, and unearthed it the moment everything else failed. But she found that with her daughter unconscious, she was indeed one of those people.

She stepped into the empty chapel at the hospital, and the wooden door thudded closed behind her. Light shone through the stained glass windows, reflecting various shades of red and blue on the wooden floor and the pale walls. As she attempted to settle into a pew closest to the altar, she froze and watched her mother lift her bowed head.

"Dunni." Her voice had an unusual delicate pitch. "Hello."

"What are you doing here?" Dunni asked.

"I'm saying a prayer."

"For who?" The most obvious answer didn't occur to Dunni, not when it involved her mother.

"My granddaughter, of course."

"What granddaughter?" she scoffed. "The one you've never acknowledged? The one you treat like she doesn't exist?"

Her mother's mouth opened, but didn't move, didn't mold any words together.

"Just so you're aware, Austen knows how you feel about her. When she was younger, she didn't notice it. But now she does. A few months ago, she said to me, 'Mom, why doesn't Grandma love me?'"

Her mother placed a hand on her chest, and her fingers curled against the neckline of her sweater. "And what . . ." She swallowed. "What did you tell her?"

"I told her that you love her very much. And you just don't know how to show it." Maybe that was the truth, maybe it was not. Whatever the case, Dunni had pieced that explanation together and practically force-fed it to her daughter, who was too resolute. "She didn't believe me."

Her mother's face fell flat, expressionless.

The chapel door swung open suddenly, and Dunni's father stood at the entrance.

"She's awake." His deep voice echoed in the room. "She just woke up."

Dunni's heart leaped. "Really?"

"Yes. Christopher is with her now." He extended a hand to his daughter. "Come. She's asking for you."

Dunni took a hasty step forward, then paused and turned to her mother, who trailed behind her. "I think it's best you don't come. Right now, Austen needs to be surrounded by people who love her. You should go."

⁓

In the room, Dunni rushed to her daughter's side and lowered her forehead to hers, ensuring their eyes met. "Hey, baby."

"Mom." Austen's raspy voice was tiny, a quiver. "Hi."

"I was so scared, but you're okay."

"By God's grace," Iya Agba said. "Thank God."

"I'm sorry I scared you."

"Shh. It wasn't your fault." Dunni pressed kisses on her daughter's head. "It's okay. You're okay. Everything's going to be okay." She looked at Christopher. "Right?"

"Yes," he responded. "She's going to be fine."

"You see?" Dunni said, her tone confident. "Everything's going to be fine."

"Where is he?" Austen glanced at the door. "Did he leave us again?"

"Did who leave, honey?"

"My dad. Where is he?" Tears ran from her eyes as she scuffled on the bed. "He's gone. He left again. Didn't he?"

"Okay," Christopher said coolly. "Austen, sweetheart, you need to stay calm. She needs to stay calm." He addressed the adults in the room. "We don't want to get her worked up."

"And we won't." Iya Agba stepped to the bedside. "*Omo mi.*" She stroked her great-granddaughter's hair. "Relax, eh? You have to rest, so you can get better."

As Iya Agba soothed Austen, Dunni followed her father into the hallway.

"What are you going to do about this?" he said. "She's asking about him."

"I know, Daddy! I was there!" Dunni bit her tongue and watched him timidly. "I'm sorry. I didn't mean to raise my voice." When he nodded, accepting her apology, she released a pent-up breath.

"Since Jeremiah told me that Obinna is Austen's father, I've been trying to contain my shock and anger, especially considering the circumstances." He folded his arms over his broad chest. "But this is insane. Obinna. That small boy of yesterday is Austen's father. How?" He held up his hand. "Do not answer that."

Dunni thought it was best she didn't either.

"Anyway, I spoke to him," her father said.

"To Obinna?"

"Yes. And apparently, he only just discovered that he had a child. Why didn't you tell him?"

"I tried to, but we lost contact."

"Okay. But why didn't you tell me? I knew this boy. I knew where he lived. If you wanted to get ahold of him, it wouldn't have been a problem."

"I was scared about how you would react and what you might do to him."

"What I might do to him?" he repeated with a grimace. "He got my teenage daughter pregnant, so I would have dealt with him as I saw fit. But then I would have dragged him to America so he could take care of his responsibility."

"What?" A sudden jolt hit Dunni's core. "You would have brought him to America?"

"If that was what you wanted and if it was best for Austen, then yes." He sighed and his shoulders slumped slightly. "But you didn't trust me enough with the truth. And apparently, neither did your mother or grandmother."

Over the years, Dunni's what-ifs had created many scenarios. But there was one what-if she had never asked, one alternative she had never considered. What if she'd told her father everything? He presented the possibility of that alternative, and she wished it were something she could still grasp.

"I'm sorry, Daddy. I'm so sorry for not telling you. It was stupid of me."

"You were a child, Dunni. You did something stupid because you were only a child. I understand that. What I don't understand is how your grandmother and your mother kept this from me."

"Based on some information I gave Iya Agba, she thought she was doing what was best. It wasn't her fault."

"And what is your mother's excuse?"

Dunni shrugged. "She never liked Obinna. She never wanted us to be together."

"So she decided to act like he didn't exist—like he wasn't the father of your child?" He rubbed the stubble along his jawline. "Your mother baffles me. I've tried. For years, I've tried to be patient with her. I've tried to understand her. I've tried to help her, but . . ."

"Help her? Help her with what?"

"Nothing." He blinked sharply. "Don't worry about it. What you need to do right now is talk to him." He looked over her head, and she followed his gaze to where Obinna stood down the hall. "Go and talk to him. He seems to have a good head on his shoulders, but be sure of that o. Do not bring any man into my granddaughter's life who will disappoint her. Do what is best for Austen."

Dunni nodded and approached Obinna.

"Hey," he said, pulling his hands from his pockets. "I heard she's awake. How is she doing? Is she okay?"

"Yeah. She is."

He released a long breath and looked at the door that led to Austen's room. "Can I see her? Would that be okay?"

"Obinna, can we talk?"

"Um . . . okay."

They sat on a bench. Dunni kept her knee straight, preventing it from leaning against his.

"Will you . . ." Obinna cleared his throat. "Will you tell me about her? What's she like?"

Dunni smiled. "Well, she likes soccer. She's very good and very competitive."

"What else?" he nudged. "Tell me more."

"She's smart. And I'm not just saying that. She's really smart—like book smart, street smart. She has it all."

"Who took care of her while you were in Nigeria?"

"Emily, my friend. She has two girls about Austen's age. They all go to the same school."

For a moment, they were quiet, and then Obinna exhaled.

"You told her I was dead."

"I thought it was better than thinking her father was alive and just chose not to be with her. I didn't want her to feel abandoned or unloved."

He nodded because he understood that.

"She asked about you," Dunni said. "When she woke up, she asked about you."

His head snapped up. "Really? Then she wants to see me." He shifted on his seat, and she placed a hand on his leg, preventing him from rising.

"I think seeing you might be too much for her right now. She's still healing. I don't want her to get worked up."

"Oh. Okay. Well, when do you think I can see her then? Maybe in a few hours. Maybe tomorrow? Maybe—"

"I don't know, Obinna. I have to speak to her and make sure she's prepared, in every sense, to meet you."

He nodded.

"You should go. You've been here since last night. Go get some rest."

"I'm her father. I want to be here. I want to be in her life—not for a few days, but every day. Always." He stared brazenly into Dunni's eyes. "I want a life with the both of you in it. And I'm going to fight for it and do whatever it takes.

"I'll leave Lagos and move to Seattle. I'll give up everything I've built there in a heartbeat because you and Austen are worth everything to me. And I'll be patient while you work through these doubts you're having about us." He pressed a kiss to Dunni's forehead and stood. "I don't want to upset Austen, so I'll go. I'm staying at the Hilton. I'll be there for as long as it takes. When you get the chance, tell my daughter that I love her."

He walked away, and Dunni felt compelled to go after him. Instead, she sat and watched him leave.

CHAPTER FORTY-TWO

Dunni had forgotten that before her daughter got into an accident, she had a life—a job, a home, friends. Now inside her town house, the walls embraced her with a familiarity she slowly became reacquainted with. Her home, with its teal-and-cream palette, appeased the unrest in her; it promised that normal was still within her grasp and she would soon fall back into the routine of juggling a career and motherhood.

She had learned to do it all alone, especially after Iya Agba returned to Nigeria. *Alone.* The word, although familiar, didn't bring Dunni much comfort. Once, alone had been equivalent to independence, and she had taken so much pride in that. Now, more than ever, the word highlighted everything Dunni and her daughter lacked. She stood in the living room, her eyes roaming, and wondered if her home was even that.

A knock at the front door drew Dunni from her thoughts.

Suddenly more alert, she gripped the bag in her hand and continued filling it with things she planned on taking to Austen. She shoved an iPad inside and scanned the room for its missing charger. The knock sounded again, and she groaned. After flinging the door open, confusion replaced her annoyance.

"Mother? What are you doing here?"

"I came to see you." She fiddled with the pearl pendant on her gold necklace. "I wanted to speak to you."

"Speak to me about what?" Dunni shook off her curiosity, realizing there were more pressing matters. "This isn't a good time. I just dropped by to take a shower and pick up some things for Austen. I have to go back. I'm heading out right now."

"Your father and grandmother are with Austen. She's fine, so just spare me a few minutes. Please."

Dunni assessed her mother, who was unnaturally timid. Despite being eager to return to the hospital, she stepped aside and allowed her in.

She had been in Dunni's house only a few times, but never on her own—always with her husband. Usually, she would sit in silence and observe the space and the people within it with an air of discomfort and detachment, as if she were a stranger and not family. Now, she stood in the center of the living room in the same manner, and Dunni lost her patience.

"Look. Mother. I really have to go, so if you—"

"Can we sit?" She settled on the sofa and waited for Dunni to do the same.

"I don't have time for this—whatever this is." She suspected it was a plea to take Christopher back. Or perhaps she was upset

Obinna had been at the hospital. With her mother, the subject matters were limited.

"I need to tell you something important, something that isn't easy for me. So please, Dunni. Just sit."

Tentatively, Dunni sat on the couch, a cushion apart from her mother.

Seconds merged to form minutes. The refrigerator hummed; the sound pierced the silence.

"I was . . ." her mother started. "I was married before."

Those words hooked Dunni's attention and drew her in completely.

"To another man. We met at university."

Again, seconds extended to minutes. Deep, controlled breaths filled the silence.

Dunni noted her mother's intentional breathing was the sort prescribed for managing anxiety.

"I loved him. It was the most overwhelming feeling—so big it consumed me, filled up all the spaces inside me with him." She paused and considered. "But loving someone like that can be dangerous, especially if the feeling isn't reciprocated."

"He didn't love you?" Dunni asked.

"Not like I loved him. But he loved me enough to propose, so I said yes. My parents didn't approve. We had just graduated from university. They believed he was too poor. He had nothing. His family had nothing."

Dunni leaned away from her mother, recognizing a startling similarity in them that surpassed their physical appearance.

"They thought he couldn't take care of me, even with his degree, ambition, and dreams. I didn't listen to them. We got married without their approval. It was a court wedding. But we were so happy."

Dunni sensed another *but* coming, the interruption of happiness.

"Shortly after the wedding, I got a good job at a marketing company. His search for a job was harder. So, he started an importing business with some friends from school but it failed. He pitched other business ideas to company executives, but they turned him down.

"This went on for months. I took care of all our expenses. I didn't mind. But he did. The fact that he wasn't providing for us put a strain on our relationship. He resented me."

Dunni wanted to reach out and touch her mother. Though she wasn't bold enough to do something so out of character.

"I felt guilty for going to work every morning. He would look at me like I was doing something wrong. I hid my accomplishments from him—successful presentations, praise from my boss, a promotion. I made myself small so he could feel big."

Again, silence. The refrigerator hummed, the heightened sound earsplitting.

"He started drinking. I would come home every night to find him drunk and angry." Her eyes reddened, strained from holding back tears. "The first time he hit me—"

"What?" Dunni blurted. "He hit you?"

She nodded, and her eyelids fluttered. "The first time it happened, I was making us dinner. It had been a long day, and I was an hour late. I was still in my work clothes, quickly chopping onions. Then I felt a sudden heaviness on my face. At first, I didn't know what it was. It took me a moment to realize it had been his hand."

Dunni stifled an outburst, curses that crammed her closed mouth and stung and fought for release like a swarm of bees.

"He beat me because I was more successful than him, and he wanted to feel like more of a man." Finally, the tears she had been holding back fell, flowed, drenched her cheeks. "He beat two pregnancies out of me."

A tightness in Dunni's chest made her breaths short. She didn't think twice about navigating the boundaries between her and her mother. She shuffled to her and took her shuddering hands. "I'm so sorry."

"Two pregnancies," her mother repeated. "And still, I stayed with him. I hated him, but that love was still there—like a poison my body had slowly adapted to.

"Three years into our marriage, he was still jobless, and I had learned to cover my bruises with makeup and clothes."

"When did you leave?"

"The night I knew he was going to kill me. I saw it in his eyes, so I fought back and got out of the house. It was the middle of the night, and I just kept running. When I stopped, I caught a taxi and went to my parents'." She wiped her wet cheeks, and mascara residue blackened her skin. "Two years after the divorce, I met your father. He was a good man. I told him about my past, and he was so patient with me. He allowed us to move at my pace—to do things only when I was ready. I loved him, but it differed from what I felt with my first husband. And that was a good thing."

Dunni remembered the way her mother had once described love. Constant, sensible, reliable, and safe. It was that kind of love she hoped Dunni would have with Christopher. While Obinna represented a different kind of love, the kind that had destroyed her.

"Obinna was—"

"I don't hate him," her mother interrupted. "I never have. The first time I saw both of you together, it triggered my past. I saw the way you looked at each other. And then I saw where he lived. The similarities terrified me. I didn't want history to repeat itself. All I could think about was protecting you."

"There was nothing to protect me from," Dunni said. "There never was."

"But I didn't see it that way. My trauma wouldn't let me. It had been years, but I was still dealing with the aftermath of what happened. My trauma manifested in ways I didn't understand and couldn't control."

"What ways?"

"I had nightmares. Constantly. And there was this anger inside me. Anything could set it off, and I couldn't control it. When you were four and Jeremiah was six, you both were fighting over a toy. Jeremiah pushed you. You started to cry, and I just lost it. I hit him. He was just a baby, and I hit him."

She looked at their clenched hands, as if expecting Dunni to pull away. She waited, then met her daughter's soft gaze.

"When your father came home from work that night, I told him everything. I told him I didn't trust myself to be alone with you both, so he got us help—nannies, maids. And I left you both in their care. Because you were better off with them—safe."

"That's why you were never there—why you traveled constantly."

She nodded. "I didn't want to hurt either of you. I thought you were better off without me."

"Why didn't you get help—see someone, talk to someone?"

"Like a therapist? No. In those days, Nigeria wasn't like that. There weren't therapists. There was church. You prayed your problems away in church." Cautiously, she raised her fingers and stroked Dunni's cheek in a way she hadn't before. "It killed me to be away from you and Jeremiah, to create distance rather than a relationship. But it was all I could think to do."

Dunni leaned into her mother's touch—the silken texture of her skin, the floral notes in her scented lotion, the warmth that comforted something that had gone unnurtured for years.

"The day of your graduation party, the incident with Obinna." Her hand fell away from Dunni's cheek. "I need you to know that wasn't me. I didn't mean to push him, to hurt him. When the anger cleared and I realized what I had done, I felt sick. The guilt ate at me. And then when I first saw Austen, I saw him. I couldn't look at her without seeing him, and the guilt was too much."

"It's why you couldn't be around her."

"Yes. And because I worried I would hurt her. I didn't trust myself like I didn't trust myself with you and Jeremiah." Worry lines framed her pinched lips and tugged on the corners of her downcast eyes. "Now she thinks I don't love her, but I do. Dunni, I swear I do. I'm just carrying too much pain and anger. And I don't know what to do with them. I'm fed up with myself. Even your father is fed up with me. I don't know what else to do."

Dunni thought of a broken vase suddenly—the large shards that are picked up and mended together. Then she thought of the specks, the ones that go undetected, that slip between the spaces in a wooden floor, that hide in narrow corners, that are considered insignificant and are never retrieved. Without them the mended vase still appears whole, but with a thorough look, the missing fragments become visible—the chips, the inadequacies, the brokenness. Dunni's mother had so many missing fragments. She'd left a terrible marriage, she'd pieced herself together, but she was far from whole. Perhaps those specks of herself would have enabled her to be a better mother and grandmother. Perhaps taking the right steps to collect them, piece by piece, would have made a world of difference.

"Mom." She hadn't called her that in years. But *Mother* seemed ill-fitting for the moment. It seemed too harsh—too sharp around its edges, so she filed it down and smoothed it out to *Mom*. "You need to get help. You need to see a therapist. Not a pastor, a doctor. We'll find a really good one. Promise you'll go to every session. For me. And Austen. And Daddy. And Jeremiah. And yourself. Promise."

With tears in her eyes, she watched her daughter. "Okay. I will. I promise."

Again, Dunni acted without navigating the boundaries of

their relationship. She leaned forward and wrapped her arms around her mother. She couldn't remember ever hugging her. It seemed like the first time, so she captured the details of the moment—the scent of her mother, the feel of her body, the warm hues of dusk that shone through the windows and filled the room—and stored them away among other cherished firsts.

They pulled apart and regarded each other.

"I am so sorry, Dunni. For everything. The list is long, and I'm sorry for it all."

"I know you are. Thank you for telling me. For explaining everything."

"I owe the same explanation to your brother. And to Obinna. I mistook him for someone else. But I've been watching him at the hospital." She smiled, a wary, rueful expression. "That boy loves you, Dunni. I will not stand in the way. Never again. Be with him if you choose."

For the first time since Dunni met Obinna, nothing stood in the way of them being together—not parents, a country, a misunderstanding, or a secret.

The only obstacle Dunni had to oppose now was herself.

CHAPTER FORTY-THREE

Vibrant colors and doodles of animals covered the walls in the children's hospital. Dunni had missed this detail until now, as she walked down the hallway to Austen's room. She leaned against the doorframe and glanced between her sleeping daughter and Tiwa, who sat in a chair and stared at her phone. When she cleared her throat, Tiwa's head snapped up.

"Oh. Hey. You're back." She stood and walked to the door.

"Yeah. Where's my dad and my grandmother?"

"They went to the cafeteria to grab some food. I told them I would stay with Austen." She scanned the corridor. "I haven't seen your mom though."

"She isn't here. She went to see Obinna."

"Oh." Tiwa's eyes settled on Dunni. Her lips tightened to a pout. "So. Obinna."

They still had not addressed this subject, and Tiwa hated being kept in the dark.

"Why didn't you tell me?" she whispered, glancing at Austen. "You told me her dad was a random guy you hooked up with when you first came to the States. How could you not tell me the truth?"

"Well, it wasn't like you knew Obinna back then."

"Yeah. But what about when you learned that I did? Huh? Why didn't you tell me then?"

"It wasn't that easy, Tiwa. It was a complicated situation. It was a complicated time. I had to figure things out first." She swung the travel bag in her hand and watched her friend sheepishly. "But I'm sorry. I know we tell each other everything."

"No, I tell you everything. You only tell me what you choose."

"Yeah. You're right. But I'll tell you what happened between me and Obinna. I promise."

"Okay." Her peeved expression softened. "But you're obviously dealing with a lot right now, so tell me whenever you're ready. Preferably in the next week or two, but no pressure."

Dunni laughed. "Thanks."

"So. You and Obinna. Are you two together now?"

"I don't know. I'm still sorting through some things. Right now, I just want to focus on Austen." She hugged Tiwa. "Thank you for stopping by. And for hopping on a plane the moment you heard."

"Of course. She's my goddaughter."

"Well, I appreciate it, and I love you."

"I love you too. I'll call you later."

After Tiwa entered the elevator, Dunni stepped into the room and sat beside the bed. She watched her daughter sleep, content with just observing, oblivious to how much time passed. During the first weeks of Austen's life, Dunni would watch her sleep for hours, even when she was exhausted or had to study or write essays. Back then, nothing else mattered. And things had not changed.

"Hey, baby," Dunni said when Austen's eyelids fluttered.

"Mom?" One eye opened completely and then the other. "Were you watching me sleep?"

"I was."

"That's so weird."

Dunni noted her daughter's hoarse voice and grabbed the water bottle on the table. "Here." She angled the straw to her mouth.

"Thanks," Austen said after a long sip. "How come you were gone for so long?"

"I went home to grab some things, and then your grandmother dropped by."

"Oh." Her tone flattened.

"She's coming to see you tomorrow."

"Why?"

"Because she's your grandmother, and she loves you. And she wants to tell you that in person." Dunni studied the apprehension on Austen's face. "Will you do me a favor? Will you just give her a chance? Please."

"But, Mom, do I have to?"

"It would mean a lot to me."

Austen thought deeply, then grumbled. "Fine."

"Thanks, sweetheart." Dunni's hand moved over her daughter's dark, curly hair, stroking the stray strands flat.

"Mom, when you were gone, I thought that maybe . . . um . . . you were with my dad."

Dunni shifted in the chair. "No, sweetie. I was just grabbing some of your things. I brought your iPad." She gestured to the bag on the couch. "And some books. I could read to you if you like."

There were no signs of excitement on Austen's face. She clearly didn't appreciate the subject change. She frowned at her mother, her thick eyebrows bending in the same manner as Obinna's. "Why did you tell me he was dead? Did he not want me? Is that why you lied?"

"No. Of course not." She took her daughter's hand. "Austen, the truth is, he didn't know about you. When I was pregnant, I tried to tell him, but we lost contact. So he never knew. But if he had, if he had known about you, he would have wanted you. He would have loved you. He would have done anything for you." And Dunni knew that without a shred of doubt because she knew Obinna. "When I went to Nigeria for Auntie Tiwa's wedding, I saw him again after so long. That's how he found out about you."

Tears filled Austen's eyes.

"He wanted me to tell you something," Dunni said. "He wanted me to tell you he loves you."

"He loves me?" she asked, sniffing. "How can he love me? He doesn't even know me. He's met me once."

"He doesn't have to know all the little details about you. He doesn't have to see you a hundred times. He loves you how I loved you when I first saw you. That kind of love is automatic. It's the best kind."

"Is that how you loved him?"

"What?" Dunni asked.

"Before. When you two were together, before you lost contact. Didn't you love him?"

"Yes. I did."

"Well . . ." Austen's eyes grew big, eager for information. "What was it like? Was it automatic?"

Dunni thought briefly on what it had been like the first time she'd met Obinna. She'd felt something. Though it had not been love. It had been a strange and aggressive certainty. That had been automatic. She had tried to rationalize that certainty, but it had been pointless. It just existed, having no true base. On that first day of school, she had looked at him, shaken his hand, and felt sure that Obinna was hers. Something beyond her grasp, yet firmly rooted in her confirmed it.

Now Dunni looked at the scar that split across her palm; the sight of it prompted doubts and fears. But for the first time in so long, that certainty was louder—as aggressive as it had been when she first met Obinna. But unlike that time, years ago, she didn't try to rationalize it.

She simply trusted it.

CHAPTER FORTY-FOUR

Dunni had a new kind of faith. Not in her religion, which she practiced irregularly. And not in science—in her study of cells and tissues. She had faith in something that had no name or explanation, something so far-fetched it straddled the space between myth and delusion. There were no books devoted to understanding it, no scholars who had mapped its workings, no hypotheses to inspire intellectual speculations and sensible conclusions. And yet Dunni had faith in what she could only call *something*—the reason she loved Obinna, the reason for that unshakable certainty. *Something* was perhaps an unseen force, pulling the heartstrings of teenagers, tethering them together, and fashioning soul mates.

She thought of this something and the blood oath, comparing the two. Before one, the other existed. While both were equally unexplained and far-fetched, Dunni's faith lay in only one.

With her daughter's hand in hers, she knocked on the hotel room door and waited.

It broke open, and Obinna stood before them with a phone to his ear. He blinked sharply, then squinted. "Um . . . Dave." He cleared the kink in his throat. "Let me call you back." As the phone left his ear, his stare shifted from Dunni and settled on Austen. "Hi," he said.

"Hi," Austen replied.

Dunni watched the interaction—their first since meeting two weeks ago.

Since Obinna left the hospital, he'd called Dunni twice a day to ask about Austen. And although she had detected the longing in his voice—to see his daughter and her—he'd never asked. He'd been patient and respectful, even with the toll it likely took on him. He'd set his needs aside and put Austen's first, allowing her to be in a better place, physically and emotionally.

"So . . ." Austen clasped her hands together. "You're my dad."

Obinna laughed, then crouched, leveling their eyes. "I am. It seems like I've been waiting a lifetime to meet you."

"Yeah. Same." She rocked back and forth on her feet. When her weight shifted from her heels to her toes, giving her some height, she extended her arms and threw them around Obinna's neck.

The sudden contact shocked him. Though he adjusted quickly and held her tight, lifting her off the floor as he stood. He pressed his eyes shut and exhaled deeply. When Austen loosened her hold, he lowered her down and let her go.

"Can we order room service?" She rushed into the room and grabbed the menus on the coffee table.

"I'm sorry it took us so long," Dunni said. "This is a lot. I had to make sure she was ready. Thank you for being patient."

He took her hand and squeezed it. "I would have waited for as long as it took. But thank you for cutting my wait short. I missed you." He tugged her gently toward him. "I love you."

"I know." She aligned their faces and whispered against his lips. "I love you too, Obi."

They watched each other, a glint in their eyes as they stepped inside and closed the door.

When Obinna's phone rang, he declined the call. "It's just my Realtor," he explained. "I'll call him later."

"Realtor?"

"Yeah. I'm looking for a place in Seattle."

"Really? You want to move here?"

"Of course. I told you I would." He studied her tense expression. "Isn't that what you want?"

She shook her head. "I want to go back home. I've been homesick for twelve years. I'm ready to go home now. With you and our daughter."

So that they could stop grasping at an imagined future and stop jumping over hurdles. They had been doing that for too long. They were exhausted.

"I'm ready for bam." Dunni slapped her hands together just as she said "bam," and Obinna laughed.

"Yeah," he said, bringing his lips to hers. "I think we've earned it."

ACKNOWLEDGMENTS

First, I am so grateful to every person who buys and reads my books. It still amazes me that people take the time to read the stories I write. It means so much. Thank you. A lot goes into publishing a book—so many people help the book reach little milestones. To my agent, Kevan Lyon, thank you for all your support throughout this process. To my editor, Kate Seaver, thank you for loving this story as much as I do. To the entire team at Berkley, thank you for everything you did to get this book on shelves and in the hands of readers.

Writing this book was an interesting and unusual experience for me. I felt Obinna and Dunni's story so intensely, connected with it more than anything I've written before. At times, I joked it was my story—something I lived in a past life. It sounds crazy, but I can't totally reject that possibility. If writing this book has taught me anything, it's that it's okay to rely on the unexplainable, on things our minds can't grasp and reduce to logic. After all, isn't that what love is—something illogical yet powerful enough to completely turn our world upside down? I think to believe in love, you have to place faith in the unexplainable. I learned this recently, not just from writing this book, but from living and unexpectedly meeting someone who, within a matter of days, completely turned my world upside down.

I think the best part about being a romance writer is constantly studying love and exploring the different dimensions of it. And at the same time, exploring all the things love isn't. While Dunni and Obinna are a beautiful example of what love is— kind, respectful, selfless—the relationship between Dunni's mother and her ex-husband shows us everything love isn't. It was important that I depict this disparity, so one isn't mistaken for the other. If an expression of love isn't kindness, then it isn't love. It's something else. And I hope anyone who has experienced cruelty or dysfunctionality camouflaged as love gets the help they need to heal.

To everyone in my life—my mother, my sister, my brother, and You—who have shown me the many dimensions of love, thank you. Your continuous support means everything. And to God, who loved me first, whose love is overwhelming, neverending, and reckless. *Uwese.*

WHERE WE END & BEGIN

Jane Igharo

Discussion Questions

1. What are your thoughts on Iya Agba's gift—her ability to predict future tragedies?

2. What do you think of the oath Obinna and Dunni made? Do you really believe it was a driving force in their relationship—the reason they were so connected?

3. Have you ever had an experience where the line between the natural and supernatural blurred—where things didn't totally fall under the category of rational?

4. Obinna experienced various types of rejection throughout his adolescence. How do you think this affected him as an adult?

5. What are some instances where Obinna's and Dunni's different socioeconomic backgrounds came into play in their relationship?

6. If Obinna and Dunni had committed to the plans they made—a future in America—what do you think their life would have looked like? Do you think they, naive and hopeful, could have weathered all the challenges of life?

7. Based on Dunni's mother's experience, what are the different ways you think untreated trauma can manifest?

8. When they were teenagers, Obinna explained to Dunni that he wanted "easy love." In turn, Dunni told him she wanted the opposite—love with obstacles that prove it's worth fighting for. What are your thoughts on this?

Photo © Borada Photography

Jane Abieyuwa Igharo was born in Nigeria and immigrated to Canada at the age of twelve. She has a journalism degree from the University of Toronto and works as a communications specialist and voice-over actress in Ontario, Canada. She writes about strong, audacious, beautifully flawed Nigerian women much like the ones in her life.

CONNECT ONLINE

JaneIgharo.com

AuthorJane.Igharo

VictoriousJane

Jane_Igharo

Ready to find
your next great read?

Let us help.

Visit prh.com/nextread

Penguin
Random
House